Trozas

B. Traven

Trozas

Translated from the German by Hugh Young

IVAN R. DEE
CHICAGO

Library of Congress Cataloging-in-Publication Data:
Traven, B.
    [Troza. English]
    Trozas / B. Traven ; translated from the German by Hugh Young.
        p. cm.
    ISBN 1-56663-044-4
    I. Title.
PT3919.T7T813 1994
833'.912—dc20   93-33404

Trozas

1

  "And you, what are you called?" the contratista, Don
Remigio Gayoso, asked the young Tseltal Indian in
front of him.

"Andrés Ugaldo, your humble servant," answered the young
man politely.

"Good. Y de qué sabes trabajar, muchacho? What sort of
work have you done before? Work with the machete? Or have
you worked with the hacha, the ax?"

"No, patrón, for some years I worked for Don Laureano in
Socton as a carretero."

"Then you know about working with oxen?"

"Yes, patrón, very well."

"Boyero!" said Don Remigio, turning to the capataz, the
overseer, who was following him like a sergeant, carrying a
notebook.

The capataz poked his chewed-up bit of pencil into his
mouth, looked at the blunt point for a moment, and finally said:
"Name, puerco sucio, you dirty swine?"

"Andrés Ugaldo."

"Su humilde servidor, jefe—that's what you have to say when

I ask you your stinking name, you shitty worm. Get me? Now then. Name?"

"Andrés Ugaldo is my name," said the young Indian, obstinately refusing to use the same polite expression to the overseer that he had readily given to the contratista. The contratista, the real boss, would have taken no notice and said nothing about it if the youngster had just told him his name without adding any form of compliment.

It is only the little pipsqueak that always demands definite recognition from a defenseless inferior, because he is not himself certain of his own real dignity, and indeed can't really be certain of it since he has so little. People who never forget to stick their medals on their chests are not quite sure what they are worth.

"What's your name, you skunk?" bawled the capataz.

"Andrés Ugaldo."

"Your most obedient servant, sir, you've got to say when I ask you something," shouted the capataz, his face turning deep red. "Now, one more time. What's your name, you swine?"

"Andrés Ugaldo of Lumbojvil." The young man's face was quite expressionless. He stood there calmly, as if he were carved out of some brown wood. Even the look in his dark eyes betrayed nothing of fear or anger. Coldly, firmly, he looked up into the capataz's face, which seemed to be bursting with rage.

"I'll soon teach you to obey me, you insolent toad, you just wait until we get alone together, just you and me," said the overseer as he wrote the name down in his notebook and added "boyero" in the next column.

Boyero meant drover.

When he had finished writing and looked happily at what he had written, very proud of being able to write so beautifully and so fast, he looked up at Andrés again. He was thinking of bellowing another violent warning into his face when Don Remigio called him: "Hi, Ambrosio, you goddam leper, you lazy dog, what are you up to with all that goddam writing?

Come here and write this fellow's name down. He's worked on wood with an ax. The next one, put him down as a machetero. Says he can work well with a machete. Only four weeks then we'll give him an ax."

"A sus órdenes, jefe," shouted the capataz the moment he was called, and fell in dutifully one pace behind his boss. "Here I am, Don Remigio, always at your so valuable command."

"Write, then, and don't spout so much rubbish. Get a move on, you idiot. Every hour I spend here unnecessarily costs me a whole sack of gold. Heaven and hell, Madre Santísima en el lado de Dios, why did I ever get myself condemned to taking on caoba contracts? Every day in this desert, surrounded by savages, costs me a whole year of my fine healthy life. My poor mother—and she was a saint like none other—she'd turn in her wretched grave if she knew how I have to slave here, what I have to suffer in this sweltering heat to be able to eke out a miserable existence and earn a couple of crooked centavos just to lead a decent life."

Don Remigio had reached the end of the long line of the caoba men who had been recruited for work in the jungle and had just arrived. He had asked for sixty men, but the recruiting agents had been able to send him only fifty-five. In a letter which the capataz brought him, they had told him he was very lucky to get so many men. Other contractors had had to put up with a smaller number, and the agents, Don Ramón and Don Gabriel, had made better arrangements for him only because they knew he never made a fuss about the commission for the recruits and was always ready to redeem the advances made and to pay the commission.

Don Remigio had asked each one of the line of montería workers, mostly Indians, with a few mestizos, what their names were, compared them with the names on the lists the agents had sent him, and then begun to divide the young men into the working groups in which they would be most useful for his contract, according to their bodily strength and fitness or their experience in particular kinds of work.

When he got to the end of that uncommonly heavy and responsible task, he had a good time complaining about his fate and bemoaning his miserable existence. Since no one else in the world ever felt sorry for him, there was no other way to arouse pity in the circumstances than to pity himself.

2

This checking of the recruited caoba workers and breaking them down into working groups went on over the whole territory of the Caoba Exploitation Company. The area was a peninsula formed by two jungle streams which met there and then flowed as one, winding a long way through jungle and bush and finally joining the great Uskumacinta River. Whether it was a matter of winding for a hundred or two hundred or even four hundred kilometers was something nobody knew, because distances were never measured; nobody had time for it or even wanted to do it. No one was interested in scientific research, still less did anyone care about any of the beauties of nature.

The area was flat and overgrown with dry prairie grass. From about eight in the morning until five in the evening a suffocating tropical heat weighed down on the whole region, more and more killing off the already meager grass, almost scorching it. There were just a few trees and bushes growing apologetically here and there, as if they were ashamed to exist amid all that dry grass. The more the grass was burnt, the more the sandy soil was exposed. From that scorching soil the screaming heat bounced back into the baking, shimmering air, so that if you were out in the open you were afraid to draw a deep breath for fear your lungs would suddenly dry out.

The administrative buildings, the Central Offices, were no more than the ordinary Indian huts of tropical America, only built on a large scale. A number of strong tree trunks were driven into the ground. A roof truss, also made from rough tree trunks, was laid over them and then bound to the vertical trunks with lianas. Only axes were used and no nails of any sort. The roof was covered with palm leaves. The walls were built of thin tree trunks, lined up close to one another, stuck in the ground, and then bound together with thin lianas. The doors were rough-cut thick boards of mahogany, hanging on hinges roughly worked from some other kind of hardwood. Each one of the buildings was put up like that.

Within each of those buildings rooms had been partitioned whose walls similarly consisted of no more than thin trunks. The doors leading from one room to another, insofar as there were any doors, consisted of rough planks or of little trunks woven together with bast. A bit of grey cardboard was pinned to some of the doors, with the name of the contratista or the employee whose office it was written on it. Some of those bits of cardboard were also marked "Private." Anywhere else such a notice would have looked ridiculous, ironic; for little or nothing that could have been called private could have been carried out in that building or in one of those partitioned rooms without anyone who was anywhere near being able to see and hear it just as distinctly as if it had been carried out in the open air. But there the word "Private" had the purpose of making it known that those buildings were genuine, civilized office buildings and not just, as a visiting newspaper reporter might think, just huts in which cannibals found shelter.

On tables consisting of roughly cut mahogany boards lay office books of the same sort as you can come across anywhere else in the world where business is carried on. Only there was not much ink to be seen. And the little that was to be found anywhere within a hundred miles was in the private office of the administrator, where it was used for signing checks. However, even that ink was more often dried up than liquid. All the entries in books or on lists were made in indelible pencil or ordinary pencil, whereby they lost nothing at all of their value; for if there was something that anyone didn't like, he could just come and make it better.

In certain weeks and months of the year the books could not be left on the tables or on the rough shelves at night but had to be hung up from the beams on string soaked in creosote. If that was neglected, it often happened that in the morning the book could not be found, or only a few chewed shreds of it. Ants, beetles, or cockroaches had found the book on their explorations and either eaten it or dragged it away in little bits and stored it in their nests.

Even greater care had to be taken with envelopes. Every bit of the envelope that was gummed was eaten. But even when the envelopes were successfully protected from insects, they could still become useless in the rainy season when they stuck together, and stuck so well they could be opened again only by cutting them.

One of the buildings had been modernized and had come under the influence of a futuristic architect. The building in question was the one that served the administrator as head office and also as his villa. In that modern building the tree-trunk walls had been smeared with mud, which stuck to the trunks as soon as it was dry, made the walls nontransparent, and even, looked at superficially, simulated the appearance of cement walls. The Company, especially of course the administrator, was as proud of that building as a New York insurance company is of its sixty-story skyscraper. Some imitations of that villa were added in due course; they were given the name of bungalows, not villas.

It was the administrator's one wish to be able to paint the house with red or green paint. But there was no paint available. He could of course have ordered the paint from one of the trade caravans. But he always forgot the order when the opportunity occurred, and only remembered what he wanted when the caravan had left. If he did think about the order at the right time, then he was generally drunk. And, drunk or sober, he had a great deal of trouble working out how much paint he would need for the building. In one of those mathematical calculations he had once reached the figure of fourteen thousand kilograms of paint needed for the painting of the house. And that high figure for a house twelve meters long and eight meters wide, with just one ground-level story, so horrified him that for a time he gave up working out the amount of paint he needed.

And always, when he had forgotten to send off the order for the paint by the caravan, or when his calculations told him that a caravan of four hundred mules would be necessary to bring the paint all that way into the jungle, he cured himself by giving himself a lecture or a sermon, and declared that painting the building would simply be a degenerate kid's luxury, and that real men don't need luxuries. But that was only one conclusion. The true reason was that neither he nor any of his staff reckoned to spend enough time in that beastly godforsaken desert to take any serious interest in what the house they had to live in looked like.

The Oficinas, the Administration, as the whole group of the different buildings was called, gave any newcomer the impression that it had been laid out and built to serve the occupants for only a short time, six months perhaps as a work camp and shelter, like the buildings in an area where oil borings are to be made. But, as in all the other monterías or mahogany camps, it always turned out that the provisional arrangement was a permanent one and often had to serve the management and employees for five, even ten years as living and working quarters.

Although the number of buildings was quite small, the estate could quite well be called a town. The inhabitants of the town generally got used to the conditions very quickly after they arrived, and they were so indifferent that it never crossed their minds to improve the town with good, sound bungalows fit to live in.

3

The administrator, the accountant, the secretary—they were all people of a certain education. They still missed their good houses and good beds and clean environment. But under that blazing sun which beat down on their heads day in, day out, and in the middle of an army of Indians who for the most part did not even speak Spanish, only their native tongue, and lived in their native fashion, and moreover twenty days' ride from the nearest small town: in such surroundings and under such conditions it cost them too much mental effort to work out plans for a civilized town, and would cost them far more mental effort to carry out such a plan. The less they were obliged to think, the better they could bear the life.

Moreover every one of the staff, from the administrator down to the youngest wages clerk, believed that maybe tomorrow something would happen that would give him the opportunity to leave the place and return to civilized life with the next traders' caravan. But since all the staff were there only because they had to live on their pay, and they had taken the job only because they couldn't find anything better anywhere else, there were only two unlikely chances for them to leave. The first was getting news that they had been offered a better job in a town. They waited for such news month after month, occasionally tried to save up to get a little capital and so be able to live for a little while until there was another job available. They hoped so long for such a change that in the end they either left in a caravan at the end of their contract with no thought of the disagreeable economic consequences, or else were mercilessly struck down with fever. Even that was looked on as a release.

All the employees had gone there voluntarily, but only as voluntarily as any individual compelled by the economic situation. Hardly anyone went to the monterías out of a pure sense of adventure. When that did happen, tempted by splendid stories of the jungle that told of a colorful and exciting life, the adventurer was ready after four weeks' stay to sell his soul to anyone who would help him get away. By that time he was convinced that it could be no worse in hell than it was there.

It was much harder for an office worker to decamp from a montería than for an Indian. And even an Indian only did so if he could see no other way of protecting his miserable life. To walk for fifteen days through the jungle, even to ride, was so hard that it was not attempted by anyone who knew what it meant. You needed riding animals and pack animals. To buy such animals and feed them you needed money. But the administrator gave no money to people who were leaving, only a check for the total amount due, which nobody there could cash. And you couldn't buy a riding animal or pack animal even for a thousand pesos. All animals of any use belonged to the management. The administrator would not, and could not, lose an employee as long as he had no replacement for him. That was why he sold no animals. But if the fugitive had stolen an animal and fodder, three capataces were sent after him on good horses, and he was brought back in less than two days. The administrator was not only the senior but actually the sole judge; and if he wished he could also be the executioner as well. When someone who has been robbed, who has been harmed, who has been provoked, is judge and executioner at the same time, then it is senseless to allow yourself to be captured by him; it is better to find another way to free yourself from his sphere of influence than by a badly organized escape.

4

It was a genuine town, a pueblo, that had been built up there. The Company's buildings were of course the biggest houses, but they were not the only ones, nor were they the majority. Here and there on the estate there were more than thirty other buildings. Some of them were houses put up in the style of the

Company buildings, only a good deal smaller. Others were most wretchedly built, with no care and no waste of time.

Others again were no more than palm-leaf shelters set up on the ground, so low that those who lived there could only get into them bent double or sliding on their knees.

Living in those houses were people who were not working for the Company, who either carried on some trade of their own or operated for the Company in some way without having a contract as employees or workers. There were Indian and half-caste women who did the laundry for the office workers, kept their clothes in order, mended their shirts, darned their socks, and cleaned and repaired their shoes. Then there was a barber, with a boy, who carried on his business there. Also living there were the artesanos or manual workers who worked for the Company but were still independent in many ways, and worked rather as they wished than under the orders of the management: the smiths, the saddlers, and the cayuqueros or canoe-men. There too, as inhabitants of the town, came the crowd of zacateros, the young men who looked after the oxen, horses, and mules, the animals on which the steady progress of the Company's operations depended. Also living there were members of the workers' families who had followed them into the jungle because they had no home except the place where their son or their husband found work. Many of those relatives carried on some small trade. They owned a tiny shop for things that the Company's tienda didn't stock because their sale didn't pay. Others sewed clothes for women and girls or shirts and shorts for other independent people in the town.

And then there were the parasites living there, the kind who are found wherever workers want some sort of diversion in their spare time. That was a postscript to the wartime army. It was that dubious gang—dubious yet tolerated because it was indispensable—that finds its way to gold-mining settlements, oil-fields, mining towns, as soon as people have begun to work hard there. Where that gang comes from, by what means it finds out about the newly discovered oilfields, how it is assembled and organized in such an incredibly short time, and how it actually takes the risk of making any profit in the place, that seems to be as secret as the appearance of vultures over a corpse only an hour old.

There was no question in the montería of the sort of profits possible in goldfields or oilfields. But even the wretched wages paid in a montería seemed to have enough attraction to ensure that the battlefield did not remain free from hyenas.

Mescal and comiteco were dispensed without paying tax. That was strictly forbidden, for only the Company had the right to sell spirits. But the biggest profits are made everywhere on things that are forbidden or are highly taxed. If one of those bars was discovered, the administrator ordered the hut to be destroyed and forbade the occupants of it to stay on the estate any longer. A man who was expelled made no trouble. He packed up and moved to another montería, where he set up his bar until he was turned out from there too. Once again he went off to another montería, where after another profitable stay he had to shift the business again in the same way. In many of the monterías it was not taken so seriously, and there had to be a real scandal, aggravated by one or two murders, before he got an expulsion order. After some months he might try to get back to the first montería. Either there was a new administrator there, or the administrator had had to expel so many barkeepers in the meantime that he did not remember the one who was coming back; sometimes he just pretended not to know him.

There were illicit barkeepers of this kind in every capital of every montería, often as many as half a dozen. It was remarkable, or it might seem remarkable to the uninitiated, that such illegal bars could last even a single day without the administrator hearing about them. The reason why nothing got out about them was that those who knew, and visited, an illegal bar kept their knowledge of its existence as the deepest of secrets. Those who could not get on without the existence of the illegal bars even included office workers, the very people who actually made up the administrator's staff. And not infrequently the administrator himself was to be found in those huts, either pretty drunk already or simply determined to get so disgracefully fuddled that he was convinced that being the administrator of a montería was the most enviable thing a man could achieve in all his life.

Often the reasons for his tolerance were to be found less in his generosity than in the fact that the bars either paid him a toleration tax or that the bills which he made out for himself in the bar were never submitted for payment.

The liquor bars carried out a further task besides their purely social object. The customers came not only to fill themselves up with cheap but highly intoxicating comiteco but also in search of another kind of excitement that cannot be enjoyed alone. There is no pleasure in just gambling the contents of your left trouser pocket against the contents of your right. The pleasure and the excitement only materialize if you lay out your own money in order to win that of the other customers. The more customers are prepared to win from each other, the more exciting is the game and the less you feel you have been wasting your time. So it was quite natural that in those bars there was heavy and eager gambling. Every possible game was played that their experience told them they could win or lose at. To make a change they sometimes introduced newly invented games which were fashionable for a week or two; then those were shelved and they went back repentantly to the more reliable and familiar cards and dice. It was the gambling mostly that led to trouble, disputes, and murders.

When in the heart of a civilized country the severest punishments and the most efficient police cannot prevent gambling for money, day and night, open or disguised in every possible way, one can hardly wonder that the administrator made no effort to suppress gambling in the camp. It was so much the harder for him to forbid it or prevent it in some way or other when he himself would not have known how to spend the evenings if there had been no opportunities for gambling. For the most part he only got annoyed, and drove all the barkeepers out of the montería if he lost too often or even regularly. Yet, like all other managers of monterías, like the Company itself, he never forgot that the bars and the gambling schools were indispensable for the orderly running of the enterprise. Without the illegal bars and the gambling huts the life of the people who had to work there often became, at any rate for a long time, virtually intolerable.

The manual workers and office workers who lived there had to be allowed what they might call a sense of life. Otherwise they would have forgotten that there was any difference between themselves and the oxen and mules of the montería. Oxen and mules did not need to drink aguardiente and gamble for money; they were content to be given their hard work and their fodder. Newly arrived office staff especially, after they had begun to get used to their new surroundings, behaved like captive coyotes or jaguars that had been chained up. They were infected with a kind of madness, tried to murder the administrator or the other office staff. They got hold of a horse and rode about in no particular direction, taking no food with them; they had to be hunted down and were found somewhere in the jungle, sick with fever.

They got better, with the fever permanently deep in their bodies, began to work and at the same time to drink and to gamble. Under that unchanging sun burning endlessly in the sky, which seemed to be steadily melting, and in an atmosphere like boiling steam, they carried out their work half asleep, feeling as if there were a lead weight on their heads. With nothing else to divert them, after a few weeks they fell into a state in which all day, from the time they got up in the morning, the whole interest of their lives was concentrated simply on drinking spirits and on the evening's gambling.

On top of that they forgot all about saving, forgot their longing to get back to a civilized town, to get married there and live a well-ordered life. Everything was immaterial to them; all they found important was that there should always be enough aguardiente, cigarettes, and tobacco in the tienda and, of some interest, the amount of money they had lost or won the evening before and how much it would be that evening.

Making the men forget everything there was, or could be, outside their present surroundings was an advantage to the Company, just as it is useful to a dictator when he wants to suppress the people he governs so much that they become completely uninterested in political life and feel themselves lucky because it is no longer necessary for them even to think or take on any kind of personal responsibility. The sheep feels best, safest, and happiest in the flock, where it has nothing else to do but graze, grow wool, and give birth to lambs. Once the new office workers had reached that stage, when their intellectual capacity and their ambition had become like those of sheep in a flock, that was when they had begun to be useful and reliable pillars of the Company they worked for and which paid them their salary.

5

The ciudad, the town, would not have been complete without the cantinas' additional appeal. Aguardiente and gambling alone could not be enough to gratify quite completely a man with a brain in a confused state. You could no more expect a sheep to be happy when it can only graze and grow wool. Do not stop a man from meeting his sexual needs but reward him for the active gratification of his desires, and you have a contented and obedient citizen who will make no sort of difficulty for you in your lust for power. But the question is not just of craving for power but also of craving for money. Both cravings are of course identical, only they display a different outward face. One who has power has all the money at the same time; and on the other hand, one who has enough money has got that power he wants. In this particular case it was the barkeepers who carried out a further social task. They took the trouble to satisfy the men who had to work and live there so that their capacity and readiness to work were not too greatly impaired, something that would certainly not have been in the interests of the Company.

There were always women in the cantinas who did their best to make the men's life less monotonous. They endeavored, on their own account and with the assistance of the cantineros, to keep their real profession dark. Some of them worked as waitresses. They brought the aguardiente to the men at the roughly hewn tables, and when they put down the glass that had been ordered, they put another glass on the table beside it, for themselves. The second glass of course contained only colored sugary water with a drop of comiteco stirred into it. But the glass was charged for as if it were real comiteco. The waitresses got no pay, just a small commission on the glass of sweet water which they drank themselves. It was an understood arrangement that for every glass the customer ordered, three were credited to the waitress. If the man finally got drunk, on every additional glass he ordered six to ten were credited to the friendly waitress. Meanwhile the man had lost his power of judgment so much that he saw the waitress, seldom under forty-five years old, as a young, fresh, lovely blossom of the female sex. The price was agreed, and the man and the woman left the bar looking for all the world like a bridal couple leaving their wedding breakfast, to find out at last whether it was worthwhile or whether they had got it wrong.

Sometimes the nurse came back after an hour to look after another invalid who might need treatment. Often she didn't even come back but was not seen again in public until the next day.

Other women, whose charms were rather less than what was required of a waitress, women who, at least in appearance, had left their first half-century behind them, who were often covered with pockmarks, had twisted, crooked mouths and only the witch of Potzcuaro knows how many warts and superfluous beards, all those women had to work in one way or another before the critical eyes of the world. They were cooks, menders, seamstresses, washerwomen, dishwashers, and washers-up, overtly at least. But since those jobs were no more than a pretext, they earned nothing from them, and it was the actual trade for which they had gone to the camp that was most important. As they charged low prices and only appeared in public in the town where there was no street lighting, they were never short of customers. Many of those women, not to put things too baldly, were in many ways better off than they could hope to be in paradise. Where they had been before, in a town or even a village, they had certainly led a modest and virginal life over the past thirty years. Not because they wanted to but because even if they could have paid in gold they would never have found even a poor cripple who would have welcomed their body and the heat of their desires even for half an hour. But all the men in the camp were so completely fit and well preserved by nature that they never had any idea of deviating from what was natural, still less would it occur to any of those men to get something by abnormal means that, in the circumstances, was not available in the straightforward natural way. For those men, a woman was just a woman. And since they could not have women around them such as they may sometimes have longed for, they took what they could get. The woman's looks and her age were all the same to them, for that was not what they wanted to make use of. So long as a woman had what the men wanted and needed, in good order and serviceable condition, the woman was a welcome treat in what was otherwise such a dreary life. And since those women had in any case over the last two decades abandoned any hope of achieving the glories of life, they gave all they were capable of out of gratitude, so as not to waste even a single minute of the last remnants of their earthly existence unsweetened.

Men who had some experience came to the conclusion that people who had never tried a shriveled old hag didn't know what real pleasure was. They went so far as to assert that they would not even want to have a fresh young virgin if she were offered to them on a silk cushion, for only a real expert knows how to appreciate true art.

The administrator, as the senior authority, was given the privilege of Brinco Primero, first pick, by the cantineros, admittedly in order to keep him in a good mood with the illegal bars. In many cases, one may say in the majority of cases, the administrator must have been thankful to all his gods that his right to the first pick was only a privilege and not a duty. If it had been a duty, the administrator would probably have preferred on many occasions to withdraw into the depths of the jungle and only reappear once he was certain that the creature had retreated so far from his headquarters that she could not be brought back again within twenty-four hours, even by aircraft.

6

When some new nursemaid had arrived in the town, the cantinero with whom she had been given lodgings and work sent her to the Oficina Particular, the private office of the Señor Administrador, to ask his permission to stay; for since the estate belonged to the Company as a concession, the administrator could forbid anyone he chose to live on the estate.

The new arrival presented herself, modest and smiling, dressed in her best, washed with highly scented soap, sitting innocently on the hard chair offered her and talking as elegantly and genteelly as she felt was right in good company.

The interview took place toward six o'clock in the evening, when the administrator expected to have got over the day's problems and could abandon himself to more cheerful thoughts. He looked at his visitor and asked: "What is your name?"

"Amalia Zarraga, your most humble servant, caballero."

"Have a hard journey through the jungle, señorita?"

"Oh, my God, if I'd known before, I certainly wouldn't have come here. But I didn't know what to do. I am from Puxtacan. My poor husband died two years ago." And she produced a little white handkerchief because she was ready now to shed tears.

That, according to the administrator's program, was when he had to say: "A very sad fate, poor lady." Then he stood up, came over to her, and patted her on the shoulder. That happened of course only if the woman before him understood how to make a desirable impression on him. And that depended on whether he found himself in special need on that day and at that time. Under those conditions he didn't take the girl's appearance and figure so seriously. But if he had been well looked after the day before, or if he had something better and more reliable nearby, then the greater part of the interview came to an end with the expression of sympathy. He merely said: "Who are you going to work with? With Don Prisciliano? Good. You know, we keep things in order here in this camp. No soliciting. No scandals. Or I shall have to send you back to Jovel with the next Arabian trader that calls here."

"I am so very grateful to you, caballero, for allowing me to stay here, to get over my sad loss and earn a living here in a steady and honorable job. Con su permiso, caballero, with your friendly permission, I will leave you now."

She stood up, made a humble bow, and left the office.

But when it happened that the Señor Administrador got a

certain pleasure from the woman before him, he said: "You must have suffered a lot, señora, in your life."

To which she replied: "Gracias, caballero, mil gracias, a thousand thanks for your understanding of my terrible troubles. Mi alma y mi corazón sangran, my soul and my heart bleed, caballero, for the great sorrows I have endured since my poor husband, blessed be his grave, had to leave me alone in this cruel world. Why did I not kill myself at once, on that same day, as I laid him in his cold, wet grave? But, por la Santísima Madre de Dios, that would have been a sin against God. And do not forget, caballero, I am a devout Christian and not one of those who just don't take it seriously."

Meanwhile the administrator had lit a cigarette and kept on nodding his head to let the poor girl know that he understood the world and its cruel dangers, and that he had been through the same sort of thing in his own life.

The visitor now took her little kerchief in her hand again and brushed it over her eyes, taking care that the makeup on her eyelashes and under her eyes was not wiped off. She dabbed at her mouth too, without staining the handkerchief red, for she did not have many of those fine little kerchieves—to be quite precise, she possessed only that one, which she kept for use only on the most splendid occasions.

Finally she sighed deeply, and followed the sigh with a gulp in her throat. Then she said: "I hope now, here in this loneliness, to be able to forget what I have suffered, Señor Administrador, and for all the privileges you have been so kind as to extend to me I shall be eternally thankful to you, to the end of my life, which may not be far off."

The administrator went over to the suffering woman, patted her on the shoulder again, and said: "It will all be all right." Then he slid his hand higher up and stroked her hair, a compliment that pleased the poor woman so much that she laid her head on his breast, took a deep breath, and held the handkerchief to her nose. She was so eternally thankful for this consolation that she could not resist suddenly grasping his hand and pressing it to her face. In the exuberance of her feelings of gratitude, she found herself kissing his hand ardently, so hard that she drove her teeth into his hand.

Now she recovered herself, as if she were waking from a dream, and said: "Perdóneme, señor, forgive me for my behavior, but I really don't know what I'm doing, I feel as if I were drunk. You are so kind, señor, much kinder than I deserve. I really don't know how to thank you. If I could only think of one word that would show my gratitude for your great kindness."

Now she made a swaying movement with the upper part of her body, as if she were losing consciousness.

This gesture gave the administrator the opportunity he had been waiting for, to say: "Won't you drink a copita with me, a little glass, to help you recover your strength? I have a good cognac here. Not here in the office, of course. In my living room. May I invite you?"

Now she smiled.

"Un caballero tan noble y tan fino, how could I refuse so noble and magnanimous a gentleman such an honorably intended invitation!"

She got up and went before him the way he had shown her. The first little glass was followed by several more. He moved closer to her, and she said: "Not under the arms, por favor, I'm very ticklish there."

Another little glass was filled, and then the administrator found some place where the poor woman seemed to be less ticklish, or maybe the pleasant feeling so far overcame the unpleasant that it would have been a sin to complain about the tickling.

From then on everything happened very quickly. The woman was clearly heard to refuse. She took obvious trouble to sound really firm in her refusal. No doubt she knew people, and knew what sort of man she had to seem very willing toward and with what sort it would be more successful if a little imagination were used to make the startled man believe he had boldly overcome a proud, tough woman and conquered her after a noble battle. However it was, refusals became more and more scarce and more and more feeble. The last words to be heard outside referred only to the mosquitoes which began to sting the defeated woman's hot legs.

If the administrator only had the idea that it could be worthwhile to spend an hour with one of those women, he was quite ready to let the conversation go on and on. Only if the woman appeared so played out that the administrator, even though he found it embarrassing, did not dare to hope even for a few little secret pleasures, and if he drew the right conclusion from the rest of the interview with the applicant, that apart from a lack of bodily attraction she was also short of the talent to make up for her shortage of bodily attraction by refined, highly cultivated manners, then he let her go so quickly that she never got round to telling him that she had had to leave a sick mother and half a dozen younger children, all of whom she had had to care for and who would be sure to die without all her hard work. However, in cases where either the woman he was interviewing was attractive enough to interest him, or fortunate enough to come at a time when he had nothing better to deal with, it pleased him to listen carefully to the stories and even to accompany them with words of comfort, with exclamations of astonishment or of deeply felt understanding. He knew very well that most of what was told him, if not the whole of it, was just a performance, lies or something learned by heart from some cheap novel, and might perhaps have been recited a hundred or five hundred times for the same or similar purposes. A woman who knows how to tell a good story effectively, one that sounds true, is aware that she can skillfully conceal many another fault she might have. As in the sale of houses or of cars, it always pays if the vendor can talk well. He can confuse the purchaser's judgment.

The administrator, who was the highest-ranking personage there and demanded, or at any rate expected, respect from everyone who arrived, could not just go to one of the illegal bars, thoughtlessly drink all he wanted, and then cart off one of the so-called waitresses with him to his bungalow. He would not have found a woman there who had not been had the evening before, or even an hour before, by one of the filthy ox-drovers or canoe-men because he had a peso, and who now perhaps had lice, if nothing worse. The administrator could not risk his regal dignity as easily as that. And so, if the cantineros wanted him to let them sell aguardiente and run gambling schools without saying anything about it, they took on a further tacitly recognized obligation, to send every newly arrived lady who applied to them for a job to the administrator for assessment in his house, under the pretext that they had to apply to him for permission to stay.

Every lady was trained for several hours by the experienced cantineros as to how they should behave with the administrator. The administrators were changed from time to time. And every administrator had his own special ideas about that human necessity. It was the task of the first two or three women who got through an hour's friendship with a new administrator to find out what his characteristics and his tastes were and pass that knowledge on to the cantineros.

7

The present administrator, Don Leobardo Chavero, got pleasure from a visitor only if she understood how to give him the impression that she was a comparatively decent woman. That she really was a highly respectable citizen, that was something he could not expect. Otherwise she would not be there. Still, he always wanted to have the feeling that the woman had only been compelled by some accident, in which she was not to blame, to go to the lowest market that such a woman could ever consider.

The montería was the last such market. After that there was no other. Even prisoners, who could pay for it and were occasionally entitled to such rights on health grounds, would probably have rejected the majority of those women. The more a woman visiting Don Leobardo knew how to give the impression that she had come there only through accident or ignorance, the greater prospects she had of being allowed to stay in his bungalow for a whole day, even a whole week, and of being treated by all the inhabitants of the town as if she were his wife. When that happened, Don Leobardo did not let the woman stay in the camp after he got tired of her. He waited until a trade caravan whose owners he could trust came to the montería and sent the woman back to her home town, provided with a substantial check.

But if a woman behaved badly, if she quarreled with him, then he threw her out pitilessly, cared no more about her, and there was no choice for her but to go back to the ranks of the warriors, against heavy competition.

Don Leobardo, unlike any other administrator in the monterías, was morally by no means petty. If he had one woman for weeks, that did not stop him from taking in new visitors and trying out their abilities, assuming of course they were in line with his tastes. And if it happened that one of the new visitors pleased him specially, then he took her into his house as well for a few weeks without giving up the previous woman, as long as she still appealed to him. The new assistant was taken in as a companion to the first woman. If one of the two didn't care for that sort of cozy family life, or if one of the two was quarrelsome, she was let go, with a check. It actually happened that during the sixteen months Don Leobardo spent as administrator in that montería, he once, so people reckoned, entertained one woman and three companions in his bungalow at the same time for three months and two weeks.

It was a very cheerful family life, and if things had gone Don Leobardo's way he could have stood it for a full year. But two of the office staff, who took a fancy to two of the companions at the same time and whose affections were occasionally reciprocated, just when Don Leobardo was trying to solve problems of the philosophy of life with the woman and a companion, brought strife into the domestic bliss. Don Leobardo was not guilty of the strife; he had declared himself ready to forgive both the two erring companions and the two office workers and to forget the incidents. It was the two companions who were to blame, when they discovered after three days that each of them had picked the wrong one of the two office workers and wanted to swap. That led to revolver shots, most of which missed, though two got home; of course that was no fault of the marksmen, who, as they said, had had no intention of murdering one another. Consequently Don Leobardo had no alternative but to lock the two companions in a room and keep them locked up there until he could send them off to Balun Canan with an Arabian trader's caravan.

8

Anyone who went to that town uninitiated, by mistake perhaps, a town so hastily put up in the jungle, so empty and so ugly, got the impression that it was a camp in which every building, every hut, every living creature, man or beast, served no other purpose than the production of mahogany. That was indeed the object of the town and of its inhabitants, just as in a mining district every activity is aimed indirectly or directly at the extraction of coal or ore.

What else happened in the camp, apart from the work, could be seen only if you spent weeks there—not weeks as a visitor or a journalist or one of an official inspection team, but as one who belonged there as an office worker, a manual worker, a contratista, a trader, or one of the huge army that provided entertainment and made money from the amusements, without which life there would have been hard to bear.

If the construction and appearance of the Administration buildings were a long way away from what one is used to in office buildings, even in sugar or coffee plantations, the buildings that served all other purposes were certainly a hundred times further from what one expects to see as bars, gaming houses, dance halls, and houses for feminine assistance in, say, a small seaport on the Pacific coast of Central America. In those little ports where only tramp steamers dock whose destination and ownership are not always clear, such places retain at least one spark of the glimmer and the false romance that a thirsty and randy seaman is looking for. He is perfectly satisfied, and indeed finds it normal, if the port's two or three taverns and the dance halls associated with the bars are built of old cans and petrol tins hammered out flat and rusty bits of corrugated iron full of holes. Such buildings, in their architecture and their materials, still stand for civilization in a certain way, with certain connections; for they readily call to mind those dilapidated huts you can sometimes see on allotments on the outskirts of big manufacturing towns in civilized countries, where workers spend their Sundays planting lettuces which are always picked by somebody else.

Compared with the buildings in the mahogany camps that do duty as places of entertainment, the shacks in those little seaports could really be described as palaces. For in the monterías there was not even wood from crates, not a single piece of corrugated iron, no nails, no wire, no iron hooks, nothing at all of what can be seen in the most wretched ports on the most miserable coast. Tables and chairs were only found in the office buildings, and even those had seldom been made with a saw but generally with an ax and a machete. Some of the office staff had to sleep in hammocks because they couldn't sleep on the bare floor for fear of the snakes, scorpions, and big tarantulas. Others of the staff, including the administrator and the chief accountant, owned bedsteads. Like all the furniture, those bedsteads were made of the finest mahogany or ebony. The wood was worth thousands of dollars—in New York or London, that is. In the montería, if it wasn't good enough or big enough to supply the size required for the market, it was simply used as fuel. But although the wood for the beds was the finest wood, the bedsteads themselves were put together so clumsily from chopped up planks that they would hardly have deserved the name of bed anywhere, not even in a poor peasant's house in Albania. Strips of rough oxhide were stretched sideways across the frame. On that network a bast mat was spread out, and over that a mattress, very cleverly worked by Indians out of the bast of a special plant. It was about three centimeters thick and quite soft. In European countries it would be thought to have been made from peat. Its color is like that of light peat. Good pillows were made out of cambric and stuffed with specially selected Louisiana moss known as Musgo.

Beds and mattresses of this kind were regarded in the town as the highest luxury anyone could possess. And if the administrator or one of the staff took a woman into his bungalow, it was immediately recognized that the woman felt comfortable enough and was quite sure that an English duchess could not sleep more softly. For in their own dwellings the girls slept either in a hammock or on a bast mat spread on the ground. A hammock was actually a luxury that not every woman could afford; for even if they had the money, the Company's tienda might have none in stock, and it was not certain when the next caravan would bring any. But sometimes there were Indian men or women in the camp who set up a little business in knitting hammocks out of bast thread.

The bars and gaming rooms mostly consisted of no more than

one or two rough tables set up in the open air. This style was already considered fashionable. The less fashionable drink and gambling centers were nothing but naked earth where the customer squatted Indian-style and drank his mescal direct from the bottle or from fruit shells. Even the gambling took place on the naked earth.

Some of the bars had a palm leaf placed against a tree or a post so as to give protection from the wind or, in most cases, to hide them from view from the Administration building.

Then there were other houses which consisted of a whole palm leaf, folded over on the ground with nothing to hold it up. The two open ends were blocked with dried shrubs. One end acted as the door. When the shrubs were pushed out, then the door was open; and when the shrubs were pushed back, then the door was shut. That was the kind of house the waitresses and other women lived in, where they received visitors to discuss anatomy with them.

A man must sleep; and if he has no bed, he just has to sleep on the ground. The women, like the majority of the manual workers, barmen, and laborers, had only that sort of hut to live in, simply a palm shelter not high enough to stand up in. Since many, probably most, of the occupants of those little hovels owned neither a bed nor a hammock, they slept on a mat on the ground. Everyone who woke in the morning without having been troubled by a snake or a scorpion or one of the ten thousand other creatures of the jungle considered himself as blessed by fate as a soldier who goes home unwounded after a long war.

The manual workers of course could have built themselves better huts, for they had the necessary skill. But they hadn't the time. All the time from sunrise to sunset, Sundays included, belonged to the Company. At night they were too tired, and in any case they would not have been able to do that sort of work by night. That was what things were like under the palm shelter, until one day it burned down or was destroyed by a powerful hurricane. Then they had just enough time to build a new shelter, which generally fell down quicker than the first one.

They all hoped to pay off their debts to the Company and be able to go home. Because they all hoped that would happen quite soon, everyone preferred the primitive house he'd got. But the longer he worked in the montería, the deeper he got into debt with the Company, and the more hopeless became his prospect of getting away. The debts had to be paid first before a man could leave the camp.

Of course there were houses of one other kind. In those the roof was set on pillars high enough for a man to stand upright under the roof, even leaving a little space above his head. Some of the sellers of aguardiente owned such houses. Often improvements were made to those houses, the sides lined with bushes so as to make a wall. Sometimes even a second wall was created in that way, and the landlord cut off a room which he lined with bushes on every side. That was the room where he slept with his wife or, if he had not brought a wife with him, with one of the meseras or waitresses who served in his bar, each one in turn.

Some of the manual workers, who belonged among the more intelligent, were called maestro, got well-paid work, and, because they were irreplaceable for the good progress of operations—the smith, for instance, the harness-makers, the rider who carried the post, the mayordomo of the arrieros—were independent and were respected like the office staff, and lived in huts which looked not so different from the Administration buildings, only on a smaller scale. Given the circumstances, those houses were regarded as the best that were available for the inhabitants of the town.

9

On the extreme outskirts of the estate, near where the jungle was already beginning, stood a neglected-looking building with no walls. The rotted palm roof had big holes in it in several places, and broken rafters suggested that with the next storm it was pretty certain that nothing would be left of the roof. A rotten board nailed to one of the main piles carried a faded inscription, evidently written with a thick carpenter's pencil. Some of the letters had become illegible. But anyone who could decipher the mysterious hieroglyphics might with a little patience discover that the inscription had once read: "Escuela"— "School."

The monterías were obliged by law to build and maintain schools for the children of their workers and staff and of all other people who lived there. The law had intended by that order that the monterías should fully equip the schools and arrange for the teacher, and should pay him. Since that was not expressed literally word for word in the ordinance, but all it said in the concession was that a school must be built and conducted, the Company had complied with the ordinance as the Company interpreted it.

A dozen piles were driven into the ground and a palm roof laid on top of them. To ensure that no one should make any mistake about the purpose of the hut, that board was nailed up with the inscription "Escuela Rural," rural school. No child had ever been taught there since the montería was started. Now the hut was used during the hottest hours of the day as shelter for the mules and asses, to let them enjoy a little shade. In the Company's annual reports, several copies of which had to be sent to the authorities, the school was in fact listed among the Company's assets, and indeed as a positive asset valued at two thousand six hundred pesos. Its real value amounted simply to the working hours spent on it by a few peons and amounted to four pesos and eighty centavos. Every montería had a school like that, because they had to have one according to the legal requirement. The one described here was the best of them all. The other monterías' schools had for years had neither roof nor rafters. The school at the La Tumba montería consisted of no more than a single post, which could bear witness to its former magnificence; the other posts had either decayed years ago, or it had occurred to somebody to use those that were still any good for some better purpose. It was not meant ironically, but as a statement of fact, that the one remaining pile still standing carried that board on which two letters could still be read, .s...l.. The other letters had faded out.

All those schools had not existed before the dictatorship. But now they were quoted among the number of rural schools in the reports of the Education Ministry and showed the whole world what efforts El Caudillo, the leader, had made to raise the country's educational standards. The dictator dictated, decreed, and ordained, and, look! thanks to him a new people was born and took its place among the civilized nations of the world. On paper!

2

 Sometimes it seems that time is very expensive here. It was always happening that time was used wastefully, as if absolute eternities were of no sort of value.

In many ways it was rather like a soldiers' parade ground. With a lot of shouting, threats, and thumping, the soldiers are chased out of bed at half past four. Then there is fighting, cursing, arguing for a quarter of a minute, because the sergeants give the impression that the welfare of the men depends on the company being moved from one corner of the parade ground to the other in exactly five seconds, so as to be on parade at exactly fifty-nine minutes and forty-five seconds past six.

The company commander arrives at twenty past seven, strolls up and down the ranks looking for a loose thread here, a crooked button there, discovering at last to his satisfaction that one soldier's belt buckle is pushed exactly one and a quarter millimeters too far to the left, such a world-shattering event that the sergeant has to enter it in his notebook, to record it for ever and ever.

Two hours later something finally begins to happen. The captain gives the order that tomorrow the company must fall in half an hour earlier, because today it was on parade too late. After that begins the process of convincing the soldiers little by little that they can't really walk yet, and first have to learn that in order to make them effective defenders of their country. Since the time spent in teaching young men that they can neither move their arms nor their eyes naturally nor remember what they are called, is paid for not by the captain and not even by the sergeants but by the people who pay the taxes, this crazy comedy is repeated every day for years until they become completely stupid; and an education and training that for any normal, healthy young man would be completed with absolute success in four months takes three whole years, with the result that the head men in the system seriously and enthusiastically recommend, after thorough consideration, that six years are needed to be able to achieve real success.

It was not so different at the montería. But the causes were comprehensible, even reasonable. Don Remigio had begun to curse his life and his fate for the waste of time that it took him to check the workers when they arrived and divide them into their working groups. He often felt like shooting his sergeant, the capataz Ambrosio, because he was not quick enough with his little notebook in his hand when Don Remigio wanted him.

After the questioning was finally over, despite all the hustle and bustle nothing else happened.

Don Remigio left the men, who had been on the march since one in the morning to get there from their last bivouac by midday, standing in the tropical glare of the sun as if they were blocks of stone. Whether they were seriously sunburnt or even collapsed or went off their head, that didn't seem to worry him. They cost so much of his money. He had to pay off each individual's debts, since it was on account of them that the man had been sold or peddled to him. For each individual he had to pay the president of the municipality of Hucutsin the tax on the labor contract at a rate of twenty-five pesos, so that the authorities would arrest the man if he ran away. What is more, he had to pay a high commission to the advertising agents who bought out peons from the fincas, the estates and the villages, who were in debt to their masters, as well as other Indians whose police fines had to be paid in order to bring them here. No one could expect that the enganchadores, the advertising agents, would work for nothing, still less as they were in a business in which they hoped to get very rich. Finally, a cash advance had been paid to every man recruited by the agents, the better to tempt the men to confirm their contracts before the municipal president and thus, in the eyes of the civilized world, give the impression that it was a simple labor contract such as can be concluded anywhere on earth. The old cacique knew far better than the newly fledged dictators how to conceal the true conditions in his country from the suspicions of the other nations, helped by a gagged and self-corrupting press that groveled before him. What the workers themselves said or spread abroad was nothing but lies and slander. Truth was only what was written in the labor contracts, acknowledged by the workers, and stamped by an official authority. That the Indian workers could neither read nor write the dictator did not regard as his fault. Why didn't they learn to read and write? They were too stupid for it and just didn't want to learn.

All the amounts and payments that the contratista laid out for a man he had recruited, that man had to earn back in the jungle. A contratista could not be expected to pay out all those amounts for an Indian, or even for two hundred of them, out of pure philanthropy, and then tell the man: "Many thanks for your friendliness, allowing me to pay your debts and give you an advance, which you take so you can get pissed and go whoring. Go back to your father's house, increase and multiply, and live happy and contented to the end of your days!"

What would become of a contratista who did that sort of thing? In this world, where everybody has to fight for a crust of bread, even a contratista cannot give things away without there being something at the other end. He has to work damned hard to be able to live and to make something of it. If it happens that he has nothing once he is old, then he can go begging. So he must take care of his welfare as long as he is in a position to. Wife and children at home have to live too. And if he has to work hard himself, why not the peons? They're not used to anything else anyway and do nothing but fool around. If they have no work to do, they just get pissed. Instead of thinking of something else, most of all how they can pay off their debts and escape from enslavement, they waste their good strength on nothing but bringing a crowd of kids into the world.

Besides, the people in New York and London want mahogany furniture. Why they want it has nothing to do with us contratistas. That is their business. But there is money to be made from it, a lovely mountain of money. Our jungles are full of caoba. We have no idea what to do with so much caoba. We have such an infinite amount of it that we actually make our railroad ties out of mahogany and ebony. Why shouldn't we provide a few tons of our rich excess of this handsome wood for suffering mankind? Of course, it does have to be got out of the jungle. We contratistas can't do that by ourselves. I least of all. I get great blood-blisters on my hands if I cut caoba just for three hours. Mahogany is as hard as iron, damn it. But those Indians, boozy fuckers that they are, are lucky to be able to do something for their fatherland and raise the exports figure.

This attitude of the contratistas is thoroughly comprehensible; it shows reason and a profound insight into the confused laws of world economics. Of course, the Indian thinks about it differently. But then he is only a wretched proletarian, not a director of a bank. And it is simply incomprehensible to any normal-thinking man that those goddam proletarians simply won't ever grasp how reasonable and right and patriotic are the ideas and opinions that are hatched out with so much trouble and worry and sleepless nights by dictators and factory managers, for the good of the fatherland. Goddam it all, all those proletarians should just be shot, then there would be peace in the country at last. Why is the miserable dog a proletarian anyway? It's his own fault after all. It certainly isn't the fault of the contratistas that the peons are permanently so deep in debt to their masters. The master needs his money too, and if he finally loses patience and wants to have his money, because he has to have it, and so sells the peons to the contratistas for the amount of the debt, then there is an outcry and a lot of screaming about the slave trade and slavery.

It is all so clear, so simple, so logical, so reasonable, that one has only to wonder why the proletariat won't understand it when they are dictated to. Once they understand for the first time and fully accept that everything done is done only for their good, that no dictator, no shareholder, thinks or has ever thought of impinging on the value of the worker or making him into a beast of burden, once they begin to see that people only want their good, even their best, then the time will at last be ripe when they may be counted among the reasonable, and every single proletarian will have the prospect of actually becoming a factory manager and chairman of a board of directors. But as long as he does not, or will not, understand, he must keep his mouth shut and let himself be managed and dictated to.

Everything here was therefore going right. No one was treated unjustly. No one had any cause for complaint. All the business, that of the advertising agents, of the contratistas and the companies, was carried on, always and in all circumstances, within the framework of the law. If gaps showed in the legal network, there was a dictator who mended those gaps with a signature. And what the dictator did was always right, for all his activities were confirmed by the Cámara de Diputados. If by chance one of the Diputados raised an objection, he ceased to be a Diputado, because he was hindering the order and the well-oiled progress of business. Only yes-men were accepted in the Cámara and the Senate. It was a joy to live, and anyone who didn't like it had no right to live, and was shot. If there were moderating circumstances, then he went to the concentration camp, El Valle de los Muertos, an area fenced in with barbed wire, in the middle of the best-chosen fever swamp in the south of the state of Veracruz. He went there never to return. It was the golden age of dictatorship.

2

While the caoba men stood in their ranks and, with their questioning over, waited to be told what to do, their contratista, Don Remigio, went into the tienda, where he sat on a crate, groaned over the hard work he had been doing, and ordered a bottle of comiteco. He began to drink at once and gradually began to feel better again. He had led his horse under a tree, in the shade. The men didn't concern him. They were sensible and knew what to do. But what they did without specific orders was always wrong, and the capataz went up to them and hit half a dozen of them in the face with his whip.

3

Ambrosio, the capataz, had gone over to one of the illicit bars because he knew that he could get spirits cheaper there than in the Company's tienda. Of course, in those bars there was only the usual mescal, while in the tienda you could get the good Añejo comiteco.

Ambrosio had three girls beside him, helping him to drink so as to make the check bigger. Of course he didn't know that the women were drinking only sugar-water. Consequently he was quite astonished that they were able to drink him under the table so easily and so quickly.

Under the table is not quite right, since there was no table. Ambrosio sat on a board lying on the ground, which in all the huts there was called la silla, the chair. From that chair Ambrosio began to slide, because he could no longer see it clearly; his eyes blinked, more and more dull and misty.

But he remained conscious enough to get into a bet which had been suggested by one of the girls in order to stop him drinking. He was to guess which of the girls had the fattest legs above the knees. He bet a full bottle of aguardiente that he could guess right. Then he grabbed each of the girls under her skirt so as to find out whether he had won or lost. The girls were also sitting on chairs like the one Ambrosio had. They were wearing nothing under their skirts except a short shirt. That made the bet really enjoyable and screamingly funny. Of course he lost, because he had long since lost the ability to make a correct estimate.

It didn't end with that one bet and one guess. The girls had a very extensive program for their performance.

"I'll come and pick you up later, chula," said Ambrosio to the fattest.

"Come, why not. How are you fixed for silver, caballero?"

"Don't worry about that. Mi jefe—Don Remigio is my jefe, as you know—gives me as much advance as I want. He can't do a stroke of work without me. If I weren't there, he wouldn't get a single man out to the trees."

"What a great man you are!" The girl said it ironically, but Ambrosio took it seriously, as if it were admiration.

"You and I, believe me, we could do quite different things, and much better. If I want to, I can be contratista tomorrow, and earn montones de dinero, mountains of money. Then I'll take you with me, you can live with me as long as you like. When the comerciantes come, then just say what you would like and I'll buy it for you, just like that." He snapped his fingers to show that he could buy the entire stock of the Arabian traders that visited the camp more easily than a bottle of aguardiente.

"We'll talk about that, hombre, when you really are contratista." She turned away from him a bit and nudged one of her colleagues toward him.

Ambrosio did not notice that a different girl now at his side was pressing against his leg. He went on talking, taking no notice, and explained to her that he would take her to Balun Canan, where she could see for once, he understood, how to associate with real ladies.

"All just whores here, just ordinary Tequila-putas!" he suddenly shouted, beginning to stagger to his feet. "All of you here are nothing but perfectly ordinary whores and street women. And those two fucked-out old tarts that the administrator's got in his damned stinking bungalow, just ordinary street women whom I know very well from Tullum."

At that the barkeeper broke in: "Shut your mouth, damn it. If the administrator heard you he'd set fire to my hut and burn it down and chase me out to hell."

"Him? That whoremaster? Let him just come near me. I'd have something to say to him. Anyway, I shall go over to him right now and tell him straight to his face that he's only got whores." Ambrosio was waving his arms about. Then he yelled, as if he wanted to sing. He shook his head, wiped his face with his limp hands, and shouted: "Hey, chula, where the hell have you got to?"

"Go to him," the barman ordered the first girl that Ambrosio had got involved with. "Go to him, pat him on the legs a bit, and take him out. The administrator will have the skin off me. Tell him you want to go to bed with him. Maybe you can get him out. Then dump him wherever you can get rid of him."

Ambrosio, awkward as he was, was ready to follow her. But he had scarcely left the hut and got into the sunlight when he fell headlong.

The barman, with the girls' help, dragged him into the shade of a tree and left him lying there.

At that moment Don Remigio shouted across the square: "Ambrosio! Ambrosio!"

Getting no answer after calling several times, he yelled in absolute rage: "You fucking bastard of a boozy leper, where are you off whoring this time? Come here, damn and blast you!"

Ambrosio was definitely in no condition to hear anything, and even less able to get to his feet. Don Remigio, fuming like a rhinoceros scared out of its sleep, ran straight across the square to look for his capataz.

A girl came sidling up to Don Remigio, smiled at him, and said, "Caballero, how would it be if the two of us got together tonight?"

Don Remigio bellowed at her, "Go to hell, you bitch. I've got other things to worry about just now."

"Who is it you're looking for, señor contratista?" asked the girl, not taking the least notice of his angry manner.

"May I be damned in heaven and hell, I'm looking for that drunken parandero, that tramp, my capataz."

"What's his name then?"

"Ambrosio. Damn and blast it, I ought to call him Amurschio, the bloody loafer."

The girl knew at once whom he meant. And since Ambrosio had not been drinking with her but with other girls that she didn't get on very well with, with whom in fact she was always at daggers drawn, she was happy enough to say: "Oh, it's that one you're looking for, señor. You won't have to look very far. Just take about thirty paces, you'll find him lying behind a tree trunk. Not even a pig could be as drunk as he is. You'll really enjoy yourself, señor." Then she didn't bother about the caballero any more.

"Rosita was a lovely girl, but she had got three kids," she warbled to herself and went into one of the huts where she knew that some of the arrieros, the mule-drivers, were sitting playing cards with a bottle of aguardiente in front of them. She would much rather have spent the afternoon, the evening, and the night with the contratista. "But when you want to eat fruit and you can't get mangos, then you have to make do with bananas," she consoled herself, with a shrug of the shoulders. Then she laughed at herself a bit, because without really meaning to she had made a comparison between mangos and bananas which is always taken obscenely if it is said with the right sort of expression or with a dirty grin.

4

Don Remigio went the way the girl had shown him. And there he found his capataz, stretched out on the ground, with a face so deep red in color, so bloated, that it looked as if it might explode any moment. The man moaned in the depth of his sleep as if he were dying. To be completely and severely drunk on that kind of aguardiente, prepared from maguey or mescal or from sugar cane, quite possibly from a mixture of all three, is an intoxication that knows no equal. But to be drunk on spirits of that kind early in the afternoon in a tropical country, and then to lie for a long time under the burning sun, almost without shade, that will turn even the most confirmed drunk into a helpless, pitiful lump.

"You drunken swine of a sinvergüenza, you shameless, depraved swine of a mugger," shouted Don Remigio when he saw the state Ambrosio was in.

He kicked him in the ribs, mercilessly, as if he wanted to break a hole in his body. But the man didn't move, didn't even change his attitude. He seemed to be in a deep narcosis. Once or twice he gurgled as his tongue shifted in his throat. Then he grunted a groaning "Sí, jefe."

Don Remigio stood there for a few seconds, then he spat on him, turned round, and looked at the building where the tienda was that he had just come from.

He felt like going back there and regarding the whole day as wasted. Slowly he strolled across the square. After some paces he stopped and looked in another direction. There he saw the men, lying down in groups. Some were lying by the trees, others in the shadow of the huts. Some of them were asleep, others sat side by side talking to each other. Others again were stirring pozol into fruit shells with water they had fetched from the river.

Don Remigio went over nearer to them, counted them, and shouted: "There's eight or nine of you missing. Where have they got to?"

"Down to the river, to bathe. Their feet are bleeding," one of the young men called out, half standing up as he spoke, out of politeness.

"Call them up here. And then all of you come over to the tienda."

Don Remigio went on. After a few paces he turned round and shouted: "Bring your packs with you, in case they get stolen. You never know how many rogues and villains there are around here."

At that moment a woman came out of one of the huts. She was barefooted, her hair tousled, and she was wearing only a skirt and a dirty, flapping, torn blouse which was so wide open that her breasts hung out from it. She was not one of the women who worked in the camp but probably one of the many women who once lived there with their husbands.

"Oiga, señor!" she called, her arms akimbo, and stretching out her stomach, which was actually already swollen. "Listen, nobleman, we're not villains here, we're not bandits. We're more honest here than you are."

"Yes, I know, and shut up. No one has ever wanted anything from you, you crazy old crone. And I'd be the last to come to you." Don Remigio had only half turned toward the woman as he said that.

The woman gabbled something and began to grow really

agitated, stamping on the ground with her naked foot, making threatening gestures with her arms, but Don Remigio didn't understand a single one of all the hundreds of words she screamed after him.

"Who's that old cow mooing there?" Don Remigio asked the salesman in the tienda, when she finally left him.

"That is Doña Julia. I don't know what else she's called. She's a bit touched in the head. One of the barkeepers originally brought her here with half a dozen other women. When she wasn't much good anymore, I mean of course when she no longer did anything for the barman, a canoe-man cropped up whom she liked, and she lived with him in Tres Champas. The man had an accident with his canoe one day and was drowned. Then she came back here with a family. She's only been in our camp for eight weeks. That's why you don't know her, Don Remigio."

"Why doesn't she go back to her pueblo, then, where she comes from?"

"There seems to be something against it. If I heard it right, she stabbed another woman, out of jealousy. And since the police were after her, it struck her as very convenient to be able to go with the barman in the monterías."

"That stabbing must surely have been three or four years ago," said Don Remigio, pouring himself a brandy from the bottle the salesman's assistant had put on the counter.

"Certainly four years," the tendero confirmed.

"Then enough grass has grown over it for the incident to have been forgiven and forgotten long ago." Don Remigio poured himself another.

"She seems to feel at home here. We think she doesn't want to go back." Now the tendero poured out half a glass for himself.

"There must be something else, I'm sure," said Don Remigio. "She's ashamed to face her family, or her former husband has got married in the meantime. So that's the best thing she can do, make the whole world believe she doesn't exist any more."

"I think you're right."

"Listen, Don Telesforo!" Don Remigio changed his tone, as if to say that the affair no longer interested him and he was now getting down to business.

"Bueno, what is it?"

"My men are coming. Open an account for each of them for, say, fifty pesos."

"With pleasure, Don Remigio."

5

Meanwhile all the men had gathered in front of the tienda. Don Remigio stepped into the doorway and spoke to them. "I make you all open an account here. For fifty pesos each. To start your account. You can buy what you want or what you need. For the next twelve months we don't come here to the Oficinas any more. We stay out in the selva, in the jungle. But you will only be given enough for one peso's worth of aguardiente each. You have to know that."

The men began to fidget and to start lively conversations among themselves, discussing with one another what they needed. It was the newcomers most of all who wanted to find out from the experienced men what was needed, and whether in fact anything was needed.

Best known to be the most experienced man was the Chamula Indian Celso Flores, son of Panchito Flores of Ishtacolcot. Celso already had two years of work in the monterías behind him. On the three weeks' march through the jungle he had made himself well liked among his companions by his friendliness and helpfulness. He seemed to be a really good friend. As a result of some fights, he won their respect. The newcomers looked up to him as their leader and adviser, the weak ones as their always helpful comrade, and all of them recognized him as their leader and spokesman. And now too Celso gave good advice. And nearly all the advice he gave could be summed up in the same sentence: "If you don't definitely need it, in all possible circumstances, don't spend a single centavo. The earlier you've paid off your debts, the sooner you can hope to go home to your mother or your wife. You don't know what a hell this place is. But after a week you'll get to understand why I give you this advice. And now, do what you like. Why should I bother about your wretched problems."

6

Don Remigio picked up his list and called the first man up to him. He read out his name and the tendero entered the account in his book. At the same time the assistant asked the man: "What is it you need?"

Both contratistas and tenderos knew from experience that when his account was opened in this way, every man bought goods to the value of the whole of his credit, fifty pesos in this case but seventy or a hundred pesos in other cases. These accounts were not opened and offered so generously in order to make the Indian workers happy or to do them a favor. Happiness, gifts, favors—those were things that might perhaps be used as bait in recruiting, but here in the jungle no one knew the words anymore, still less their meaning.

The accounts were opened for the good of the Company and the advantage of the contratistas. The bigger their account, the longer the men had to work there. They were never free until all the debts that the agents had paid for a man they had recruited, all the advances, taxes on contracts, and commission for the agents, had been paid off. As long as his accounts were not cleared, a worker who tried to run away was arrested by the authorities and taken back to the camp as a deserter. The entire cost of his arrest and transport back to the camp was charged to the fugitive, on his account. For running away he was liable to special punishments which loomed over the man, according to the mood of the contratista, up to five hundred lashes with a whip, or even a thousand, spread over several weeks. Even an attempt to run away was severely punished. The bigger the account that had to be worked off, the longer the Company and the contratista could be sure of their labor force. But the Company made a profit through the accounts in a double way. For all goods sold in the tienda, the Company's shop, without a single exception were five times, eight times, even ten times higher priced than in the nearest village. The Company's tienda alone had the right to sell to the workers, and all workers were obliged to buy only from the Company's tienda.

Independent traders also came to the monterías, of course, mostly Arabs. But those traders were not allowed to sell anything on the Company's estate without the Company's permission, or only such trifles and petty objects as were not stocked by the tienda because they were worth so little. Such things included little hand mirrors with a saint or the Holy Virgin on the back, pocket combs for women, glass beads, rings with great glass jewels, earrings of the trashiest kind, silk ribbons of the cheapest artificial silk, buttons, cotton. Naturally the traders also offered more expensive goods of the same kind or even better, and at lower prices than they could be bought for in the tienda. And it was over those goods that the real battle went on. They included trousers, shirts, sun-hats, sandals, rawhide, dresses, woolen ribbons for belts and for the hair, cotton wool, satin, printed cotton, calico, cheap silk, mosquito nets or material to make them, cigarettes, tobacco, and above all aguardiente. Good Añejo comiteco, brandy, and whisky, which could be got from the tiendas, were bought only by the administrator and the office staff and were available only in small bottles. They were too dear, and both the administrator and the staff as well as the contratista and the agents, when they spent a few days there, often preferred one of the better brands of comiteco, which was far cheaper than brandy and whisky and generally cost only a fifth of the price of brandy. That was the brand going by the name of Habanero, or sometimes Mexican brandy.

Trade and industry were free in the republic. But no one had the right to set up his shop or lay out his goods on another man's estate which he had not either bought or leased or rented. Wherever the traders went, they were always in the domain of some montería where the Company, which owned the concession, had sovereign powers.

Often it happened that one tienda or another was scarcely interested in goods, or at least in certain kinds of goods. Then the workers were given permission to buy those goods from an independent trader as long as one came. But no one in the camp had any cash, or if they did, then very little. No one needed money, for everyone there bought from the tienda on account. Moreover there were vouchers issued by the Company for the accounts. So that anyone who wanted to buy from a trader could pay only with the Company's vouchers. It was those same vouchers that circulated in the camp as cash—gambled with, spent on aguardiente in the illicit bars, and given as cash to obliging women. The value of those tickets was determined by the Company in such a way that for forty pesos in vouchers the Company entered fifty or even sixty pesos on the account. No one can borrow money for nothing. The trader could do nothing with those vouchers in his home town; they had no value there. So he had to cash them with the cajero, the Company cashier, in the camp before he left. He didn't get cash for them, because there was very little cash there. He got a check which could be cashed at the bank in Jovel or with the Company's principal agent in Jovel or Villahermosa. But when the Company bought back the vouchers from the trader with a check, it was again the Company, or the cashier, that decided their cash value, which was often five or ten percent less than the original value when issued. All those profits, the interest and the difference on redemption, came of course from the workers' pockets, for they were the only ones who bought anything and also the only ones there who formed a market of any value. No one else produced anything at all. They all lived on the difference between the two amounts, that which the worker got for felling and transporting timber, and that which the Company got from the American and British importers in the seaports. If the workers had examined the final account of their purchases in the camp, they would have found that they had bought no cheaper, and seldom any better, from the independent traders than in the tienda. In any case, if any difference could be traced it only amounted to a few centavos. But the workers were given the impression by the seemingly free dealing with the traders that they were independent in their purchases and had some influence on the fixing of the prices, because they seemed to be able to buy as they liked, from the tienda or from any independent trader there.

Often when a trader arrived the tienda bought all the goods he had brought with him, as a job lot. The tienda fixed the price. It even allowed the trader to make an adequate profit for his three or four weeks' march and his expenses for pack animals and mule-drivers. But the Company got the goods much cheaper that way than if it had sent its own caravans. For it took no risk of losing pack animals and goods on the journey. The trader could bargain with the Company's buyer, the tendero, and try to fix the best price. If no agreement was reached, the tendero simply dictated the price. If the trader did not accept that price, he was refused permission to lay out his wares. He had to march back through the jungle, two, three, or five days more, to the next montería, where he might well be offered even less. It could happen that the man had to march with the whole of his caravan and all his goods for four weeks back to where he had started, without having sold a thing. As a result of this double transport the goods were by then so dear that, however well he might be able to sell in the town, he always made a loss. That no doubt explains why a trader never refused to come to an agreement on good terms with the Administration about the price, also why a trader never refused, in big or small matters, to do anything that was demanded by the administrator or the tendero, and why he was nearly always ready to come to an agreement about profits with anyone there whose word carried any weight.

7

After Don Remigio had called out four names and the lads had come into the tienda and received their written account, he found the work too tiring. No doubt due to a sudden recollection of the girl who, a quarter of an hour ago, had laughingly tried to invite him to go with her, he had suddenly become aware that no man can make all his fortune just from tedious work, but that he felt well only if he had a girl around to help him, be it only temporarily, only for two hours. And because the good God in heaven has so decided, Don Remigio saw no reason why he should deny himself that pleasure. The woman who was waiting for him in his hut in the semaneo, the actual working camp in the depths of the jungle, Doña Javiera, was getting a bit old, sometimes began to get a bit cross, and sometimes was really boring. Nothing really pretty and plump ever came to the monterías; and the one who agreed to live with him in the loneliness of the jungle, one or two days away from the Oficinas Generales, was not always just as he would have liked her. You have to take what you can get, and give hearty thanks to the gods for it.

So—taking all the circumstances into account—it was not to be held against Don Remigio that he sometimes felt like a change. As he found such thoughts so suddenly and so powerfully rising up in him, he realized how the hard work of keeping the accounts in order was preventing him looking for the change he wanted and making friends with it.

"It's all the fault of that fucking cabrón of a drunken capataz," he yelled, and slapped the list he was holding on his knee. "Damn it, I have to sit here with this list like a lousy young clerk while that bastard sleeps off his booze the whole afternoon."

He called one of the Indians out of the group crowded in front of the tienda: "Hey, you, what's your name?"

The lad jumped up and said: "Teofilio Palacio, su humilde servidor, patroncito."

"Good. Take that stick you've got and go over to the goddam cur and beat him black and blue. Boozing the whole bloody day, and I've got to do the whole of the damned work myself."

"What cur, patroncito?" asked the young man, who seemed not to recognize that description.

"Good, good. All right. Stay here. I'll get to work on the worm myself. I'll fine the leper two months' pay, boozing and fucking about in every corner where he can see a skirt. I hope he gets the plague and the Spanish collar on top of it!" Don Remigio was talking himself into a fury, all the more now as he caught another glimpse of two girls in the distance, strolling off between the huts. The girls were barefooted and had nothing on but brightly flowered, very thin cotton dresses. They still had to walk toward the sun, which made Don Remigio furious because he was too far away to get special pleasure from it.

"Give me the bottle, man," he said to the assistant. He poured out half a tumbler of Habanero and tossed it off in a single draft. Then he made a croaking noise—it would have been hard to say whether he was trying to force down the strong drink that was burning his throat, or whether it was an expression of his satisfaction.

He leaned back in the rough chair to sit more comfortably. As he did so the butt of the heavy revolver he wore in his belt struck him hard in the small of his back and made him swear again. "The chairs you've got here," he said in a vicious voice, "are real instruments of torture."

Hilario, the tendero, laughed and said: "Don Leobardo has already ordered a club armchair in Mexico City and an extra one for you, Don Remigio."

Don Remigio looked up at the tendero and grunted crossly: "Shit, I'm not in the mood for that sort of joke just now. Who's next on the list?"

While the Indian he called up stood in the tienda ordering his things, Don Remigio seemed to be looking for a new idea to enable him to get away from this boring work. He could simply give the list to the tendero and let him call the men up. But Don Remigio trusted no one. The tendero would no doubt write in two or three more names, and Don Remigio would have to pay the accounts. The tendero could sell off the goods allegedly supplied in the camp. There were always buyers there. Especially for flowery fabrics and silk ribbons.

However, the next idea that occurred to Don Remigio was a good one and made it hard for the tendero to charge him for goods which neither he nor anyone else had taken.

He called out to the crowd outside: "Can any of you bloody gang read and write?" One or two of the Indians exchanged glances. But several of the Indians, who didn't understand enough Spanish but spoke only their own language, did not know what the contratista wanted anyway, and asked those of their companions who spoke Spanish as well as Indian. "Nothing special," was the answer.

Celso said half-aloud to Andrés, who was sitting beside him, "You can read and write."

"Of course I can. I was encargado, caravan leader, with Don Laureano."

"Quite right not to tell him," Celso nodded to him in a friendly way. "I can tell you, if anyone does volunteer, I'll smash his face in this evening."

There were maybe two or three others in that crowd who could read and write, even if only very badly. But no one volunteered, even though none of them had heard that Celso would be sorting out any volunteer later.

"Of course not," said Don Remigio angrily. "Who could have that sort of luck here? Not me, that's certain. Out of half a hundred of them there's not a single one that can write. All the better. Damn it, I really should like to go over there and thrash that cursed bastard with my whip until he sobers up. But that won't do me any good. In the morning he'd go on strike, and I need the drunken swine too much to allow myself the luxury of tearing the shreds off his bones."

So there was nothing left for him to do but sit there, call out the names, and check the accounts.

"Never get out in front! Make that one of your most important rules here," Celso advised Andrés. "No one should ever push to the front anywhere in life. Only when it's a matter of your own pot. You don't get anything out of it. Only twice the work and a kick up the arse when it's over. No one catches me anymore with sweet words, not even with a flattering smile on their lips. Not me, manito, mate. But listen, you could help me learn to read and write. I know a bit already. I can write a capital I, that's just one line. And I can do the capital L, that's just one line with another line under it, and capital T has one line with a roof on it. I'm not as stupid as you may think."

"Why not? Como no! I'd like to show you. I taught my mujer, my wife, to read and write too."

"Where is your wife now? With her padres, her parents?" asked Celso.

"No, she hasn't got any parents now. She's all alone in the world. She has only me. And I've been sold here for my father's debts and can't do anything for her. Not even write. I don't even know where she is now. I advised her to go to Tonala. That's on the railroad. She can work there as a maid with some family. She's called Little Star, Estrellita. That's her name. I gave her that name. When I found her she hadn't got a name. Maybe some guy will come here sometime who is from Tonala, and then maybe I can get to know whether she went there and works there." As he told that to Celso, Andrés felt an extraordinary pressure in his throat and felt his eyes growing moist. When Celso looked at him he smiled and said: "Do you know, I've got sweat in my eyes. It's damned hot here, real hell."

"Not yet, mate," Celso corrected him. "You'll know hell in two weeks, when we're in the semaneo and working on the trees. Then you'll have no time and no thoughts about your Estrellita, where she is and what she's doing. Then you'll be thinking about yourself and nothing else in the world."

8

Just then Andrés was called by the contratista to go to the tienda and make his purchases.

"Fifty pesos account, young man. Confirmed, Andrés Ugaldo?"

"Sí, patroncito. Correct and confirmed. Confirmo," answered Andrés.

Don Remigio demanded confirmation from each of the men: that is to say, the man, in the presence of the tendero and others standing there, must testify verbally that he had received fifty pesos on his account. Since the men could neither read nor write and didn't even know how to reckon in big numbers, they had to testify by word of mouth to the correctness of their debts, the advances, and the accounts. The Indians were never cheated in this; for that would have been illegal. The amounts named were always correct. The exploitation and unfairness arose in the shameless raising of prices. Raising the prices, which amounted to infamous profiteering, was legally permissible. A merchant surely had the right to fix his prices as he felt necessary in order to balance his books. But at the montería there was no competition. The workers had to buy in the tienda, for only there could they obtain goods without having any money in their pockets. The high prices were simple to justify; and no profiteering law, even if such a thing existed, would have made any difference in such cases. For even in the towns interest on capital of fifteen, twenty-five, and forty percent was permissible. The prices were justified by uncommonly high transport costs, with the risk of loss during transport and the risk of loss if, for example, a debtor died without anyone being able to find a guarantor for payment.

"What do you want?" the assistant asked the Indian.

"I need a mosquito net."

"Good. Twelve pesos." The assistant pulled the thin cloth out of the shelves where the nets were piled up. It wouldn't come out quickly enough, and a piece of the cloth was torn. In any other shop no customer would have accepted a net like that. A hole in the mosquito net lets the mosquitoes in so easily, and in such numbers, especially if the sleeper is sweating, that he might as well not have a net. The hole must be well sewn up. But then it is a repaired net, and every customer who pays for a new net has the right to insist on a net that has not been torn and repaired.

The assistant looked at the long tear. "That makes no difference, mate, you can fix that with a needle." He gave Andrés two small safety pins.

Andrés knew that as an Indian and worker dealing with a Ladino, a Mexican, he would not have been treated fairly if he had refused to accept the net. So he said nothing. Like all his companions, he was so used to that sort of triviality that he didn't even notice it and neither grew angry nor pulled a wry face.

The assistant rolled the net up and threw it to Andrés, who caught it and pushed it under his arm.

"Un pavillón, one mosquito net, twelve pesos, Andrés Ugaldo," repeated the tendero as he wrote the entry in the account book on the page with the man's name on the top line. He wrote in indelible pencil. Everything was written in indelible pencil, because ink did not remain liquid in the heat of the sun.

"Confirmed, Andrés Ugaldo?" asked the tendero.

"Sí, patrón, es correcto."

A cheap mosquito net of that kind cost three pesos in the nearest town. At the nearby railroad station in an ordinary tienda it cost two pesos, or even twenty-five centavos less, and it was wrapped in paper and tied up.

"What else?" asked the assistant.

"Un petate, a bast mat, muy barato, very cheap," Andrés demanded.

"El más barato, the very cheapest we have in petates, cost three pesos sixty centavos," said the assistant, lighting a cigarette.

At the Saturday market in Jovel a mat like that would cost forty centavos. It was thick, rough, woven from ordinary bast, with none of the decorations that are woven in by the Indian mat-makers.

Andrés knew the prices quite well, just as he also knew the real price of his kind of mosquito net and of most of the items in the tienda. He had been carretero for years, had carried goods worth tens of thousands of pesos from the railroad station in the caravans, two hundred and three hundred kilometers to poor and godforsaken districts in the interior of the vast state, had visited all the markets that he came across on the way, and so had picked up a rich knowledge not only of prices but also of the quality and usefulness of every item you could think of.

"But this mat is very dear," he said, fighting for the pesos he had not yet earned.

The tendero glanced up from his account book and had a look at the man who dared to speak. In all monterías and in all the monterías' tiendas it was looked on as severe lèse majesté if an Indian worker opened his mouth to voice anything that sounded like any sort of opinion. It was not only like that in the monterías but in the whole great republic under the dictator that no worker, neither in factories nor on estates and above all not on coffee plantations, sugar plantations, and in chicle forests, was allowed to utter a word unless he was addressed. Moreover he accepted the judgment of the most unwashed of his superiors without contradiction and with the reverence and humility of a priest in church.

But the tendero seemed to be in good temper, or he didn't want to get excited, perhaps because he was looking forward to a different kind of excitement in the evening.

After he had looked at Andrés for a few seconds in surprise, he glanced over at Don Remigio, who in the meantime had poured himself another hefty Habanero and was obviously taking no notice of what was going on.

The tendero laughed briefly and probably wanted to make a joke about Andrés's objection. But when he noticed that Don Remigio was looking over the square in a different direction, where more flowery cotton dresses round naked bellies were strolling about again, he decided to keep the joke for another occasion. In monterías good jokes are expensive, much longed for and much stolen, and Hilario didn't want to waste the joke he had thought of—which he thought was a good one.

So he only said: "Look what a smart guy we've got here. Too dear. Too dear for you. I'll sit on my bottom and make you a special mat for five centavos. Wouldn't you like me to knit you a pair of woolen stockings too?"

"No, I'm not asking for that, señor," answered Andrés in a tone as if he were just saying it out of stupidity. But other lads standing nearby caught the mockery that lay behind Andrés's words, and laughed out loud.

That infuriated the tendero, and he bawled at Andrés: "Chín-gate tu madre, you cursed cabrón and son of a stinking bitch, if the mat is too dear for you then shit one out of your stinking arse if you can get it cheaper."

"What the bloody hell is going on now?" shouted Don

Remigio. "By all the devils and saints, Don Hilario, do me a favor at last, for Almighty God's sake, and get a move on with those men there. I'm sick and tired of sitting here on my old arse and reciting the names like a stupid rosary, damn it. Get a move on or I'll move off with my men without opening any accounts."

"A sus órdenes, Don Remigio, at your esteemed command," said the tendero, intimidated now. Quarreling with a contratista, that was something he could not allow himself. A really terrible row would break out over him if Don Remigio were to leave without charging any goods on account and the administrator learned about it.

Less violently than before, he now said to Andrés: "If the petate is too dear for you, then of course you must try to do without it. We don't have any cheaper ones."

"All right, give it to me then, jefe, I must have one."

"One petate, three pesos sixty centavos, Andrés Ugaldo. Agreed, young man?"

"Correcto, señor."

"What else?" asked the assistant when he had told Andrés to take one of the mats that stood rolled up in a corner. "Three packs of tobacco," ordered Andrés.

"Take six, young man," intervened Don Remigio, "you probably won't be back here for eight or ten months when we really get down to work."

"All right, six then," said Andrés. "Or give me eight."

"Damn it all," cried the assistant, "do you want six or eight? Say what you want."

"Eight."

"Hey, Andrés, oye, listen," Celso shouted at him, "they'll go moldy if you take so many."

"Shut your dirty mouth, you there!" shouted the tendero to Celso. And as he entered the figures in the account, he read out: "Nine sixty, one twenty for each pack. Agreed?"

"Cierto, señor," replied Andrés.

"What else?" asked the assistant, throwing Andrés the tobacco packs from a corner.

"Nada más, nothing more," answered Andrés, and prepared to leave the tienda.

"How much has he taken, then?" Don Remigio looked up. Don Hilario added it up and said: "Twenty-five twenty."

"You can have twenty-five more, young man," called Don Remigio.

"Gracias, patroncito, muchas gracias, many thanks, but I don't need any more."

"No shirt, no pants?" asked Don Remigio suspiciously.

Andrés was naked down to the waist, like all the`men. They all had to carry their heavy packs on their backs and wanted to take care of their shirts, which otherwise would have been worn out on the march.

"I've got my shirts in my pack, patrón."

"Your pants are all ragged, though, not a bit of them that doesn't need mending."

"I have another pair in my pack, patroncito, with your kind permission," said Andrés in a modest voice.

"Just as you like, young man," said Don Remigio. "Next. Gregorio Valle from Bujvilum." And turning to the tendero, he went on: "Don Gabriel caught this one for me. Don Gabriel, you know, used to be Secretario Municipal in Bujvilum. Very thick with Don Casimiro, the Jefe Político up there. Now he's Don Ramón's socio, his business partner. He, Don Gabriel I mean, he's a damned rogue. I'd never travel through the jungle alone with him."

"Don't know him," replied Don Hilario, "but what I've heard about him is not very good but pretty bad." Turning to Gregorio, he asked: "What do you want?"

"Nada," said Gregorio shortly and a little obstinately.

"Nothing?" repeated the tendero.

And "Nothing?" asked Don Remigio at the same time, in an astonished voice.

"No, nothing," said Gregorio again. "I want to work off the fine that Don Gabriel inflicted on me for a row that I had, and then go home to my wife and children."

"But you can get fifty pesos' worth of goods here on account," Don Remigio reminded him.

"I know, patroncito; but then I shall have to stay here many months longer to work off the new debt, and my wife and children are waiting for me."

Don Remigio grunted to himself, then shrugged his shoulders and said to Don Hilario: "If he doesn't want to take anything, why should that worry me?"

He was about to call up the next one when Gregorio said in a rather hesitant voice: "I'll take six packs of tobacco."

He had seen the eight packs of tobacco under Andrés's arm, and as he brushed against him on entering the shop the aromatic scent of the fresh, clean, untreated tobacco caught his nose. Now it revived his longing for tobacco. The six packs he wanted were handed over to him, he confirmed the amount, and when he was asked again whether he now wanted anything more, he said firmly: "No, patrón, gracias."

"Celso Flores," called Don Remigio.

And "Celso Flores," repeated Don Hilario, writing the name in his account book. Celso went up to the counter and, without being asked, barked out: "Six packs of tobacco."

When he had taken them and confirmed the sum, he turned round sharply and was going to leave the tienda.

"Hey, you," Don Remigio called out to him, "is that all you're taking?"

"All, patroncito," said Celso and went out to his comrades. Don Remigio jumped to his feet and looked at the tendero. "What's all this, then? What's going on here?" he asked furiously. "Just look at this." He pulled the book over to him, turned it

round so that he could read the accounts, and flicked through all
the pages on which new accounts were written. He took a look
at the accounts and then said to Don Hilario: "But that is—not
one of them has taken more than thirty pesos."

"That's true," answered the tendero. "Generally the fifty
pesos aren't enough for the account, and we often go up to
eighty to give everyone what he asks for."

Don Remigio stayed by the counter, cast a look at the list,
then called up the next one.

"What do you want to take, then?" he asked him as soon as he
came in. "Maybe only three packs of tobacco?"

"With your kind permission, patrón, I should like to have
four," said the lad, his head lowered humbly between his
shoulders.

"And nothing else? Is that right, you son of a fucking whore?"
asked Don Remigio, showing his teeth in a scornful grin.

"Con su muy amable permiso, patroncito, with your very
kind permission, that is right, I don't want anything except four
packs of tobacco," replied the Indian.

"And only rags round your filthy body," shouted Don Remigio
in a fury. "Yet you haven't got a single decent rag in your pack. I
know that."

"If you will kindly permit me a word, patroncito, I have a
mosquito net in my pack and a mat that is still good. And I
shan't need shirts and pants in the semaneo. I work naked."

Don Remigio lifted his arm and struck him right across the
face. The young man stood stock still for a moment; then, when
he saw that the contratista was looking at the book again and not
thinking of hitting him again, he turned round, tucked his four
packs of tobacco under his arm, and went out, where he
disappeared, crawling between the men lying on the ground.
When the next man too asked only for three packs of tobacco
and nothing else, Don Remigio burst out: "Por la Madre

Santísima y por Jesu Cristo, this is murder! This here is really absolute murder!"

"Don't get so worked up," the tendero soothed him. "That's nothing new, Don Remigio. It often happens that the men don't buy anything because they often bring enough from the feria in Hucutsin."

"I don't know—" responded Don Remigio, becoming thoughtful. "That may be. May be. Has happened before. But in this case there's something wrong. Where is that goddam bastard of a capataz? He'd deal with them all right, they'd forget to say a word here. But the swine is pissed, lying in his own shit and waltzing around with those cursed whores."

"Next one! What's your name, then?" Don Remigio had quite forgotten to look at the list and call them up in order. He just dragged up the one standing nearest to him and asked him his name.

"Santiago Rocha, su humilde servidor, patroncito," said the young man, and went into the tienda.

Don Remigio calmed down when he heard that Santiago not only took six packs of tobacco but also bought a mosquito net and so many other things that he nearly reached the fifty pesos that each man was allowed.

"How high is your account with me, then?" Don Remigio asked suddenly.

"I only have the fifty pesos that Don Ramón reckoned for the enganche, the recruitment. I joined the group on the way here."

"No contract, then, with the authorities in Hucutsin?"

"No, patroncito. But now I have nearly a hundred pesos on my account."

"Bueno, good, now clear out of the tienda and let the next one in."

Don Remigio called out another name.

Santiago Rocha, who had been a carretero like Andrés, found himself among the impressed workers because he had had to run away after hitting the seducer of his wife, owner of a tienda, with an aguardiente bottle. On his escape he had met with the troop of enrolled caoba men and had joined them in order to reach the area of the monterías, where no policeman would ever look for him. And because he had not been able to carry much with him, having decided so suddenly that he must take flight, he was now obliged to buy what he most urgently needed. On those grounds he excused himself with Celso, who had advised them all to take as little as possible on their account, and now he believed that Celso might show himself angry with him for having bought so many things.

Celso understood, however, and said it was all right and did not reproach him. "It is good anyway that you should take more than the others," he went on to say. "Otherwise the patrón would have noticed much too easily that we have agreed something here among ourselves, and it is better if he doesn't notice anything."

9

When all the purchasing was over at last, Don Remigio said to the tendero: "Let me just have a look at the account book."

The tendero turned the book round so that it was in front of Don Remigio. The contratista went through the pages and shook his head. Turning the book round again, he shrugged his shoulders and assumed a thoughtful expression.

The tendero commented: "Yes, I find it remarkable too; there has never been so little bought on account in a new contract. Is there something wrong, perhaps? What do you think about it, Don Remigio?"

"What can be wrong, then, I should like to know?" answered the contratista. But there was an uncertain sound in his words which Don Hilario, the tendero, interpreted rightly; for he came to the conclusion: "I don't believe there's anything to worry about. The men are willing and obedient, and if sometimes they have their aguardiente and take too much now and again, they are as contented as the angels in heaven."

"That, Don Hilario, is just what attracted my attention. They've hardly taken any aguardiente. It's hardly worth mentioning. Other times, when I started a new contract, they could never get enough liquor. They really wanted to cart off whole barrelfuls into the jungle. Give me a good strong one now. No, not just a thimbleful, Dios mío, give me the whole tumblerful. A teaspoonful is just not worth the trouble of picking up."

Don Remigio tossed the whole drink down, grunted, shook himself, went halfway out of the tienda, and stood there, looking thoughtfully over the group of men who were lying down at their ease and chatting to one another.

"Hey, you!" he shouted at the lad lying nearest to him. "What's your name then?"

"Luis Campos, a sus órdenes, patroncito."

"Come here!"

The young man, who had got up off the ground when he was asked his name, fell in front of Don Remigio.

"Would you like a trago, a good drink?"

"Just as you like, patroncito."

"Pour him out a copita, Don Hilario, the ordinary stuff," said the contratista to the tendero.

The lad put the whole glass down in one gulp, wiped his mouth with the flat of his hand, and said, making a little bow: "Muchas gracias, patroncito!" And straightaway, after waiting a few seconds for new instructions, he began to slip off in such a smart way that one got the impression he wanted deliberately to avoid some task.

But Don Remigio did not bother any more about the young man. He watched him go back to his pack without calling him back and without explaining why he had called him up and asked his name. He looked after him with vague eyes which stared not only past the young man but over the whole gang, as they lay there, as if there were nothing there but air.

He turned to Don Hilario: "Give me another big glass. I can't get my wretched dry throat wet today. Caray, I should like to know what's wrong with me. I'm not what I was, believe me, Don Hilario. The calentura, the damned paludismo, jungle fever—it's got right inside me, and that goddam poison just won't leave me. That's what my trouble is. I'm afraid this is the last contract I shall run."

"Yes, I know, Don Remigio. How many last contracts have you actually run already?" Don Hilario laughed as he spoke. The contratista looked at the tendero, laughed too, pulled up his belt, squared his shoulders, pushed his revolver to the front, went one pace toward the door, and shouted to the resting men: "Los, adelante, boys! Over to the bodega!"

10

The gang began to move. The young men got up, threw the straps of their packs over their shoulders, and marched in the direction Don Remigio pointed with his arm, over to the bodega.

The bodega was the store in which all the equipment, harnesses, clamps, chains, climbing irons, axes, machetes, and other tools used in the montería were stored. The manager of the bodega was Don Mariano Tello, an employee of the Company, who kept the stocks in order with the help of two Indians, kept the camp's books, and, when there was nothing to do in the sheds, supervised the work of the smiths and the harnessmakers. He always had plenty of spare time, and so in the first week of each month he was asked to help with the drawing up of the monthly accounts.

The books had to be kept, and it often occurred to the administrator that a monthly account was demanded by the Company's headquarters at Villahermosa only when he remembered that he was already in the middle of the last week of the month and no entries, or only one or two, had been made since the first of the month. Then a positive storm broke out in the Oficinas from six in the morning to nine in the evening, to prepare the monthly report. And that was the work in which the bodega manager had to play a big part, helping to sort out three weeks of the office staff's idleness. Every time the clerks, accountants, and other staff found themselves sitting before a huge, neglected mountain of files, minutes, notes, shavings of mahogany with figures and hieroglyphics scratched on them, as happened in every last week of every month, they swore they would work more steadily next month and never let a day go by without having every entry, every settlement in the right place every evening.

But when, after much groaning and sweating, the monthly report had finally gone off with the post riders, they felt so exhausted that they had to rest for a whole week to recover their strength. During that week there was so much drinking, gambling, and whoring that the poor devils had to recover from their efforts in the week after and so couldn't do any work. So then they needed the last week of the month, in which as usual they had to work like supermen, to get the report ready.

That irregular pattern of work reached its highest degree during the rains. Then the riders could neither come nor go with the post, because the horses would be sunk in bogs and morasses. Such mountains of work piled up then that the papers and files filled a big room from floor to ceiling; every job was put back from week to week and from month to month, and they all comforted themselves with the thought that, on account of the eternal rain, it would not be possible to send any reports off, and no one could come from headquarters, and they could happily wait for the four or five monthly reports until they saw that the rainy season looked like it was coming to an end.

Although the number of jobs that the bodega manager had to cope with made a deep impression on everyone to whom an account of those jobs was given, it must still be said that the bodega man was able to lead a very tranquil life. Perhaps that was the reason why he behaved in such an uncommonly nervous and excitable way when a group of workers came to his bodega to ask for tools. Then he began to shout and swear at his two Indian youngsters in a way that could be heard over the whole country. The things were thrown to the workers with howls of rage, and if they were not quick enough to give their names he threw whatever he had in his hand in their faces.

First came the hacheros, the fellers. Every hachero received two good steel axes. Inferior axes could not be used on that iron-hard wood. The axes were entered on each man's account. The amount charged to the fellers for each ax was three times the price for which the ax could be bought in an ironmongery shop at the next railroad station, where, compared with the prices in the big towns, they were in fact already very dear. Of course, the feller brought the axes back after the expiration of his contract; even if they had been damaged in the course of his work, they would be credited to him on his account. Yet however carefully the men handled the axes, it was often quite unavoidable that one or even both their axes were lost. The jungle is no meadow, no cornfield, no cultivated pine forest. It can very easily happen that the ax flies out of the feller's hand and drops in a river or into a deep gorge that is so thickly overgrown that the man might thin out the bush all day and still not recover his ax. Or, during the rainy season, the ax could fall in one of the great morasses. If the feller had not seen precisely where the ax fell, it would take an all-day search, often a vain search, to find it. Quite often that cost the man his life, because in the course of his search in the bog he lost his footing on the soft ground.

After the hacheros came the macheteros, who each received two machetes, similarly on their account.

Then climbing irons were issued, which always called for a

particularly small line, because not every man used such irons every day, only under special conditions.

Although the prices of all their tools and equipment were substantially higher than the amounts asked in the towns, it cannot be said nevertheless that the prices were excessively unjust. Even a very strong and well-trained mule could hardly haul more than four meters of strong chain on those long trails through the jungle. Four picks or six axes generally made a good load for a beast.

It seemed unjust to make the workers personally responsible for the tools and equipment. But it should not be overlooked that, quite apart from the price, the tools were irreplaceable in the jungle. They were as precious there as the diamond for a well-borer or a coal miner. If the diamond breaks off, days have to be spent recovering it. If tools broke, the full amount of work could not be done; and, according to the season and the nature of the jungle tracks, it might be months before the lost tools could be replaced.

After the men had finally taken over all the tools and the manager of the store had howled for the tenth time that if a single man came to him with a complaint that his axes were too light or too worn or too blunt, he would shoot the man at once, and what's more he was dying of hunger and must have a good drink now it was evening, he shut the rough door with a padlock and said to the contratista: "If you need anything else, Don Remigio, come tomorrow morning."

"That suits me. I'm entirely of your opinion. I need a big drink just now. My throat is like an old dried-out hosepipe. Just feel it here, Don Mariano."

"I don't need to feel your gullet," answered Don Mariano in a sympathetic voice. "You should only look at the inside of mine. It's completely fossilized, and I can tell you, Don Remigio, if I don't soon get away from here and among civilized human beings, you can fix a chain round my neck and tie me to a tree. I can tell you in confidence, I'm well on the way to turning into a gorilla here. Believe it or not, in the last four months I've dreamt three times that I was a gorilla and thumped on my chest like crazy, and I've shouted in my sleep so loud that the two clerks who live in the same bungalow as me got up and poured a bucket of water over my head. I scared them so much in my sleep, they were afraid I'd eat them alive."

"And talking about eating, Don Mariano," said the contratista, "I'm enormously hungry. Apparently that goddam heathen of a Chinee has forgotten to ring for dinner."

As if the Chinese had only been waiting for that complaint, and perhaps felt it in the air that someone was going to yell at him, Where's the dinner tonight? he came out of his kitchen and swung the big handbell as a sign that all the caballeros should come to the comedor, the dining room, where he was ready to reveal what magic tricks he was capable of.

3

  Good food can cheer up a dreary existence with happy interludes, just as a good cook can make an unhappy marriage tolerable. In the La Armonía montería, however, even the food helped to dim life and to make residence and work there each as much of a penalty.

Two Chinese had taken over the catering for the staff in the Oficinas under a contract. Each employee paid one peso fifty centavos a day for three meals to be served to him by the Chinese.

No one expects the Chinese cooks in oil camps, in mining areas, in coffee, sugar, banana, henequen, cocoa plantations, in chicle camps and wherever else it might be, to show similar skill in preparing human food as, say, the chefs in big French restaurants. If you have to depend on those Chinese camp cooks, if you have worked in several camps and amassed a fair amount of experience, you pretty quickly come to the conclusion that Chinese cooks must surely all have their training in the same kitchen. In all camps, even if they are two thousand miles apart, there is always the same food, in the same form, in the same order, with the same taste, even with the same lack of salt or pepper in the same dishes. The bread those cooks bake in every camp, wherever it may be, has exactly the same greasy flavor. That greasy flavor comes from some oil or fat that is put in the dough to keep the bread firm, soft, and edible for a little longer in the tropical heat.

The food is always plentiful enough. So much must be said. For the price the Chink charges for providing the meals, he can't put caviar on the table, still less offer hors d'oeuvres with real salami, truffles, and liver paté. Even where three or even five pesos are paid for three meals, he can only put the usual food on the table, because the prices he has to pay for the ingredients are so uncommonly high that his own contribution is only a little higher in order to stay within one peso fifty centavos a day. Those Chinese become prosperous only through their skill, their patience, and through an economy in their trade so skillfully devised that the famous feeding of the five thousand with five loaves and two fishes can surely not be regarded as a miracle.

It was just the same there as it was in all other camps: the two Chinese limited their purchase of goods to the minimum. Anything they could produce themselves, they prepared in such time as was left them in the intervals between cooking. They grew all the vegetables themselves in a little bit of field, which took a third of their working time to water. They kept hens and pigs and goats. They had brought them all through the jungle by themselves, with incredible trouble, not losing a single hen or kid. They could not allow themselves to sleep in peace at nights as they deserved but always had to watch over their hens and kids so that they were not stolen by the undesirables living in the camp.

At every meal there were biscuits, fresh hot soda biscuits such as are to be found on every table in America. At lunch and dinner there was always pie, warm puddings filled with pineapple or bananas or apple purée or plums. Where the Chinese got such things was a puzzle even to the members of the staff. Given the special conditions, the preparation of the nicest things was in any case possible only with help from canned goods. But there they were. And if it happened they weren't there, then there was a terrible row in the comedor. The cook was accused by the infuriated eaters of wanting to make himself a millionaire out of their hunger and misery. And they threatened that, if he didn't have a proper civilized meal on the table next day, they would tie both cooks to a long rope and duck them in the river until they turned green.

For breakfast, for the caballeros, that is to say the office staff and the contratistas, there was some kind of fruit, generally papayas, grown in the camp by the Chinese. If there were no papayas, maybe there was the heart of a young palm, gathered by Indian boys in the jungle. Or there was porridge. Or shredded wheat. Or one of the other kinds of the many American corn foods which are to be found on an American breakfast table and which enterprising American manufacturers disseminate in cans and packets all over North and South America, and have established so well that you can find some of those wheat or oat products even in the shops of the smallest Indian villages on the border of the jungle.

For the next course there followed a pair of eggs, fried or boiled or scrambled or as an omelet, made to order. Every wish was taken into account. After that came rice with braised cubes of dried meat. And then coffee, with canned milk, sweetened with raw sugar.

Many of the well-known canned goods, as well as coffee and sometimes also tea, were on sale in the tienda and could be bought there. But only when the cooks were severely embarrassed and positively had to have the things did they buy anything in the tienda. They ordered everything they needed for their kitchen from the traders, with whom they agreed on prices in advance.

Anyone who wanted them could also have frijoles, black

beans, for breakfast. There were frijoles at every meal. They formed the basis of every single meal, as they do everywhere in Latin America and in the greater part of the United States. In the States the dish differs from the same thing in Latin America only in that, every so often, besides the black beans there are also brown or white beans.

After breakfast the staff went to work, or pretended to do something they called work. Sometimes they went fishing in the river or shooting in the jungle. The booty was sold to the Chinese or to other inhabitants of the montería town.

But often the office staff worked harder. That was when they were given the job by the administrator of riding out to the distant semaneos to inspect and record the amounts of felled timber available. The semaneos, the areas deep in the jungle where the mahogany was felled, sometimes lay a full day's hard ride away from the Oficinas. So it could easily happen that the administrator or one of the staff, when he went to visit the semaneos, could be away for a week or more. For the administrator or the staff, riding on those inspections, although it did mean a certain vacation from the dreary monotony of life in the Oficinas, was a real torment.

2

The jungle looked just the same everywhere, with no sort of variety for the eye or the mind. In the thick, wet jungle vegetation the heat was more oppressive and more tiring than in the Oficinas. The dark green twilight, which never grew any lighter, weighed heavily on mind and spirit and gave one the melancholy feeling that everything on earth was pointless.

Even the great monkeys springing from branch to branch in the tops of the trees, which followed a rider, howling for half-hours at a time and throwing broken rotten branches down on him, lost any sort of interest for the rider after half a day, they were so common.

It was as good as impossible for the rider to talk with the Indian who accompanied him, because the young man spoke only Indian and the rider only Spanish and generally knew only the most essential Indian phrases and expressions. Not uncommonly, the administrator or the staff members came back from those rides broken in health forever, their bodies full of ineradicable fever and their minds half rotten with dislike of their work and general sluggishness of thought and movement.

Coming back from such a ride the empleado, the staff member, found the meals of the Chinese real gifts of God for a whole week, and the pineapple tarts which he had declared four weeks ago he couldn't smell without being overcome with disgust he now regarded as the most precious thing that Chinese or any other human art of cookery could conceive.

It may be assumed with justice that those rides actually helped the caballeros to accustom themselves to those permanently unchanging meals so greatly that they would probably have lost their appetite if the menus had ever been subjected to the slightest alteration. That was never to be feared, of course, because only in a serious attack of mental disturbance would the Chinese have been able to increase by one or two the ten recipes they knew how to follow.

3

The midday meal began with soup as the first course. The soup was always the same brew in its basic constituents, sometimes flavored with dried meat or with the meat of a wild boar or a wild turkey or a sacrificed hen, but often with fresh pork or goat's meat. Nonetheless, whatever kind of meat the soup was cooked with, it was always equally tasteless and watery, so that it would have been uncommonly difficult even for an expert to say for certain what animal or bird had imparted its basic qualities to the soup.

However, in order not to let this similarity be too evident, a frequent change took place in the solid component of the soup. This solid component was made, according to the day of the week, from rice, brown beans, tomatoes, noodles, or garbanzos, big peas which will never go soft. The Chinese also conjured up green vegetable soups, about whose origins all kinds of rumors circulated in the camp.

For the second course a pair of eggs was served. Each individual was asked, when the soup was served, how he would like his eggs. After the eggs a dried steak came to the table. This steak was so tough that it had to be cut into quite small pieces, which after a short but fruitless attempt at chewing were simply swallowed whole, in order at least to have them in the stomach and so give oneself the sensation of having eaten a steak. Often in fact there was wild game instead of the steak—a hen, a wild turkey or a kid.

If the eaters sometimes knew little about the origins of the green vegetable soup, they knew just as little in almost all cases about the origins of the dried meat and the fresh meat. The toughness of the dried meat could easily lead to the conclusion that it might well be the flesh of worn-out mules and asses which had trotted into the Kingdom of Eternity by themselves and were found soon enough before they were too cold to be used as healthy meat. Then there was the possibility of animals that had fallen and had had their throats cut a moment before they passed away. And finally there could still be mules and horses which perhaps had been attacked by a puma and which might have defended themselves well enough to get back near the camp and receive the coup de grace there.

With all well-salted dried meat it is hard to say what sort of animal it comes from. If the taste seemed suspicious to the men eating it, they generally called out to the Chinese: "Mira, Chinkies, what dismal sort of meat is it today? Surely you haven't bumped off an old mule?" On which the Chinese held up his hasty serving routine, clapped his two hands over his breast, smiled the beautiful smile of a contented fat Buddha and said: "Caballelos, oh gentlemen, don't you know this exquisite meat? What a sin against the pleaching of Confucius! That is the meat of a totally good stlong wild boar. A plesent flom heaven in this dly bit of land. Another nice slice flom the leg joint, caballelos?" To go with it there was white bread and hot soda biscuits. Also tomatoes as salad. And rice with chiles. On rare occasions a little plate of highly economically laid out pieces of potato or baked potato slices.

After that came the inevitable black beans, either whole or ground and warmed up as a mash, known as frijoles refritos. Whatever had been missing until then for the healthy filling of the stomach was made up with the frijoles. They were the heart of the meal, as of every other meal of the day.

The water that stood on the table in clay pots was plain water scooped out of the river. It was often yellowish, often reddish, and often it was greenish. It was drunk just as it had come from the river. If anyone had suggested boiling the water or filtering it in some way, it would have been taken for granted that he had a screw loose. The glass of aguardiente that was quickly put down after the coffee was just as good as boiling and filtering the water. And if this old camp means was refused, there was plenty of room a kilometer away from the camp where the water-drinkers who had refused that form of filtration could be buried. But never mind about such trivialities, it all comes out the same in the end.

After the frijoles came the pineapple tart or banana tart or a tart made with some kind of jam whose origin remained as obscure to the eater as the origin of the green vegetable soup and some of the dishes made from dried wild boar meat. The piece of tart was washed down with a glass of cold tea or hot coffee. The tea was offered by the Chinkie with "Té helado, caballelo?" That was meant to mean: "Iced tea." But since there was no ice, the tea so boasted of was lukewarm. With half a lemon and a lot of sugar it acquired some flavor. The wise man preferred hot coffee with a good dash of American canned milk and two or three huge pieces of raw sugar.

When even that was ended, the luncher grunted, stretched, wheezed, yawned, lit a cigarette, staggered out into the shade of the overhanging roof of his bungalow, and there collapsed in his hammock.

4

At that time of day they had at least some excuse for not working; for what idiot will ever be so demented as to sit over account books in such tropical heat? The books would have gone soft all through from the rivers of sweat that streamed off their foreheads.

After a peaceful sleep of three or four hours the tormented clerks got up from their swinging hammocks and, first of all, put back a good quarter of a bottle of aguardiente with the observation that they must wash the sleep out of their stomach and at the same time disinfect the water they had swallowed.

Then they wandered a little around the camp, just to find out whether all the women were safe and sound. You had to be concerned with their availability on account of the long evenings. Reassured, they strolled back to the main buildings and now began seriously to sit in front of their books. After everyone had opened his book, he grumbled for a while, then lit a cigarette and sharpened the indelible pencil which he had finally started to use. When the indelible pencil was ready for use, the clerk remembered that there were other things necessary for a proper digestion as well as disinfecting the stomach. He found himself an old newspaper and marched over to the smallest room where he decided to read the paper in peace and with serious interest, so as to be properly informed on the political events that had taken place in the world four months ago. For that was the latest paper he had. And because it was already four months old, the reader did not react to it and so his healthy digestion was not damaged.

Every one of them spent an hour on those necessary and interesting occupations. But if the newspaper was full of a long murder story or a provocative marriage drama, another two hours were devoted to the care of the digestion. One must honor and respect one's body as long as one possesses it; for once it has passed on, there is no longer any point in worrying about one's digestion.

Leaving the smallest room, the empleado noticed that it was getting dusk, so it must soon be six o'clock. He had to work until six. That was in his contract.

So now he hurried back to the office where one or two of his colleagues seemed to have already tried to do the same sort of work, and had only waited until there was a loo free to be able to bring themselves up to date on politics at home and abroad.

Once he was back the man became very active. He wrote in his book like mad, hurled notes and files all over his desk, and swept all the papers together, so that if the administrator came in at that moment he could observe with satisfaction the industriousness and endurance of his subordinate.

The administrator was seldom to be expected any earlier. He had his own office, separate from the others. However, whether he worked in his office under the strain of all his intellectual gifts or occupied himself with this or that or the other of his hobbies while summoning up all his physical qualities, it was not one of his subordinate's jobs under his contract to look into that. That was what the administrator was there for; he had the right to decide for himself which of his duties had to be fulfilled most urgently, and at what time.

And it went without saying, however remarkable it may seem to the innocent, that it was always at the very moment when the administrator came into the office and found all his staff writing furiously in the account books with thick sweat pouring from their hot red foreheads, and he could be satisfied with such discipline and such keenness, that the handbell was rung with whose tempting notes the Chinee called the caballeros to dinner.

4

"We'll finally get something in our bellies," said Don Remigio to Don Mariano. "I couldn't drink more than just a cup of coffee at lunchtime. I couldn't spare the time, I wanted to get the men organized first."

"We can wash our hands here," said Don Mariano, as he walked up to a rough wooden stand with an enamel bowl of water standing on it; a piece of ordinary yellow soap lay beside it and a badly washed, grey hand towel was hanging over a rail.

The two caballeros washed their face and hands, combed their hair with a pocket comb, and went on to the comedor.

The dining room was a big room under a palm roof. Three sides of the room had the usual walls of thin tree trunks bound together. The fourth side was only partly closed. The greater part was open.

In the middle stood a long, roughly made table of thick mahogany planks—they ought really to be called boards. The boards were unplaned, only hacked. On each of the long sides there was a long bench, also of mahogany and just as roughly made. The floor was deeply covered with zacate, long jungle grass. As a result one could walk in the comedor as if on a very thick, soft carpet. Under the zacate, on the naked earth, lay a thick layer of ash, to hinder reptiles and insects from creeping in.

On the walls, partly attached with big wooden pegs, partly stuck to the posts with chewing gum, hung bright posters of cigarette factories, breweries, comiteco distillers, the remains of out-of-date calendars from business firms in the bigger towns, a framed picture of Nuestra Señora de Guadalupe, of the Mother of God, and three unframed and badly torn pictures of Saints Anthony, James, and John the Baptist.

All those decorations owed their presence to the artistic sensitivity of the two Chinese, who over the years since they first had the restaurant—café, they called it—had gradually decorated the walls in that style.

Stretched all over the dining room were red, green, yellow, and blue paper garlands which had been hanging there since the Señor Administrador's last birthday, when a huge banquet had been held in the room, with dancing and all the rest that occurs on such occasions. Those garlands had caused a lot of work and cost the Chinese no end of money; they looked pretty and gave a friendly atmosphere to a room otherwise so dull, and a better appetite to those who ate there. So they had been allowed to stay hanging, and everyone was content. With time they would wear out and fall down by themselves.

There was a green oilcloth on the table, so worn at the corners and the edges that you could stick your hands into the holes. This tablecloth gave the staff at their meals three opportunities a day to complain about the miserliness of the Chinese, and the Chinese had to accept it as they served them. And every time one of the employees declared that he would certainly pull the cloth off after the meal and burn it in front of the comedor, because he had had enough of the disgusting thing and wanted at last to see another cover in front of him, in another color, the Chinee said: "Velly good, caballelo, muy bueno, then eat off the bare table. I ordered a new cloth ten months ago, I swear that by all my most honolable and noble ancestors. But when the petaches, the calavans, don't bling the cloth, what can I do about it? It's the fault of fate and of plovidence, not my fault."

"Shut your jaw, Chinkie," called Don Leobardo across the table. "Bring that lousy pastel at last and the coffee, or else we'll be sitting here in three hours' time. And if you don't get a new tablecloth soon, goddam it, I'll tear your hide off you and have it tanned and laid on the table so that we can have a decent tablecloth at last."

2

The caballeros settled down comfortably at the table. The younger employees hitched their uncomfortable chairs nearer, after the Chinese had put plates of hot soup in front of them.

Don Leobardo looked at the contratista who was sitting next to him and said in a soft voice, as if he found it hard to speak: "Gentlemen, yes, I mean you down there, we do not want to overlook the customs and usages of civilized woodcutters even under these very difficult conditions, in the loneliness of the tropical jungle, surrounded by tiger cats, mountain lions, and wild Indians. Please, gentlemen, tonight we have a guest among us, Don Remigio. Maybe we should take care for a while at least that we have trousers on, even if filthy dirty, and not go about in shirts like the Caribs."

Irritated by the inconvenience, the young clerks concerned took their widely stretched arms off the table. One of them said to his neighbor, half aloud: "Oh shit, the old man's going to play the mouth organ again." Then they gulped down their soup after breaking their bread into it to give it a bit more solid consistency.

"You will be most surprised, Don Remigio, at the great news I am going to announce," said Don Leobardo.

Everyone sitting at the table listened.

"I really ought to know any news before you do, Don Leobardo. I was talking to Don Ramón and Don Gabriel two days ago, the ones who got me the new men for the contract. They didn't say anything about any special news."

"They didn't know about it. I've had it in a letter from the Company."

"Then you must have had it here for some days, Don Leobardo."

"Right, but there hasn't been the right occasion to talk about it before.—The Company has sold the montería."

Everyone sitting at the table, even Don Remigio, forgot to put the mouthful they had forked into their mouth.

After a moment the contratista asked: "Sold it to whom?"

"To the three Montellanos."

"To those coyotes?" said Don Remigio, astonished.

"Yes, to those robbers. What do you say to that?"

"What's the Company up to?"

"The directors of the Company have decided to reorganize themselves completely. I take it they have a first-class political nose. They certainly smell something. Maybe that old fogey up there, the dictator, is tottering on his little chair and the Company wants to withdraw from the concession in time. If new rulers take over it could easily happen that the concessions and contracts approved by the dictatorship will be declared invalid and a new agreement won't be given to the previous concessionaires, or only under new conditions."

"Don't worry," said Don Rafael, the senior accountant. "Don't worry, caballeros, that old cacique up there is sitting more firmly in the saddle than ever before, especially now he's begun to take on new men with modern ideas and to give more liberty to people who are against the dictatorship."

"The best sign that the old fox sees his glory beginning to fade," said Don Leobardo. "That's just the reason why now, at the last moment, he wants to prop up the collapsing structure with new pillars. It's too late; and I think the Company knows more than it lets us think. The state of Tabasco, especially the capital, San Juan Bautista, has always been rebellious against the old guy. I shouldn't wonder if it began to burn in San Juan Bautista overnight."

"Then is the Company withdrawing from the caoba trade altogether?" asked Don Remigio.

"I presume so."

"What can those three Montellanos pay with?"

"They've made a heap of money as contratistas, on the other side of the river."

"Yes, I believe so." Don Remigio nodded and picked at his food. "I've never met such brutal contratistas as those Montellanos. The poor men who fall into their hands have good reason to say that they know what devils are like and don't need to go to hell to find out. A man can make a fortune easily enough in a couple of years like that. But I shouldn't want to have that fortune on my conscience."

"I know them," Don Leobardo told him. "I know them from the time I was administrator at the La Costancia. The Montellanos were contratistas in El Rompido, near our montería. That any man from their contracts ever got home alive I just can't believe. Of course, it was so only because they butchered their men without mercy or compassion. I'm convinced that no other contratista in the country has got through so many men as those three have. Every month the agents brought up new gangs, and every one was taken by the Montellanos because they were always short of men. When a new gang arrived, half of the last gang taken on by the Montellanos were already decaying under the ground."

"One thing I do know, Don Leobardo," said Don Remigio, "if it's really true that the Montellanos have bought the Company, I'm not going on with them. They can pay me my expenses for the contract and they can have the men. But I won't work with them and help to make a fortune for them. Dios mío, I've just been waiting until I could decide to get out of the monterías with credit and run a decent business in a town among civilized people. At last I shall make my wife and children happy, being there all the time. As things are now my wife is a widow, my children are orphans. Now I've got a good reason to finish with it here. Now I don't need to believe that I'm retiring from this business because I'm about to collapse and can't take it any more. I could take it well enough for another three years. And the money I could earn in those three years would be welcome enough. But to work with the Montellanos, no señor, sooner with demons."

"The firm is already established in San Juan Bautista," Don Leobardo revealed. "It's called Montellanos Hnos, Montellanos Brothers. Fine brothers!"

"I'm convinced they aren't really brothers," said Don Mariano. "I know them well enough and I'm sure they're not brothers. Each of them speaks a different Spanish dialect. They're Spaniards, but each from a different province. So their brotherhood is most suspicious."

"But very convenient," Don Rafael intervened.

"Well said, Don Rafael, very convenient!" laughed the administrator.

"What will you do now, Don Leobardo?" asked the contratista.

"I'll stay with the Company. They've already offered me a new position, with more salary. The Company has a big henequen plantation in Yucatán. You'll be able to meet me there in my new office, gentlemen," said Don Leobardo, turning to the whole table. "If any of you wants to come with me, you may tell me."

The employees had not completely recovered from the astounding report.

"You can't all come with me," Don Leobardo told them. "It would depend on how many office staff and how many field managers I need. But there is room enough for all of you. The Company has taken over two banana plantations from the Montellanos as part payment; the Company also owns four banana plantations of its own, and two cocoa plantations. If any of you doesn't want to stay here, there are other good places he can get a job if he wants to."

"When are the Montellanos taking over the montería here?" asked Don Mariano, the stores manager.

"On the first of April. And you'll be interested to hear that the Montellanos have bought two other monterías and will be taking them over on the same date, La Estancia and La Piedra Alta."

Don Remigio rinsed his mouth out with a glass of water, gurgled, spat the water out in a wide arc toward the door, and then said: "So it seems that the three noble brothers are thinking of setting up a monopoly here."

"It doesn't only seem so," said the administrator, "it is so."

"One more reason, and the decisive one, gentlemen, why I cancel my contract with the Montellanos on the thirty-first of March. I'll accept what they offer for the men I have."

"Careful!" laughed the administrator. "They're offering you a quarter of what you paid for the men. But don't give in. Insist on the full amount and twenty percent more for your alleged loss. The brothers will pay what you ask. Without men they can't get anything going on the montería. They need men just as much as they need caoba. Without caoba no profit, without men no caoba. If you insist on it and say you'll take your men away to Quintana Roo and take over a chicle contract there unless they pay you the price you ask, the brothers will sweat blood and pay up without a word."

"That's right, Don Leobardo, they need my men more than I do. I'll arrange my price accordingly. Perhaps I'll make a good thing of my departure from La Armonía."

"So now at last we have a chance to think about having a

drink and celebrating the good fortune of our old friend Don Remigio, oiling him so that he can slip away better," said Don Leobardo with a loud laugh. He called the Chinese who had begun to clear away the glasses: "Chinkie, run over to my hut and bring the bottle of Añejo comiteco, the old stuff, understand. It's the bottle with a red capsule on the cork, the one not opened."

"I'm lunning, Don Leobaldo," said the Chinese and hurried out into the dark. He was back in a minute.

"I've been saving this bottle for some special occasion, caballeros," explained the administrator. "And that festive occasion has finally arrived: departure from the desert. La Armonía montería and Leobardo Chavero will never see each other again. Salud, caballeros!"

5

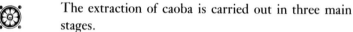 The extraction of caoba is carried out in three main
stages.

The first stage is the felling of the trees. A contratista
undertakes this work on his own account and at his own risk,
and with his own capital. He is independent, like an independent businessman. He delivers the trunks to the nearest dump
where he is paid ten pesos in gold for every ton, sometimes
rather more, sometimes less, according to the market price of
the timber. The field manager or the administrator of the camp
will show him the area within the concession where he must cut.
Every contratista works a different area, which is often two or
even three days' ride away from the Oficinas where the administrator and his staff have their headquarters.

The second stage is the floating off of the logs, an operation
conducted and supervised from the Oficinas. For from the
moment the logs are stacked ready for floating off, the contratista
has no more responsibility. The caoba now belongs to the
company.

The third stage is the arrangement and shipping of the timber
to the purchaser. Up to a certain point on the river the timber

floats freely. All the logs bear the brand of the company to which they belong; for all the companies, even if they have their monterías on a number of smaller streams, must finally use the same main river for rafting. At the last station, where there may be some motorboats on the river and the freely floating logs might damage the traffic, the logs are hauled out of the water and identified by the companies' representatives by their brands. There the logs are bound together to form great rafts and taken by highly skilled raftsmen to the seaport, where the rafts are broken down again until in due course they are loaded into ships. This third stage, beginning at the third station where the logs are floating freely, as far as the final loading, is conducted and supervised by the headquarters. The headquarters is found either in the seaport or in the nearest reasonably large town in the area.

2

The Montellano brothers, Severo Gurria Montellano, Félix Gurria Montellano, and Acacio Gurria Montellano, had decided when they bought the monterías that each of them would take on the manager's post of one of the three stages. Severo, the eldest, was to manage the third stage, the most important side of the business; Félix was to be administrator in the Oficinas, and Acacio, the youngest and most tireless, was to be the senior contratista and, as head of the contratistas, supervise their work.

The plan was good, even reasonable. But when it came to putting it into practice, there were so many obstacles that it simply could not be carried out. Don Mariano had mentioned in that conversation at table that he doubted whether the three brothers were really related to one another, with the same mother and the same father. As long as the three of them worked together, each as an independent contratista, they had always got on well. But now, when they had pooled all their money to buy monterías, they had become suspicious of one another.

Presumably they must have known one another well, have known what each was worth and what he had done, before they got together to become brothers. If one has a name that crops up fairly often in police reports, court cases, and prison registers, then one does very well, if only as a matter of self-preservation, to get rid of it and look for another which is less well known and well worn. Life after that is more comfortable, provided one doesn't find oneself facing the need to slough one's skin again. A new and usable name is always much more secure if you can produce a brother or a sister or, even better, a father. It may be that the three brothers Montellano had looked up the names of their parents in a telephone directory in Barcelona or Madrid and taken the name of those adopted parents when it was necessary in the course of business to win greater confidence. Of course, if the Montellanos' mother had suddenly come to Mexico she would certainly have been extremely surprised to discover three sons of whose existence she had not until then had the slightest inkling.

Because each of the three Montellanos knew very well why each of them had found it fruitful to become the brother of the other two, some mutual distrust might certainly not have been unfounded.

To leave Severo at the seaport as chief cashier, where he sold the timber and banked the money, while the other two sat deep in the jungle—that didn't appeal to those two greatly. Anyway, they didn't much care to be separated. To leave Félix by himself in the seaport was awkward because, as Severo and Acacio declared, in their opinion he did not understand business and would probably have sold the good timber for less money than it had cost. That was of course just an excuse not to have to say frankly that they could not trust him with all the cash.

Acacio, in the opinion of the other two, was too young and too inexperienced to be left alone in any case.

Finally, after long negotiations which had sometimes come

near to being settled with revolver shots, they agreed that all three should go to the jungle together to start by cutting enough wood. Then all three should float the wood down river together, and finally all three should settle in the seaport and look for the purchasers there.

That was a very extravagant division of labor. When all three of them were in the port, the contratistas could do what they liked, make a mistake about the wood with the company's brand and sell it to other companies, or even float it off on their own account, with the help of people who waited at the raft site for opportunities to get "wild" wood below the proper price.

What is more, the contratistas of other companies with concessions could break into the three brothers' concessions during their absence and fell trees for some months without being disturbed. It might also happen, while the three brothers were working in the jungle, that the price of caoba in the port rose very high and there were so many purchasers that it was possible to pick out whichever was paying the highest prices. And when the brothers finally reached the port to sell, the prices might be uncommonly low, with possibly not a buyer to be seen, and the timber would eat up more in storage costs than could be earned from it. Yet their mutual suspicion prevailed, and all three worked among the trees as contratistas as they had done before, only with one difference, that now the total profits went to them, and not only ten pesos in gold for every ton delivered, but thirty, fifty, eighty, perhaps as much as a hundred and twenty and even more per ton. Who could guess, who could foresee how high the price of caoba might rise?

3

It was not only that mistrust prevented the brothers from running the business as they had originally planned. The stocks of caoba already in port belonged to the Company and had not been included in the sale. The price the Company demanded for them had been too high for the Montellanos. The Company was strong enough to put off the sale of caoba until the price offered seemed most favorable to them.

The La Armonía montería was far from cheap when the Montellanos bought it. The district that included the concession for exploitation was big, about three thousand square kilometers of tropical forest. That the area of the concession was rich in caoba and, looked at closely, not greatly exploited, the brothers knew very well. As experienced contratistas they knew where the rich districts were. Long before they thought seriously about buying the montería, they had investigated the district through all the reports, so as not to buy a pig in a poke.

But there is more to a montería than just the concession. A montería, according to its size, has a hundred, two hundred, maybe three hundred oxen; it has horses and twenty or thirty strong mules used to plowing through swamps, and so very expensive. The buildings were part of it; however primitive they might be, they still represented a substantial value. The tienda belonged to it and had to be supplied with goods all the time. And the equipment for all sorts of operations, the axes, picks, machetes, chains, hooks, saddlery, yokes, field smithies, were of great value to the potential user. If a purchaser had not bought those items, the company selling the montería would have given them to him; for they would cost more to transport than they would fetch if sold in the nearest town. But the purchaser was helpless without that equipment and miscellaneous articles.

Severo Montellano, the eldest of the brothers, had not left the money he had earned as a contratista lying idle. He had lent it out. Of course he didn't lend his money to honest working planters but only to people whom he knew were gamblers or who would squander the money in some other way. He didn't lend his hard-earned money to get interest on it. That would not have been a high enough profit. He lent it with the idea that the ranch, the plantation, or the house where he lent it would deteriorate and so come into his hands. That was how he and his brothers, who had followed his advice and done the same thing, had come to possess the big banana plantation that had been given in payment when they bought the montería.

In that way they had succeeded in acquiring the montería for a price at which, reckoned in hard cash, the Company would never have sold. The Company had of course been relatively well paid by the transfer of the plantation as part of the price.

The ones who had bought far below the price were the Montellano brothers, who had been able to acquire plantations for a tenth of their true value and now gave those plantations in payment at their full value.

Since they had not taken over the Company's stock of wood in the port, the brothers now found they had no stocks of caoba at all which they were ready to sell and ship. That had been an additional reason why all three brothers had decided to go to the jungle, to start by building up new stocks of caoba. As long as there was no caoba in the harbor, they couldn't sell any.

It had of course been mentioned in the negotiations that sales at the port could be carried out by agencies, so that the three brothers could concentrate on production. But that same distrust they felt for one another they also felt about other people, in this case about the agents, who in the brothers' opinion were all swindlers; so it could work out that they would simply be working for the agents.

4

The Montellanos began their activities in the montería by first of all going very closely through the salaries of the office staff and then the pay of the manual workers, the caravan arrieros, and all the other people who were directly employed by the Company and belonged in the main camp. That included the assistants in the tienda and the stores; the youths who cleaned the bungalows for the staff and kept them tidy; the herds for the oxen, when the oxen were sent out to graze on the prairie; the canoe-men; the peons whose work was to till fields of maize and beans to feed the hundreds of men and boys who worked there; the peons who fed the pigs and goats to provide meat and in their spare time tanned and worked the skins of slaughtered animals to be able to use them for harnesses.

The pay for those peons varied between one real and six reales, or sixty-five centavos, per day. The pay of the manual workers was between seventy-five centavos and one peso sixty per day. The office staff received salaries in accordance with their activities, their experience, and their age, from sixty to two hundred pesos a month.

Although the wages and salaries might be described as very moderate, in view of the fact that the men had to live in the jungle and that every item of clothing, everything they needed from day to day, cost three times, five times, even ten times the normal price, the total amount spent in a year on salaries and wages was high enough to give the Montellanos a fright when they had worked them out. What is not paid is saved, and money you can keep in your pocket is money earned. That was how the Montellanos thought. And they went on to think: the quicker we stop this expenditure, the quicker we start saving and earning. The easiest and most certain way to reduce the expenses of a business is to cut down on salaries and wages. That hurts the cutter-down very little. As for those who don't like it, they can make their own arrangements.

When the office staff were informed of the cuts, they all made their own arrangements. They pointed out that they had a contract only with the Company, not with the new proprietors, that moreover their contract specified their salaries at definite levels, and if those salaries were not paid they had no obligation to observe their contract, even if the contracts were included in the sale.

The three brothers conferred and came to the conclusion that nothing would suit them better than the resignation of all the office staff. Those employees were idlers and spent their time drinking and whoring, and Don Severo could do all the work by himself. Reports and accounts would no longer have to be drawn up and sent off, because the three brothers themselves were the company and didn't need to write reports on themselves. Next time Don Severo went to San Juan Bautista he could look round, and he could maybe get hold of two or three half-starved vagabonds who would know how to deal with the books and accounts and would think themselves lucky if Don Severo promised them forty-five pesos a month. They couldn't eat three times a day for fifty centavos; once was enough. After long unemployment they would have got used to eating less; and if they still got hungry they could cook for themselves and go out hunting sometimes. He, Don Severo, would give them such a fascinating description of life in a montería, deep in the jungle, surrounded by tiger cats, pumas, great apes, and herds of tasty wild boars, that they would almost be willing to work for nothing to be able to lead the life of Robinson Crusoe.

So the question of the office staff was solved. The main question, a substantial one, the biggest problem that they had on pay, was cleared up and could be recorded as their first profit. Don Severo, whom his two brothers willingly granted to have the best head and the greatest skill in dealing with financial problems and always solving them in their favor, now took on the pay lists of the manual workers and peons.

The three brothers discussed which of the manual workers and peons could most easily be dispensed with. When those men had been identified they were called, and Don Severo told them the outcome of their discussion. They did not seem to take it as too great a tragedy. That struck Don Severo as suspicious, for those men lived from hand to mouth and would be hardly better off in the town than they were here.

"How much pay have you still got due you?" asked Don

Acacio, the youngest and least experienced of the three brothers. He had been given the job of sacking the men whom Don Severo and Don Félix had described as superfluous. The first man said twenty pesos, another said twelve, a third eighteen. Don Acacio wrote a comprehensive check for the men, and Don Severo signed it.

It was remarkable how quickly the men arranged their packs and got on the march. They were just leaving when Don Félix looked at his brother Don Severo and then said to him, shouting: "Pero hombre, you stupid idiot, have you checked in the tienda to see whether these men have got a great mass of credits and advances, and now they're disappearing with them?"

"Damn and shit!" roared Don Severo. With one jump he was outside and two seconds later he was with the little group.

"Stop there, you bloody robbers, where is that check? Let's have the check or I'll shoot the lot of you like lame bloody rabbits!"

The men put on an ignorant air, as if they had never known anything about a check.

But then Don Acacio came up to them, went up to one man and yelled at him: "You, you stinking dog, you've got the check. Give it here!"

He had drawn his revolver as he ran up and now held it pressed against the man.

"I haven't got the check anymore, jefe," said the man. "I gave it to Eulalio."

"Eulalio! Eulalio!" shouted Don Severo across the square.

From one of the drinking huts a woman staggered, her filthy cotton blouse hanging down in rags. She was well under the influence. Her hair had obviously not been combed for days.

When she heard them shouting the name of Eulalio, some recollection clearly stirred in her. She put both hands on her hips, bent over to give her lungs more strength, and then bellowed out: "Eulalio, that cabrón, that incestuous beast. I still have to pay for his drink here that he boozed with all those other women."

"Hold your goddam filthy tongue," shouted Don Félix.

"Hold my tongue?" screamed the woman and stuck her tongue right out. "Me, hold my tongue? That son of a whore has got the money and he's halfway to Hucutsin already on his horse."

"What's that you say? Chinga tu matrícula, puta vega!" shouted Don Acacio and ran over to his horse, where it was tethered to a tree trunk.

"Ugh, puta vega, me?" the woman screamed back at him. "You'll get nothing out of me, tu puto." She swung round, lifted her skirts right up to her shoulders and shouted: "Come here, then, if you want a taste. You call me a puta vega? I have to hear that said about me by a green son of a whore like you!" She turned her head round to see whether anyone was accepting her invitation, indeed whether anyone was looking. But nobody took any notice. Things like that happened ten times a day, every day, and had lost all charm of novelty. When she turned round too far so that she could see every corner from behind, she lost her balance, fell over, and lay there in front of the entrance to the hut with her skirts pulled right up.

Don Acacio needed less than a minute to saddle his horse. Then he leaped madly into the saddle and disappeared into the undergrowth.

In the evening he brought Eulalio back. He had taken the check off him on the path where he caught up with him. He took the check to Don Severo who looked at it and then tore it up.

5

The two brothers who had stayed behind, Don Severo and Don Félix, had spent the rest of the afternoon most of all on the accounts of the men who worked in the camp, checking on the advances made to them. They knew their brother Don Acacio well enough to know that he would bring the check back all right, even if it involved a murder or even two. And if Don Acacio himself was found murdered, he would have the check as certainly as if it had never left his hand. The man was not yet born who had stolen a check from the Montellanos and been able to get away with it, cash it in peace, and enjoy the money.

"There simply isn't a single man in the whole camp who isn't deep in hock to us," said Don Severo when he got to the end of checking the accounts.

"We couldn't really expect anything better." Don Félix leaned back in his chair. "Anyone of the whole gang that's superfluous, he's fired."

"You don't mean that literally," Don Acacio intervened.

"Of course not."

"Anyone who isn't needed here anymore can earn his living working on the trees. And when he's wiped off every centavo and not borrowed anymore, then he can go."

"That's what I meant. That's exactly what I thought, Severo," said Don Félix. "We didn't come here to do good deeds and give away liquor to drunks. We came here to work."

Don Acacio went over to the door and looked over at the bungalows of the office staff. "I hope they'll leave tomorrow. I need a bungalow of my own."

"Day after tomorrow, cachito. Day after tomorrow they'll be off with their nags and their pricks. Let's hope they don't take all the whores with them and leave us at least a couple of the better ones." Don Severo poured himself a comiteco and put it down in one.

Just as Don Acacio was filling his glass, Don Julián came into the bungalow in which the three brothers had installed their Oficinas and their bedrooms for the time being.

"Good evening, caballeros," he greeted them. "I wanted to ask you to come to dinner if you are ready."

"Muchas gracias," said Don Severo, speaking for all three. "We should just like to wash our hands."

Don Acacio, who still had the comiteco bottle in his hand, invited Don Julián: "Stick a good drop of hooch behind your teats first."

"I can use that to make me look contented," said Don Julián, laughing.

When he had drunk, he chuckled. Then he gave a loud belch, looking quite delighted.

"Caray, damn it, that's better than the scrubbing brushes we have to swallow."

"Give yourself another, amigo," cried Don Severo. "If that's all, we haven't got anything else either but what the Turks bring. How often do the Turks come anyway?"

"Every three months," said Don Julián. "Often it can be as much as five if the road is too bad."

"Ready, you two?" Don Severo asked his two brothers, who were doing their hair with a pocket comb. "Bueno, off we go then."

6

    In the comedor, where the caballeros ate, the Chinese had laid two more rough tables, because not everyone who had come to dine that night could sit at the one table that was usually there.

At the two tables, which had been set sideways against the ends of the main table, sat the office staff, while the administrator sat with the contratistas at the big table, where he had had three places left free for the Montellanos.

When the three brothers came in, with a "Buenas noches, caballeros," the administrator was at the washstand by the entrance, washing his hands.

"Chinkie," he called to the Chinese, "show the caballeros their places."

With his bespattered apron the Chinese wiped one seat clean on the one bench and two seats on the other bench by the long table. He did it as if he were taking pains not to wipe off any more dust than had settled on the one bench and the two seats opposite. That he wiped the three seats at all was more to show the three newcomers where they should sit than to display any special politeness to them.

The three brothers sat down. Don Severo, as the eldest, sat next to the administrator, while the other two brothers sat opposite those two caballeros.

Some of the contratistas and some of the senior members of staff, the chief accountant and the stores manager, had already taken their places at the table some time before. It seemed that a good number of the men had already eaten half an hour ago, or even longer, and had been chatting, for the room was absolutely full of tobacco smoke, even though the wall was half open.

While Don Leobardo dried his hands and combed his hair, he shouted through the opening in the wall: "Hey, Chinkie, listo! Bring the food, and if it's not de primera tonight, very very good, then tomorrow morning I'll break all your pots and pans over your head."

"Glacias, Don Leobaldo," called the Chinese from the kitchen, "many thanks for the tlouble. But the food the velly best that I ever cooked in all my life."

"Lucky for you!" shouted Don Mariano, the stores manager. "Lucky for you, Chinkie, I'm telling you. If it's not the best on our farewell day, then you won't see the sun rise tomorrow. I'll have you shot and leave your skeleton to rot in the selva, in the darkest spot in the jungle."

The Chinese put the first plate on the table, went over to Don Mariano, bent over him confidentially, and said, his two hands crossed over his chest: "You can shoot me, Don Maliano, nothing I can do to stop that. But you can't leave my skeleton to lot in the selva."

"Oh, and why not, hijo celeste, son of heaven?"

The Chinese laughed mischievously, raised his eyebrows high, wagged his forefinger without taking his hands off his chest, and said: "No, Don Maliano. You see, I have bought an insulance and paid all the plemiums in advance; and if you shoot me here, then the insulance in San Flancisco will send my bones to

China, to buly them beside my most venelable ancestors with evely honor. It is all paid."

"Hell and the devil, you cursed Chink, will you now serve the soup at last! Or shall I first swing a club up between your legs?" shouted Don Leobardo and banged angrily on the table with a spoon.

"Estoy volando, Don Leobaldo, I'm flying."

When he came in with the next plates of soup, Don Severo took his arm and drew him nearer.

"Do you know, Chinee, your soup is very good." Don Severo and his brothers had already begun to spoon it up without waiting until everyone at the table had been served. "Muchas glacias, caballelo, many thanks."

At last everyone had gotten their soup. Don Severo had actually reached the end of his when the Chinese brought the last plate. Now the Chinese stood behind the diners for a little while, waiting to take away the first empty plates. Don Severo turned round to him and said: "Chinee, you can stay here as cook."

"I don't think so, caballelo. There's only thlee of you, and that way I can't earn enough to feed myself. I think I go to Yucatán with Don Leobaldo and open my new café on the henequen plantation." He picked up the three brothers' plates and took them quickly into the kitchen.

The contratistas and the office staff gave him a look, then glanced surreptitiously at the brothers to see what sort of expression they had assumed. The Chinese had said that he would have to cook only for three if he stayed, and that meant that no contratista and no office staff had the prospect of staying to work with the three brothers.

The brothers behaved as if they had not grasped that. Or maybe they had realized already that everyone there would leave.

2

There was very little talking during the meal. There was just the noise of champing, the clatter of the utensils, and occasional requests to pass the salt or the ketchup or some other sauce, and now and then one picked up a half-lost sentence about some incident in the camp.

On other days the men got up straight after eating and went over to their bungalows or the drinking huts. Often they just sat there, to gamble or chat in an idle way.

Today, however, everyone remained sitting at the table. Though not a word had been uttered about it, everyone knew that a discussion would now take place. The contratistas, who came to the Oficinas only for a few days every three months, each in his own time when it was most convenient to him, had all come together today without having been sent for. They knew that today the brothers were coming and would be taking over the montería.

At first sight it looked as if the contratistas had all come together on the same day from their remote districts, to be able to greet their new proprietors and receive their instructions.

But it was not like that.

There was nobody there who did not know the three Montellanos; and even the most junior members of the staff, who had never seen any of the brothers in person, knew their reputation, their activities, and their greed. The Montellanos were intolerable as colleagues or as fellow contratistas. Yet to have them as superiors, as directors and proprietors of the company they worked for, that was something everyone who had ever heard of them would refuse.

The Company had four contratistas who, with their men, produced mahogany for the Company. All four had refused to continue in their contracts. The Montellanos didn't ask any of the four to stay and work for them. To start with, they knew that would be useless. Second, and this was the decisive factor, they were only too glad to accept that no contratista would remain. They themselves were experienced contratistas and needed no one to help them. They had already made their plans to run the montería in such a way that all the money they would have to pay to the contratistas went into their own till. The only thing that now remained to be settled with the contratistas was the annulment of their contracts. What the Montellanos were interested in was to take over their contracts as cheaply as possible. That they, the brothers, were so greatly disliked for their brutality, their greed, and their quarrelsomeness, half hated, half feared, they did not consider to be a disgrace or even a disadvantage but rather a very valuable advantage for their negotiations. None of the contratistas would work under them, each one of them wanted to cancel his contract, and because he wanted to cancel it the Montellanos knew that it was quite possible they would be able to buy the contracts cheap.

The discussions that had been arranged during the afternoon, in the presence of the administrator, Don Leobardo, were all about the price they should demand. They had decided to adhere firmly to their prices and not to give way.

3

For a quarter of an hour after dinner only small matters were talked of at table. Everyone knew these were only embarrassed conversations to allow the heart of the discussions to mature.

But then Don Severo could no longer apprehend why he had come to dinner here anyway. He could just as well have eaten in his bungalow alone with his brothers. "Don Remigio," he said suddenly, in the middle of a trivial conversation about the harbor traffic at El Carmen, "Don Remigio, have you drawn up your contract for me?"

"Certainly, Don Severo." Don Remigio produced his account book and a number of lists. "I have here all the names of the men I have in my contract. After each single name you will find what the man cost me, how much he has taken out on his account in the meantime, how much he is paid each day, and how much he has earned up to the day of the takeover—tomorrow, that is. The individual contracts of each man, with the names of the guarantors and the stamp of the municipality, the administrator has in his Oficina."

"Bueno, Don Remigio?" asked Don Severo.

"I have eighty-nine men in my contract. The muchachos' total debt today, after deducting the pay they've earned, is twelve thousand two hundred forty-seven pesos. The stock of caoba that I've got comes to eighty-seven hundred pesos in round figures. Far more has been felled, some six hundred tons, but I won't include those because they have not yet been hauled."

"So that would be altogether, Don Remigio?"

"Altogether twenty-seven thousand nine hundred forty-seven pesos."

As Don Remigio was speaking, Don Severo had scribbled the figures down on a piece of paper.

"That's right, Don Remigio," said Don Severo, and drew in a thick full-stop behind the last figure he had written. "That would be what I have to pay you, then."

"A bit more," said Don Remigio.

"What, more still?" broke in Don Félix.

"You keep quiet, understand?" Don Severo snapped at him.

"It's my money too," Don Félix defended himself.

"Your money, shit! It's mine too, and Cachito's. And keep your mouth shut!" the elder brother shouted at him. "Just be glad you're here with us and can listen when people who understand something about money discuss it with each other."

Then he lit a cigarette.

As soon as dinner was over Don Leobardo had several bottles of comiteco brought over from the tienda, and drinks were continually poured from them.

Don Severo now gave himself a huge glassful and put it down

in one gulp. The bottle went round, and if it didn't arrive anywhere in time, the thirsty folk poured out from one of the other bottles. The younger employees, out of politeness to the older caballeros, always cried "Salud!" before they drank. The contratistas and the three brothers thought that unnecessary because they didn't want to waste time. Drink when you want to drink, and don't talk too long. It does no good to you or anyone else.

When Don Severo had belched loudly and then grunted, he said, as if he had not heard properly: "What did you say, Don Remigio? A bit more? What bit more is that?"

"That is surely very simple to understand, Don Severo. Twenty percent extra on the total, for the payoff."

"I should pay you twenty percent more? But, man, we're not meeting here to commit blackmail, extortion, against each other."

Don Remigio shrugged his shoulders. "There's no blackmail there. I've had the trouble of getting the men here. Of course the agents get them down here, but without my instructions, without substantial expenditure by me, there wouldn't be a man here. I have to train the men; none of them know anything about work in a montería."

"No reason to demand twenty percent." Don Severo scribbled on the paper again.

"Maybe not," said Don Remigio, "but I will only settle for that amount. You can take it or leave it."

"I leave it," said Don Severo shortly. He paused a little while, hoping the contratista would begin to bargain. When no answer came, he asked: "What will you do with the men, then, that you're lumbered with?"

"Don't worry about that, Don Severo." Don Remigio laughed and reached for the bottle.

He uncorked the bottle and held it in his hand to pour out for himself. As he held it and twirled the glass round in his other hand as if he were wondering whether he should drink or not, he repeated: "No trouble. I'll go to Quintana Roo with my gang. Then I can get a chicle contract. I only need to say yes. The American chewing-gum firms are paying very good prices for chicle just now."

"That may be," Don Severo considered. "But the journey would certainly take four weeks, maybe five or six. I know Quintana Roo. During those six weeks you won't earn one crooked centavo. When you're on that long road and you come to villages, there's every chance that half your muchachos will walk out on you. And getting into chicle like that, overnight, as you think, that doesn't happen. You have to bargain with the jefes of the Indians there to be given districts. The negotiations could last three months before you can be sure of getting going. The jefes take their time, they're in no hurry, just waiting for the one who pays them the highest percentage. I know chicle, Don Remigio. And because I know it, that's why I'm here in caoba."

Don Remigio knew that Don Severo was right. He had hoped that Don Severo would be upset when he threatened to move off with the men. But the Montellanos weren't so easy to catch. They were Spaniards, and until today they had still not met any Mexicans who would have been smart enough to get so much as a peso out of the Montellanos' pockets without their agreement. Don Severo, apparently working out sums on his paper, kept a continual eye on Don Remigio. He felt that the moment had come when Don Remigio would become doubtful and begin to wonder whether he could not cut the chicle business short. It could very well happen that all the contracts had been awarded by the time he arrived in the area, and no districts were available where the profits might have been worthwhile; the districts he might get might be so deep in the jungle that he would have to search for the roads to them; then he would be without food and it would be several weeks before housing was put up and provisions obtained and production could be started. If there had been the occasional telephone or telegraph, he would have been able to make inquiries in advance. But since there were no means of acquiring such advance information, a contratista must run the risk of marching along with his men, to get either a fat contract or a mean one or even none at all. He had good connections with the big chicle buyers and agents, but they would only be useful at that moment if he could have telegraphed them. To send a messenger with letters took three, perhaps five weeks; and before the answer came another five weeks could have passed. Don Severo seemed to know all that very well, and that was why he had Don Remigio so well in his hands that he could play with him.

Don Severo stopped his scribbling. It was hard to guess whether he had really been working anything out or just putting a lot of figures down here and there, to create the impression that he had to calculate how much he could pay to the nearest centavo, while in fact he was only waiting for the moment that betrayed his opponent's weakness to him. Maybe not even his two brothers could have said exactly what he was doing and how he was thinking.

"Bueno, Don Remigio," he said now, throwing the pencil he had been writing with hard on the table top, "bueno, I pay you a round sum of twenty-five thousand pesos for your contract."

With the addition of twenty percent which the contratista had asked for, the amount he was expecting came to thirty-three thousand five hundred thirty-six pesos, so there was a difference of some eighty-five hundred pesos.

Severo did not wait for an answer. He pulled his checkbook out of his hip pocket and said: "I'll just write you the check, Don Remigio. What is your apellido, your surname? Oh yes, I remember, Gayoso, Don Remigio Gayoso."

"But listen, Don Severo," said the contratista in an astonished tone, "I'm not giving away the contract for that."

"Good, muy bueno, Don Remigio, then keep it. It's too dear

for me." Severo shut his checkbook again and pushed it back into his hip pocket.

Don Remigio, who had believed for so long that the Montellanos must give in to him, now saw himself compelled to negotiate. He did so almost halfheartedly.

"As I have said, Don Severo, with the stocks of caoba the contract cost me about twenty-eight thousand pesos. I won't say any more about the twenty percent surcharge. But the twenty-eight thousand must be paid."

"Now we're getting a bit nearer," said Severo. "I don't need to buy the contract. I send my brothers off, and you can believe me, Don Remigio, in ten weeks' time they'll come back with a hundred and fifty muchachos who cost us barely half of what you've paid for your boys. We know how to get the men we need."

"You sure do know that," Don Leobardo said now.

"You don't need to say that so sarcastically, Don Leobardo," responded Severo calmly, pouring out a glass for himself. "If I need muchachos, then I've got to have them. It's the same with you. Without muchachos you can get as little caoba as we can. When a king wants to go to war, he needs soldiers, and if he can't get the soldiers with fine words like "having to fight for your honor, for the fatherland," then he gets them with threats that he'll have them shot if they don't volunteer and give three cheers for him and for the war. We have bought the montería and all the concessions, and we need muchachos as a king needs soldiers. What's the difference? Tell me that, Don Leobardo. The muchachos don't come by themselves and ask if they may work here on the caoba. And since they don't come by themselves, we have to bring them here, one way or another."

"There are different ways of bringing them," said Don Rafael, the senior accountant.

"Right, señor, quite right. Therefore I am quite willing to buy the contracts here without asking how the muchachos got here, whether they came voluntarily or not." Don Severo looked at his brothers who were sitting opposite him. They leaned toward each other, and all three put their heads close together and whispered.

It was only play-acting, since Don Severo was doing what he wanted without asking his brothers for advice. But it had to look as if he could now accept Don Remigio's offer the more easily, without sacrificing his commercial dignity.

"You mustn't think, caballeros, that we have come here to cut all your throats," he said, referring to his new proposal.

"One can't be so certain of that," put in Don Leobardo sarcastically.

"What do you mean by that, Don Leobardo?" asked Severo.

"What I meant was, we don't really know why you have come here, to cut our throats or to strangle us."

Don Severo did not seem to be upset by that. Maybe he even regarded it as praise.

He said: "Don Leobardo, you would be the last person I should ever strangle."

"Right," laughed the administrator. "I don't have to do business with you. I'm just handing over to you what the Company has sold you; and because the contratistas are still contratistas to the Company, I naturally have some interest in how the hand-over is carried out."

"You say," Don Severo turned back to Don Remigio, "the true value of the contract, in round figures, is twenty-eight thousand pesos."

"That's what I said, Don Severo."

"I offered you twenty-five. Now we're not here to steal your contracts, but there is just one question."

"Bueno?"

"You have two capataces, two overseers, Don Remigio."

"Three."

"They know your districts, and the stocks?"

"As well as I do."

"Are they staying here?"

"Two of them, yes. One goes with me. He is my head muchacho. He wouldn't stay with anyone else, only with me."

"So the other two are staying?"

"I guarantee it. They couldn't very well go, they're too deep in debt with their advances. One of them is called Ambrosio. Drinks when he comes in to the Oficinas, and is no use here. But he's worth his pay in the semaneo. The other is called Emeterio. Very reliable. Knows the district very well and is a good hard worker with the men."

"You mean he gets the last ounce out of them?"

"That's about what I meant. But Ambrosio is harder."

"And more brutal," Don Leobardo put in. "He is a slave-driver and was certainly once a torturer with the Rurales or one of the cacique's Black Courts."

"Glad to hear it. I need tough men to take charge." Don Severo poured himself a new glass. "Yes, I need tough men. I haven't even a stick of caoba in the port. Only what is already available here. The muchachos will really have to get down to it."

"Go on!" said Don Rafael with a broad grin. He reached for the bottle and helped himself.

"Good, then, Don Remigio, that settles it." Severo drew a breath. "In view of the fact that the two capataces can stay here and will be able to help me, all right, I'll go up ten percent. Instead of twenty-five thousand, let's say twenty-seven thousand five hundred cash."

Don Remigio said nothing for a while. He was not used to long negotiations. They made him tired. The hardest work in the jungle did not make him half as tired as an hour of bargaining with people who were not willing to pay a price he considered right. He knew he could possibly make another thousand pesos out of the contract; for the Montellanos needed the men and without men they could do nothing. But at the same time he was well aware that there would be plenty of difficulties with a chicle contract.

"Aceptado, agreed!" he said shortly.

Don Severo wrote the check out at once, to prevent Don Remigio from changing his mind.

Don Severo dealt more quickly with the other contratistas. They had fewer men, smaller stocks, and fewer advances on the accounts. Their positions as contratistas were not as strong as Don Remigio's. One way was still open to them if they did not accept the price that Don Severo offered, and that was to stay there. Since they did not want to do that, they had to give in. The idea of taking their men to Quintana Roo struck them as absurd.

As Don Severo worked out how much he had paid for the contracts, he found that in every respect he had bought at a cut price. It was not as easy as he made out to bring enough men here in a short time. It could take months. And during those months no caoba would be felled. But the actual advantage was that, together with the contracts, the Montellanos at the same time took over adequate stocks of caoba. Those stocks they had bought at the usual price that the contratista received. Once those stocks were in the seaport they would make so much that, just for the stocks now taken over, the brothers would get twice, even three or four times as much as they had paid for the contracts altogether. It just depended on the market price. Meanwhile, however, they would work and work at extracting the caoba, and since all the men had such high advances that they would have to work for a year, maybe two or three years, before they received any pay, provided they didn't increase their advances in the interim, all production from then on was pure profit. The Montellanos could well count on it that, within a year, not only would all the amounts they had spent on buying the contracts have been paid off, but so too would the cash they had put up as capital for the monterías and the concessions.

4

When all the negotiations seemed to be over, it was almost midnight.

Don Severo yawned and poured himself another glass. The majority of the caballeros did the same.

The Chinese came in and said to the administrator: "Don Leobaldo, I thought maybe the caballelos would like to dlink a coffee now. I have it leady."

"Chinkie," cried Don Rafael, "I would give you an order if I were El Caudillo."

"Not necessaly, Don Lafael, not necessaly," said the Chinese, laughing. "I plefer to make ten centavos flom the caballelos for each cup of coffee they dlink."

"Bring the coffee and chalk it up," said Don Leobardo.

"Of course, gentlemen," said Don Severo, turning to everyone sitting in the comedor, "it's clear of course that you may use the Oficinas as your home as long as it is convenient for you."

"Only tomorrow, with your permission," replied the administrator. "Tomorrow we shall bring the animals in from the prairies, organize the saddlery, and pack our baggage."

"As long as you wish, caballeros. You won't disturb us," said Don Severo again. He could easily say that, for he knew that in at most two days there would certainly be nobody else there.

5

While the Montellanos were negotiating with the contratistas, the caballeros had not been just sitting there as if they were in church. Don Severo's sermons were not gripping enough for that. At one table, pushed over to one side, the junior employees had started a lively game of cards and, careless of what was going on around them, carried on enthusiastically, interrupted only by the frequent filling of glasses. At the other side table they were playing dice. No one at the main table could hear what had been thrown, and even anyone sitting much closer, but not joining in the game, would hardly have known with any certainty whether they were dicing for certain girls or for particular mules for the ride home, the winner having first choice. In any case, one shouldn't worry so much in life about what is being played for, much more about whether the game is straight.

Don Acacio, the youngest of the Montellanos, seemed in the end to be less interested in the negotiations that his elder brother was dealing with perfectly satisfactorily, than in a different contract, which he would gladly have included in the immovable assets of the montería and thus hopefully been able to take over in the same way as the contract workers, the manual workers, the oxen, the mules, and the buildings had been taken over.

He let his brother debate with the last of the contratistas in peace. And when he saw that his brother was deep in the negotiations, and Don Félix seemed not to be paying any special attention to him, he turned to the administrator with a confidential look on his face: "Listen, Don Leobardo, what will become of the girls that you and some of the other caballeros have in your bungalows? You'll leave them here, won't you? I should like to take over the tall brunette that is with you."

"Would you, Don Acacio? I well believe it. It's a pity you haven't brought anything with you from San Juan Bautista or El Carmen or Frontera. The girls are all going to Yucatán with us. We don't know yet what it will be like that way; and we don't want to rely all that much on good luck. What you have you know; what we may possibly get there, we don't know. And what a man needs he has to have. All the more as, in the first months in Yucatán, I won't have much spare time to have a good look round for a few girl helpers. I'm taking my two nursemaids with me in any case. I'm used to them, and so they are to me.

But perhaps you could have a try with one or another of the younger caballeros who have more time and more urge to go fishing than I have. Maybe one of them is short of journey money and still has an account at the tienda, maybe he'd give up the rights he has earned and deserved for an appropriate payment. If not, you must come to some arrangement with one of the Turks, that next time he comes here he makes a delivery. That needs a deposit, but often the delivery is worth the deposit. Until then there's nothing else for you but to look around in the liquor tents and see whether there is anything there for occasional refreshment of your ability to sleep."

Don Acacio stood up and went over to the side table to talk to the young clerks.

He hadn't been there long when Don Eladio sprang up and yelled: "What do you think I am? A slave dealer? Or a patrote who deals in tarts? Leave me alone, damn you! With your goddam filth! Where do you think you are, cabrón?"

"Cabrón? Are you calling me that? You, such a fucking son of a mangy bitch! You're saying that to me?"

And with that Don Acacio had already drawn his revolver and fired two shots.

Don Eladio had been just as quick, and he too had fired twice. But the younger caballeros sitting there were used to such everyday incidents, and the moment they saw the two revolvers were out and aimed, they seized the two inflamed brawlers by the arms and tore them apart just in time, so that the bullets passed through the palm roof. Don Severo stood up deliberately, threw a scribbled piece of paper that he was just holding in his hand onto the table with a violent gesture and his pencil with it, banged on the table with his fist, and shouted at Don Acacio: "Jesus Christ, goddam and blast it all, you chirping chicken, just hatched out of the egg, can't you sit among decent caballeros for a minute and drink half a liter of aguardiente without shooting all round you like a crazy Indian? Dios sabe, God in heaven alone knows how much we may need those two cartuchos, that goddam pair of cartridges, and you shoot them here at the compañeros who are leaving tomorrow. I ought to slap your face, you burro, you wretched ass. Stick your cannon away and sit down on your arse and leave us here in peace."

"You can't order me about like that, understand?" shouted Don Acacio. "They said cabrón to me, and patrote."

"And what else?" asked Don Severo sarcastically. "They were quite right to say that to you. They seem to know you pretty well. You deserve a hundred cabrones. What were you when I picked you up, half starved, but a patrote? Sit down and keep your mouth shut."

"What's that you're saying to me? To me? You picked me up, you? Where, then? If I hadn't had the money, who would ever have lent you as much as a centavo?"

"Go to bed, you're absolutely plastered," said Don Severo, sitting down again to go on with his negotiations.

Don Acacio, in an absolute fury, grew more and more excited.

"Plastered, me? And what other drunken swine will tell me I can't drink?"

With a jerk he drew his revolver again. He waved it about wildly, careless of whom he might shoot.

He had taken several paces back and now had all the caballeros in front of him.

Don Severo was the only one who remained calm and refused to be intimidated. He half sat up in his seat, took hold of a bottle that was in front of him, and threw it with a powerful and well-aimed swing so accurately that it hit Don Acacio's hand, the hand holding the revolver, so hard that a shot went off, but only as the revolver fell to the floor. The bullet passed through the wall.

6

Don Eladio, who had been standing beside him, jumped up quickly and picked up the revolver while Don Acacio fell staggering against the wall. At that moment, from outside, came the dreadful squeal of a pig; and in the same instant the two Chinese were heard screaming and shouting: "The pig is shot, our gleatest pig is shot."

The pig had wanted to spend the night just outside the wall. There was mud there formed when all the caballeros who washed their hands in the comedor threw the water here and there near the wall when they emptied the wash basin. The pig slept in that mud every night and was very comfortable there. The spot was all the more sought after because occasionally a few tortillas, pieces of bread, half-gnawed bones were thrown out of the opening in the wall and fell by the feet of the nearby pig so that it did not have far to run to pick up the welcome scraps. The shot had gone through the wall at the lower end, and the poor pig, which was not at all involved in the quarrel, was hit in the ham. It was not a mortal wound. But for the Chinese the pig was lost; for now it could not be driven on the journey through the jungle; to load it on a mule was too difficult, and in any case it would have been absurd, and Don Leobardo would certainly have refused to allow them a strong mule to carry it.

The Chinese came into the comedor with the saddest expression he was able to put on. He waved his arms in all directions, beat the air with his hands, and danced about like an angry dervish. He lamented and he whimpered, but all he could say was: "Oh, my poor, poor pig, and he has to die so miselably. Oh, mi poblecito cochinito, and now he has to die so miselably."

Outside, obviously kneeling by the pig, caressing it and fondling it, the other Chinese could be heard wailing and lamenting. "You, our plide and all our lichness. Muchacho, oh dulce muchacho, oh sweet little one, we looked after you so well, and now you must die so miselably. Oh, muchacho, muchacho!"

"Hey, Chinkie," said Don Rafael, laughing and imitating the

way the Chinese spoke, "have you paid for the celdo, your muchacho, I mean your poor pig, have you paid for his insulance, to be bulied in China?"

"Don Lafael," answered the Chinese sadly, "I am so deplessed, and you can only make jokes about it."

"That's enough mourning!" Don Leobardo called across the table. "The pig's gone, and that's that. At best, Chinkie, you slaughter it right away and don't wait till dawn. It will have lost too much blood by then. So tomorrow morning we'll have a real farewell meal at last, as you owe us, Chinkie."

The Chinese heaved a deep sigh, as if he wanted to submit himself to the inevitable fate with the dignity of a newly bereaved widow. He took a deep breath through his nose and said: "Maybe you light, Don Leobaldo. To wait until sunlise is too late."

He went out and could be heard talking with his partner in Chinese. After a time they seemed to have agreed on something, for the Chinese came back into the comedor and said: "Caballelos, it is good, tomollow we have a big farewell meal with evelything such a good pig can ploduce. But I must warn you, caballelos, tomollow I must charge a peso for evely meal for evely caballelo. I no can do for less. But I plomise, the food that I serve tomollow will be worth much more."

"Good, we'll pay you a peso," Don Leobardo confirmed. "And now, don't do anything silly, Chinkie. Don't take the fresh meat for me on the journey, otherwise we shall have pumas all round the camp every night. Cut off all that's left over at once tomorrow morning and hang it out to dry. It won't be quite dry until the next day, but it will be safer that way. And then there will be good meals for us on the way."

"Muchas glacias, Don Leobaldo. I had not thought that. Yes, the pumas are after flesh here like flies. Con su pelmiso, with your permission, I will now slaughter the poor pig. It makes me velly sad. But I believe the bullet hurt the poor pig in the ham like my sollow in my bleast." He ran out and gave his helper the order to be quick and release the pig from its earthly torment.

7

Things had calmed down in the comedor during the talk with the Chinese. Don Acacio was sitting at the table again, preoccupied and ill tempered. He had sat at the end of the bench, probably because he knew he would find it hard to climb onto the middle of the bench without falling under the table. There was a new glass in front of him, filled with comiteco. It was already the second since the fight for his honor. But one of the staff had filled the first four-fifths with water and only the rest with comiteco. However, no one could catch one of the Montellanos out, try as they would. Don Acacio only put the glass to his mouth, then knew at once what was wrong and what the friendly drinking companion had intended. He picked up the glass and hurled it together with its contents out of the open wall. "No one here can get away with that sort of thing with Cachito. Soy muy macho, I'm a real man with hair on my chest. I know what's comiteco and what's piss!" He didn't say all that straight out but in half-sentences; but he got it in the right order. "Cabrones, hey, where the devil is my revolver?" He had reached behind him and discovered that his pistol had been taken away.

"Cállate! Shut up, Cachito!" called Don Severo. "Babies mustn't play with fire and scissors, and anyone as tight as you doesn't need a pistol anymore. Off to bed."

"I'm going to my bloody bed when I want. And I won't be ordered about by anyone, not even you, even if you really were my brother."

"One word more," shouted Don Severo angrily, "and I'll smash this bottle on your skull so that your own mother won't think it worth the trouble to pick you up again."

"Mother, shit. Weaned long ago, and the devil only knows where she is or who she sleeps with. Give me that bottle, I'm telling you. When I want to drink, then I drink, and when I want to shoot, I shoot. Next time it will be another pig, one standing on two legs."

Then he got up, walked one pace along the table, and picked up a bottle. He put it to his mouth and drank it down.

Then he put the bottle back on the table with a loud slam, straightened himself up, threw out his chest, beat his breast with both hands, and yelled: "Muy macho soy yo! A real man! And when I want to drink, then I drink. And I drink you all under the table. Look here, who wants a bullet between his ribs? Where's my gun? Goddam it! I want my gun!"

"Félix!" Don Severo called to his brother. "Get hold of that chicken and take it to its nest."

Félix stood up and went over to Acacio.

When Acacio saw him coming he lost his temper again. "One step nearer and you'll get what that pig got! I'll slaughter you. Soy muy macho y muy bravo. The bravest of you all, I am, understand, you cabrón and son of a bitch!"

"Behave yourself in front of the caballeros, Cachito," said Félix soothingly.

"Caballeros! Shit! All sons of whores!"

"You'd better get in your cradle and sleep it off, Cachito." Don Félix took Acacio under the arm to guide him out. Don Acacio shoved his brother back so that he tumbled against the wall. Don Félix did not lose his temper. He just laughed. Then he went back to Don Acacio and hit him so hard behind the ear that Don Acacio collapsed in the corner of the comedor as if felled, and lay there like a clod.

"Pick up that lump of shit, Félix," said Don Severo, "and take it somewhere safe so that maybe I can finish my business here."

Don Félix lifted the body lying on the ground and hauled it out into the dark.

"Hey, Chinkie," they heard him call outside, "give me a lantern so I can find our bungalow."

7

By now it was midnight.

The caballeros yawned and stretched. The bottles were examined to discover the last glass they might still be made to yield. There was still one more decent goodnight shot for everyone. Outside, in front of the comedor, the two Chinese could be heard dealing with their pig. It made a lot of work; for it belonged to the hairy breed whose skin is stripped off on slaughtering or which has to be peeled out of its skin if the stripping process does not go smoothly, as is usually the case.

"Hasta mañana! Till tomorrow, caballeros!" said Don Severo, as he lazily stretched his heavy body. "I shall now go and lie on my bit of mattress. Damn it all, I'm tired enough."

"Hasta mañana, Don Severo," echoed the caballeros and withdrew sleepily from the comedor to crawl over to their bungalows.

Without being invited, but following an instinct, they all gathered in the administrator's bungalow, and he got out a bottle of comiteco and invited them all to have a last drink together.

"Good types, those brothers!" said Don Mariano. "They'll make something of the montería."

"I can swear to that," Don Rafael agreed. "I can really swear to that, they will certainly make something of the montería. Por la Madre Santísima, wherever did they come from? They must surely once have been among the lowest kind of arrieros, the lowest level of mule-drivers."

"Must have been?" repeated Don Leobardo ironically. "Only have been, caballeros? They still are, and today they're no better than mule-drivers and I suppose they'll never be anything else, even if they make millions."

"I should just like to know how they want to manage the three monterías without contratistas," wondered Don Rafael.

"Easy, the way they have in mind, and with a damn good profit," said Don Leobardo. "They have brought six capataces whom they know well and have worked with very well over the last couple of years. Those six guys you've simply got to see."

"I saw them this afternoon," broke in Don Eladio. "They're not overseers, vulgar and bad-tempered as capataces may well be. They're executioners, real executioners."

"You saw them pretty well, Eladio," confirmed Don Leobardo. "Each one of them gobbles up thirty muchachos in twelve months, eats them whole. But they do produce caoba, that's a fact. And together with the capataces who stay behind and don't leave with the contratistas, the Montellanos have a good reliable staff. They pay the capataces one peso fifty a day, and then in every semaneo they have a head capataz whom they pay fifty centavos for every ton of caoba delivered, and a second capataz who gets one real per ton. They make damn sure that caoba comes in, you can be certain, gentlemen. They would have to pay ten pesos a ton to the contratistas; to the capataces they pay four reales to the first and one to the second—that's sixty-two centavos per ton instead of ten pesos. And the capataces kiss them for their tiny dividends, the dirty crusts they earn off the scrag end, and they're humble and biddable, whereas contratistas want to have their own way and not take orders."

"God knows how long it can go on like that," said Don Rafael.

"But meanwhile the brothers are making heaps of money, and if it begins to break up, they'll pull out. But what's it got to do with me? I'm going to plant henequen. Something a bit different after these years in the jungle where you just go crazy and you're surrounded by ghosts day and night." Don Leobardo had sat down on the side of his rough bed and began to take off his boots. "There I shall only have to ride four hours and I'll be in a town. It's small, it's tiny, but it's a town. Here I have to ride three weeks through the jungle before I catch sight of anything that could be a town, if the people wanted to give themselves a bit more trouble and make a town of it."

He turned to Don Remigio. "Are you taking your muchacha with you, that Javiera, Don Remigio?"

"Of course! You don't think I'd let the girl fall into the hands of those rapists, do you? She may not be worth much, and she has a pretty eventful life behind her, that's for sure, but I'd never do that to her, I'd never hand her over to the mercy of someone like Acacio."

"But maybe she'd like to stay here."

"That's her business then, of course, and I can't be blamed. But we've already agreed on the point. She leaves with me and then she stops in Jovel, where I've promised to buy her a little shop. And that shop she shall have. Where are your two favoritas, Don Leobardo?"

"They're in the little bungalow next door. Been asleep now for a long time. I'm not buying them a shop. They don't want one. They'd rather help me grow henequen."

"That's what I call faithfulness and devotion," laughed Don Remigio. Then he yawned loudly and said to his colleagues, the other three contratistas, who were there with him: "Bueno, compañeros, I think we'll lay ourselves down on our beds now. It's after one o'clock. Buenas noches, caballeros."

"Hasta mañana, Don Remigio."

2

The Montellano brothers had bought only about half the Company's mules so as to keep the price down. They would have had no use for all the animals, in the first year at any rate. It was their intention to buy young animals from Indian breeders and raise the animals in the montería, where the grazing cost nothing.

So there was a good number of animals available for those departing to ride and to carry their baggage. Don Leobardo owned six good mules of his own; Don Rafael and Don Mariano, the senior members of the staff, each owned three of their own animals; several of the juniors had a good riding animal. Don Remigio had five, the other contratistas four each.

Nonetheless, there would still not have been enough animals to carry the great number of those leaving. As well as the staff, the contratistas, each with a capataz who wanted to stay with his master and not work with the Montellanos, there were the girls who had decided to travel with the people they trusted better than their new owners.

Then there were the two Chinese, who wanted to travel with the big caravan. They were thinking of the greater safety of traveling with a big party. But that was not their only reason. The other reason was just as important to them. If they traveled with the caravan, during the journey, which might last up to three weeks, they could cook for the caballeros and so carry on their business with no interruption. Don Leobardo and Don Rafael had of course their own muchachos or mozos to look after them and would not have found it necessary to get food from the Chinese. But it was more convenient to have someone who could be made responsible for the food. The Chinese took all their kitchen gear with them, and they even promised to produce hot soda biscuits every day. How they thought they would do that was a secret. As it turned out, however, on the second day of the journey they succeeded in offering hot soda biscuits for breakfast and for dinner. The midday meal was dropped during the journey.

Don Leobardo undertook to hand over the horses and mules, as well as some donkeys which were not included in the sale, at the Company's headquarters; from there he wanted either to take them with him to Yucatán or to where they would be passed on to the Company's banana plantations.

But since the animals that he took with him on the Company's instructions, and all the animals that were owned by the staff and the contratistas, were still not enough to transport the whole caravan with all their packs and trunks, it was Don Severo's suggestion that all the animals he had bought with the montería be made available to the travelers. Generous as that offer looked at first sight, in fact it was not. Don Severo also had to send a caravan to Jovel to fetch some necessary items that he was short of. That caravan would be run by the arrieros. The animals would go completely unladen and would only be loaded on the return journey. So it made no difference if he let all the animals go just now, and it was of no importance whether they carried any loads. It was better for his men, too, to travel with the big caravan; it was less dangerous, and the road, which became overgrown so quickly that after six weeks you could only trace it if you knew it closely, would now be cleared by all those muchachos going with the caravan and would still be clear when the Montellanos' caravan returned the same way. However, although there were undoubtedly advantages to him in sending his animals with the caravan, he did not fail to make it look as if he were making a big sacrifice by his notable readiness to help his fellow citizens. It made a favorable impression on all those who were leaving; and to leave a good impression among them all on their departure could one day be of value to him. The caravan, once it reached Jovel, would praise his generosity, and he was very anxious to get a good name in that important town. It would then be easier for him to obtain credit in case he needed it. Also, he wanted to build up a good reputation in the villages of the Indians from which he hoped to attract new workers to his monterías. Without the support he was giving them with all the animals in the montería, those now leaving would get into all sorts of difficulties.

3

The original plan was for the caravan to set out very early in the morning on the second day after the arrival of the Montellanos. But that had not proved possible.

In the course of loading it was found that many pack saddles were in a very poor state. And when all the animals were counted, the arrieros found that many of the animals had not been brought in because they had strayed too far from the central camp. They had to be traced, and that took time. Many animals that had been out of sight on the prairies for weeks had wounds from the bites of tiger cats or snakes, or boils, caused by insect stings, that had burst. Those animals had to be treated to make them fit for the journey.

The arrieros had difficulties in sorting out the animals according to their work and load capacity, and they had still greater difficulties with the organization of the baggage. And then they discovered that the supplies they had bought in the tienda were insufficient, and they must make further purchases. Two of the girls cried and complained they were ill and could not stand the journey unless they were given three days to get better.

About noon on the day they were to start, everything was at last so far organized that loading could begin.

Don Leobardo went out and inspected the camp. "Hey, muchachos, you'll need at least an hour and a half to load."

"Yes, we'll surely need that, patrón," said one of the arrieros.

"Then it will be nearly two o'clock before we can start."

"That will certainly be so, patrón."

"And about five we shall have to camp because it gets dark so quickly."

"Right, patrón. It's so dark by then that you can't see anything."

"Very well," said Don Leobardo, "then it's not worth the trouble to load and set off. Have a good rest, and don't get drunk. And tomorrow morning we'll be on the march at half past five. Is that clear?"

"That will be best, patrón," answered the arriero.

Don Leobardo made his order known, and everyone was agreed.

4

But if anyone did not agree it was Don Severo.

"Amigo, oiga; listen, my friend," he said to the administrator. "If you start so early, I shall have problems."

"How's that, Don Severo?"

"Half my men will run away and go with your lot. They would be afraid to go off into the jungle by themselves. But now they have a good opportunity to run away. Can't you perhaps wait until eight o'clock? Then it will be easier for us to keep an eye on the men, and I can watch over the camp."

Don Leobardo laughed. "Don Severo, you really ought to know better the tremendous patache that goes on on the first day of a departure. I shall be glad if we're on the march by nine."

Nonetheless, Don Severo made all the arrangements to prevent his men from deserting. He called Félix and Acacio. They got out the lists with the names of all the men who worked in the main camp in the area of the Oficinas: manual workers and peons.

He got all the men together, read out their names, and he and his two brothers looked at the men closely to learn to recognize them.

Then they were ordered to assemble again next morning at five, to be divided up for work. To let them know the time, Don Félix rang a bell that hung in the portico of the main Oficina.

When the men reported for work the next morning, the whole area was in turmoil, the result of preparations for the departure.

Don Severo took all his men to one side of the area, a long way away from the swarming crowd of the outgoing caravan. Then he divided them into two groups. The first group, including the manual workers, he took into the bodega, where under his supervision they tidied up the place and learned about the stores. They were all together there, and no one could escape. The second group, mostly peons, ordinary Indian workers, Don Félix led out into the jungle, where he got them chopping tree trunks and cutting palm leaves, which were intended for a new building.

5

The evening before, the Montellanos had dreamed up a new and splendid plan. They decided to get rid of the countless little hawkers of liquor from the camp. Not of course to introduce morality and good behavior, but to stop the wages they paid to the workers from passing into hands other than their own. Everything, even the last moldy little centavo, must come back to their own pockets and remain in the family.

So a big cantina, a luxurious tavern, was now to be built to one side of the area, well away from the Oficinas. This cantina they leased to a competent cantinero who paid no rent but had to hand over to the Montellanos forty percent of all his takings, no matter what kind, in lieu of rent. Those takings included the cantina's profits from the roulette wheel that was installed and from other games, as well as the earnings of the women who wanted to amuse themselves with the visitors to the cantina.

The visitor paid the cantinero for the woman, not the woman herself. The visitor received a voucher, a so-called ficha, which he handed over to the woman as payment. The woman passed the ficha on to the cantinero later on, receiving fifty percent of the price paid as her profit. In that way even that kind of business could be so well controlled that the Montellanos could work out their share precisely and the cantinero or the woman would not be able to engage in secret activities.

Later, when the Montellanos had built up the business as they had planned, if it happened that the women favored a visitor whom they liked without a cantinero's ficha, on their own account or out of pure affection or friendship, they got a severe warning. But if they were caught cheating the Montellanos of their share a second time, the women were handed over to the Oficinas capataz to be whipped.

In their home, in Spain, articles often appeared in the local papers that praised Don Severo as a model of diligence, persistence, perseverance, and business genius, and held up this outstanding man to the perpetually dissatisfied workers of Spain, who were nothing but anarchists and communists, as the ideal of a hard-working man, a man who, bitterly poor, emigrated to Mexico, landed at Veracruz with only twenty pesos in his pocket, and by his diligence and skill had become the proprietor of several monterías and had amassed a fortune of about twelve million pesetas.

6

While Don Severo and Don Félix were keeping all the workers busy and under their personal observation, Don Acacio carried out the task of observing the departing caravan, accompanying it for half a day and then returning. He rode in front. At a suitable point he stopped and let the whole long patache go past him, all those who had left, looking especially closely at men who might perhaps be workers for the Montellanos. Then he rode to the back of the caravan. About four o'clock in the afternoon he galloped up to the front of the procession again and once more let everybody go past him, to make quite sure that no deserter had crept into the caravan. Then he rode back, observing the road carefully, with the idea of catching anyone who might have sneaked off to the rear in order to join the caravan later.

7

Don Leobardo had not originally wanted to go to Jovel with his caravan because that involved a diversion. His plan had been to head north from Hucutsin, to reach the shortest road to San Juan Bautista and report to the Company there.

But when he arrived in Hucutsin he was told that the Bashayones, whose villages and settlements lay on his road to the north, were once more in open revolt on account of the injustice they considered they had suffered in the last months from the government, especially from the Jefe Político and the minor officials.

It was certain that the insurgent Indians would attack the caravan to steal the weapons and ammunition the men carried. It was also to be expected that they would probably demand a high ransom to allow the caravan an unhindered passage through their territory. Don Leobardo felt it would be a waste of time to wait for the federal troops, who could well be already on the march for a punitive expedition. In any case, the federal troops gave no promise of safety. The Indians kept themselves concealed in thick bush. They were so skilled in their kind of fighting that they could carry off travelers and loaded mules from the caravan at will and in full view of the military escort, and disappear so swiftly into the depth of the bush that the accompanying soldiers could do nothing to prevent it. If a patrol moved off to the left, the caravan was attacked from the right and turned back. It would have taken a regiment to protect the caravan against attacks of that kind; but the soldiers were needed more urgently elsewhere, to guard the big estates in the area and protect them from attack.

Don Leobardo was wise enough not to get involved in adventures and gamble with men's lives and goods for which he was responsible. He decided to take the whole caravan to Jovel. Nearly half the caravan was making for Jovel in any case, including of course the Montellanos' patache, which had instructions to buy the goods ordered in Jovel and would not therefore be able to go north with Don Leobardo.

All the contratistas were stopping in Jovel, some of the senior staff, several of the girls, and all the men, who left Don Leobardo there because they were at home there or thought of opening a new business there or intended to go on to Tullum and Arriaga, the railroad station. The road to Tullum and Arriaga ran southwest while Don Leobardo was traveling north.

Jovel offered good hotels, civilized restaurants, well-stocked shops, and enough entertainment so that all those who were going on to Tabasco with Don Leobardo were grateful to him when he gave the order to let the caravan stop there for four days before proceeding. For all those people who had spent many months, many of them three years, in the jungle, it was as if this instruction would open the gates of paradise for them.

8

  The headquarters of the La Armonía montería, after three days of the liveliness of a disturbed anthill, now made a positively ghostly impression, with so many men and beasts finally departed from it. It really seemed as if a whole population had left. The manual workers were working elsewhere so were not visible in the landscape. That intensified the impression that the town had expired.

On the day after the great caravan's exodus the Montellanos found to their great satisfaction that not a single man had deserted them. They basked in this realization like good soldiers who have had iron medals pinned to their chests for a bloody action as a result of which sixty mothers cursed God in heaven for having ever allowed such a thing to happen. There is no single action carried out by humans that is not praised somewhere by some other humans as a commendable act.

Now, when they were alone there, the Montellanos felt for the first time that they were the real masters. And to enjoy that feeling completely they reckoned that their first job was to describe everything the Company and its manager had done there in the past as stupid, senseless, and in every way unbusinesslike. Whatever corner of the Oficinas they went into, whatever manual worker or peon they came across, whatever work they found anyone doing, everything was done wrong, and every man who had arranged this or that or the other was described as a brainless ox, no matter whether it was the former administrator, the tendero, or the stores manager.

After they came to an end of this first day's devastating criticism, the three brothers held a conference in which they discussed how everything and everybody could be improved and must be improved. Only Don Severo spoke at this conference, of course. His two brothers had the right to listen and approve what he ordered, to carry it out with force and if need be with blood. They had brought six capataces, overseers, who had already worked with them for some time and had been trained by the three brothers as they thought good capataces ought to be trained. Those capataces were now sent for. And the second conference began.

Why should the Montellanos pay the contratistas ten pesos in gold for each ton of caoba produced, when they themselves were experienced contratistas who, with the right organization, could do it all themselves without the assistance of contratistas? They could earn the ten pesos a ton themselves. Contratistas were fundamentally just parasites, especially when they had to be paid by the Montellanos.

So it was decided that Don Félix should stay at headquarters in the Oficinas. There had to be a responsible and experienced person there to keep all the departments of the widespread operations supplied. That was where the newly recruited caoba men were handed over; where the caravans brought the necessary goods; the tienda was there; the stores with all the equipment were there; the inspection clearing system was there; and it was there that all orders and reports came as long as the brothers kept no office at the seaport.

Don Severo took over the production of caoba in La Armonía.

The youngest of them, Don Acacio, took over production in the two other, smaller monterías, La Estancia and La Piedra Alta, which lay close to each other and could therefore easily be managed together.

Neither Don Severo nor Don Acacio had the ability to be in all the districts or semaneos of their monterías at the same time. Each district was formerly worked by a contratista, and because the two brothers now wanted to exploit all those districts at the same time, which until then had been managed by nine different contratistas, the main montería alone by four, the organization must be completely altered to make it possible to produce the same amount, no, double the amount that had been produced under the previous organization.

The former contratistas and experienced senior members of the staff had already suggested in their discussions with Don Leobardo how the Montellanos would probably arrange to reduce the payments to the contratistas. And that was exactly how it happened now.

2

It was very simple. The ingenuity of the plan rested on its simplicity. When the six capataces were assembled, Don Severo made them a little speech. They had only to nod and say "Sí, patrón!" Don Severo said everything else.

"Muchachos," he said, "from now on, since we have become the proprietors ourselves, you too can finally earn something."

The lads pricked up their ears, not to miss a word; for to have been promised extra pay by the Montellanos was an unexpected novelty to them.

"You're used to our working methods. You've worked together with us long enough to know what I think and how the work must be done. We men are not in the world to loaf about, to booze, to go whoring, and to entertain ourselves, but to work. And when I say we men are on this wretched earth to work, I mean of course to work hard, very hard, until the bones crack and the juice soaks us in front and behind. That is what I understand by work. Understand?"

"Sí, patrón," answered the lads with one voice.

"So I have told myself that you must earn more, because you are really good and efficient capataces. Pour yourselves a drink, now. Goddam it, not out of that bottle, out of the other one. I suppose you can still tell the difference between what is for us and what is for you, you bloody sons of whores?"

Not intimidated by this rebuke, but just made awkward, they took the bottle of ordinary aguardiente which Don Severo had shoved at them. Each one took a glassful, said "Salud!" to each of the three brothers, and knocked it back. There was only one glass for them, so it took a while before it went round. Don Severo did not let that time pass idly.

"Each one of you will take over a district. Anyone who doesn't want to can just leave. I don't need you anyway and only keep you on here out of compassion, and because you're all so overdrawn on your advances because of your boozing and gambling and whoring. I shall decide the district for each of you."

Don Severo picked up a piece of paper. He had drawn the semaneos on it. The biggest and richest of the three monterías that he had bought was La Armonía, where the Oficinas were situated. He took that over himself. The two smaller ones, La Estancia and La Piedra Alta, were taken over by Don Acacio. Those two were about four days' ride from La Armonía. Don Severo found La Armonía divided into four districts, which he maintained. He changed only their names and now called them after the directions in which they lay from the central point, North, South, East, and West. La Estancia and La Piedra Alta he divided into two districts each, the two in La Estancia called North and South, the two in La Piedra Alta East and West. He had sketched it out like that on the paper, on a roughly drawn map. All that remained to him now was the matter of appointing the right men to the districts.

"I shall be taking over the North District here in La Armonía myself, so as to be close to you. You, Pícaro, will take on South District." The Montellanos never called their men by their real names. Maybe they didn't even know the right names, or, if they ever had been called by them, they didn't really believe in the correctness of the names. To recognize a man they relied much more on the motes, or nicknames, that they gave to the men, without having to recognize his proper name.

"Each of you is the mayordomo, the foreman, in your district with unlimited powers. Do you understand?"

"Sí, patrón."

"Have another glass. Here are some cigarettes, too. Each mayordomo will be assisted by a capataz, actually the former contratista's capataz, who stayed in the area and was taken on by us. You work peacefully with them or I fire you, and before you go you'll get a goddam flogging on top of it."

"Las gratificaciones, Severo," Félix reminded him.

"Shut your mouth and sit on your arse! I'm just coming to that. You, Pulpo, you bloody Octopus, you take on the East District."

"Sí, patrón."

"El Chucho, you take the West District. The other three, La Mecha, the Wick, El Guapo, the Beauty, and El Faldón, the Skirt, you go to the other two monterías with Don Acacio."

"Las gratificaciones, Severo." It was Don Acacio now who reminded him. Don Severo at last seemed to think the time had come to talk about the rewards. So he didn't yell at Don Acacio to shut his jaw.

From the lists passed over to him by Don Leobardo and the contratistas, he had carefully worked out the exact number of all the men who worked in each district. And he had also, as far as that could be done from the Oficinas, worked out how many

hacheros or fellers there were in each district and how many
boyeros and macheteros. Without taking into account, indeed
without really knowing exactly, how difficult the terrain of each
district was and how necessary a full number of boyeros might
be, without consideration he crossed out several men from the
hauling groups and transferred them to the hacheros.

3

A feller's compulsory production was two tons of caoba a day,
properly stripped, hewn, and ready for the water.

It had formerly been the rule that a feller who was not able to
produce two tons a day, in most cases not by his own fault, had
the right to make up the missing tonnage within a week. That
meant that if on Monday and Tuesday he had produced only
three tons altogether instead of four, he could make up the
shortage provided that, within the same week, on one day rather
than two, he managed three tons, which was quite possible if he
found a tree that yielded two tons by itself. To manage two tons
a day regularly was a devilishly hard job for a man who had to
work in the jungle in tropical heat and never got a meal in his
belly that could be described as nourishing. If the hacheros did
not achieve their full tonnage they were not paid for the days on
which they had not produced their full two tons; they had thus
worked for nothing, although they had maybe actually managed
a ton or a ton and a half. But because the two tons were not
complete, the tons actually produced were not counted, or only
counted if within the same week, sometimes within four weeks
under good-natured contratistas. The total production figure for
the week amounted to fourteen tons.

There were no Sundays or holidays. That too is quite reasonable. The jungle knows no holidays either. The mahogany trees
in it, the caoba, grow every day, day and night, without caring
about the holidays on the calendar. The jungle has no time for

that, and so the caoba men have no time to indulge in such follies as demanding holidays or rest days.

If an hachero was continually below his daily two tons, it was assumed he was deliberately not trying. The contratista sent for his capataz and gave him orders to have a word with the man. The capataz knew no other procedure than to whip the lazy feller. No one stopped to think over the physical possibilities or impossibilities of the worker. Caoba can't be produced by consideration or inquiries; it has to be felled. And anyone who has been bought to fell caoba has to do that or take the consequences.

The personal talk that the capataz had with the unsatisfactory hachero was often successful. After it the man produced his two tons a day. But if he fell short, because with the best will in the world he might be unable to deliver, then he had a second talk with the capataz. The final result was one of two possibilities. The man got used to producing the amount demanded, or he died. He died either from the continual overexertion for which he had not been prepared, or he died from the wounds inflicted on him by the capataz.

In many cases the death of a worker was only a temporary loss to the contratista or the montería, and then only a loss of time. The majority of the muchachos were obliged if debts or police fines were paid for them, or advances were given to them, to name a guarantor, generally a good friend or a brother, cousin, or brother-in-law. If a muchacho engaged under contract then died, even if it was from an accident at work, before he had been able to work off the complete debt, his guarantor was sent for and had to work off the rest of the debt in the montería. Of course several months passed before the guarantor could be notified and before he reached the montería. That was generally the only loss that the montería suffered.

Seen as a whole, the treatment of the men, however hard it seems, was still not as cruel as might be supposed. Neither the administrators, notably Don Leobardo, nor the contratistas had in general any interest in tormenting their workers. They were physically, and beyond doubt sexually, full-blooded, totally fit and normal men, who got not the slightest pleasure or any secret enjoyment out of having their men whipped and gloating over it. The capataz did that to the men privately, and he thought of it not as a sadistic pleasure but as a job that he avoided like any other strenuous work. The Company and their administrators avoided any brutality as long as they could reach their target in a more gentle way. As soon as the contratistas, at least the majority of them, realized that a man, however hard he tried, simply could not manage the production, they gave him a different job as long as they had a different one for him; or they gave him time to build up his abilities so that in the end he was able to achieve what really can be achieved if one has the practice and has learned all the tricks of the trade.

But such mitigations, often applied by companies and contratistas, and mostly with no serious disadvantage to the business, could of course find no consideration in the plans of the Montellanos. It has seldom helped anybody to make millions if they gave too much consideration to the workers; and never yet has a dictator in all his power been able to declare that he saw in his oppressed subjects anything but obedient uniformed blocks of wood.

4

Don Severo looked at the list for the South District, which he had assigned to El Pícaro, the Rogue. He found on it nineteen fellers, eleven ox-drivers, four ox-boys, and two macheteros. Macheteros are the men who clear the paths in the jungle on which the felled trees must be hauled.

Don Severo cut down the ox-drivers by three and crossed out the macheteros. Those five men, though he didn't know them and didn't even know whether they would be able to wield a heavy caoba ax, he transferred to the fellers. The four ox-boys would have to take on the work of the macheteros. That way Don Severo got twenty-four fellers for the South District.

Having worked that out so nicely, he came to the gratificaciones, the rewards.

"Pícaro, as I've told you before, and as I've told all of you, I let you make money when we make money. I'm no ladrón who exploits poor Indians. I give you a living. You can all make money if you concentrate on our interests. What the Company has produced so far is just shit. I don't know what the men have been doing. They must have just fucked and boozed and slept it off. Without overexerting ourselves we could easily produce twice as much. And twice as much, that's the very least we've got to produce. When I said I let everybody make money who helps us make money, I meant exactly that. Until now we were only contratistas. Then we couldn't pay you any more than your eight or ten or twelve reales a day. But now we're the owners and can let you earn more. From the first of next month you'll all, without exception, get twelve reales a day, that's one peso fifty. The other capataces who are under your orders will also have twelve reales a day. But now we come to the difference."

The capataces drew nearer to him, excitedly. They may well have been less avaricious than the Montellanos. But Don Severo knew how to pass on his own traits to those who could help him gratify his own and his brothers' avarice.

"Pícaro, you've got twenty-four fellers in your district. Each of them of course has to produce two tons a day, as always. That's your responsibility. If you get me fifty tons a day, then for each ton I'll give you a quarter of a real gratificación, that is, six pesos twenty-five centavos a day, and your pay as well, of course. I'll give your compañero a quarter of a real for each ton. I'll give you a note for him. But if it's less than fifty tons in the day, for that day you get no pay, and naturally no gratificación."

"Pero, patrón, entonces, then I shall be working for nothing," said El Pícaro nervously.

"But with twenty-four fellers you will be able to produce more than forty tons a day. Won't you? You and I together, the two of us, have produced more. You know that perfectly well."

"Yes, of course, Don Severo, but often the trees are not so convenient, and that's what causes the trouble."

"That's why I'm turning you from a robber into a foreman, so that you can sort out the matter of the trees. I don't need to pay a capataz just to stand around. I could just as well plant a stick in the shit, or a scarecrow, if I only wanted someone to be there. And in any case that isn't all. I told you, I'm giving you one real for every ton if you get me more than fifty. But if with the same men you manage sixty tons in a day, then for every ton I give you two reales gratificación and your compañero half a real for every ton. And that is still not enough. I'll give you three reales and your compañero one real for every ton if you manage to get me seventy tons."

"Con su permiso, with your permission, how can I get seventy tons with twenty-four muchachos?"

"What you get and how you get it is your business. That's why I've promoted you to mayordomo. If you can't do it, I'll find somebody else."

"No need for that, jefe. You know I've always stuck by you."

"It's just because I know that that I'm giving you these gratificaciones. You can easily make five hundred pesos a month, it will be nothing to you. Like that, it just falls into your pocket. Pour yourself a full glass. Me too. Chucho, Pulpo, and the rest of you, give yourselves one." Don Severo turned back to El Pícaro. "How you do it, just do what you like. You've been learning with me long enough to know that those stinking Indian swine are as lazy as dung on a dungheap. Stinking lazy in their pueblos and ten times more stinking lazy on the fincas. But they have bones like iron. Dance three days and three nights on end, drinking and whoring all the time like mad, it's an incredible sight. They can work fine if you get them down to it. Your problem. I know they can manage four tons as easily as I break this toothpick. Four tons a day is nothing to them, they can do it in their sleep. But if you can't manage it, I can look for one of the other capataces to take your place. Maybe El Tornillo or El Doblado, who stayed behind from the last contratistas."

"But, patroncito, I haven't said a word about not wanting to take it on. I can use the money as well as the others; if I want to buy that rancho from Don Aureliano I need money."

"Good, then, that's settled."

Now Don Severo tackled the next one. It was El Chucho. He didn't have to explain as much as he had had to explain to El Pícaro; that was why they had all been summoned together, so that they could all hear at the same time what Don Severo wanted from them. It was only necessary to tell each one how many fellers he had and how many tons he must deliver every day in order to receive this or that bonus.

When the meeting was over and all the capataces knew where they belonged and what they had to do, they went off to the drinking huts to have one last festive evening before the long weeks of work in the jungle. Don Severo had given them all a sufficient advance to let them celebrate just such a festive night, so that the very thought of often being able to have such nights would spur them on to fulfill all the tasks he expected of them.

9

"Out, you dormilones, you dozy whoremongers! Or you'll find the sun shining between your damned black buttocks! Come on, get a move on or I'll help you with the látigo. Out, and get those oxen moving!" The capataz Ambrosio was shouting at the boyeros, the ox-drivers, in a tone of voice as if someone had insulted him.

Ambrosio, who had worked with Don Remigio for two years or maybe longer, had been left at the montería by Don Remigio because he had been continually unreliable in the last months; he seemed to be no good at anything and had moreover acquired debts and an advance which Don Remigio refused to take over when his contract was canceled. Don Severo paid for Ambrosio, as he had for all the other men, the debts due Don Remigio. Ambrosio was useful to the Montellanos because as Don Remigio's capataz he knew the districts of the montería in and out, by heart.

Don Severo didn't like the name Ambrosio. When he came to take over in the district, asked him what he was called, and heard the name Ambrosio, he roared with laughter and said:

"I'd like to know who called you Ambrosio, must have been the fucking devil wanting to make a satanic joke."

"But that is mi nombre verdadero, my real name," said Ambrosio, evidently rather hurt. At the same time he wanted to make a subservient, groveling impression on his new master in the hope of getting special precedence and payments, and so, as he stood in front of Don Severo and answered his questions, he kept wriggling and twisting submissively like a worm.

Don Severo looked him up and down, saw how he was squirming, and then said: "No, man, Ambrosio is too long-winded for me. El Gusano, the Worm, will suit you better. The saint to whom my mother prayed and to whose special protection she commanded her soul, may she be blessed from eternity to eternity, that was St. Ambrosio. You don't look like him, Gusano. So now you know what your name is, and don't forget it when I call you, or I shall be rude."

"A sus órdenes, patrón!" said Ambrosio meekly.

"You'll be better off here than you were with Don Remigio."

"Es cierto? Is that certain, patrón?" asked El Gusano with a reconciled air when he realized that some preference seemed to be in sight.

"Yes, far better. How much were you paid with Don Remigio?"

"Twelve reales, patrón."

"You'll get the same from us. But also gratificaciones, big tips for big production. You can easily get four to eight pesos a day with me, understand, Gusano?"

"Sí, señor, y muchísimas gracias!" said Ambrosio. His new name, the Worm, had suddenly lost all its unpleasantness, since it had so quickly been associated with good money. El Gusano struck him as the most splendid name he could have thought of. It echoed in his ears like the music of the spheres, lovelier than all the Ambrosian songs of praise in heaven. The songs of praise in heaven might sound beautiful, but they had no purchasing power here on earth. Yet the gratificaciones now promised him, earnings which sounded really good to him, could here on earth be converted into everything that gives happiness and enjoyment to a healthy man. What is the beautiful name of Ambrosio worth if you can't even get a bottle of comiteco with it on credit? Down with Ambrosio, then, long live El Gusano! Don't hang onto dusty old names, man, if they just hold you back in your successful life.

What he did next was to order all the muchachos to call him El Gusano from then on if they called him by name or if he was wanted by Don Severo or by Don Pícaro, the mayordomo; but in all other cases he insisted that in the future he should be addressed as "mi jefe" if the dirty, lousy muchachos had anything to say to him.

2

El Gusano was the ayudante, the assistant and understudy of El Pícaro, who had been appointed as mayordomo of the South District of La Armonía. El Gusano therefore got a share in the gratificaciones that were awarded to El Pícaro. Don Severo was an outstanding judge of character, especially where it concerned subordinates and people who wanted to be used for his purposes. To give El Gusano to El Pícaro as ayudante had really been a devilish thought; but at the same time it was an idea that he knew would bring in lots of money. El Pícaro was able to get the last drops of strength out of a worker, if not with fair words then with merciless brutality. Don Severo knew that from experience; he had trained El Pícaro well and worked with him long enough to see how successful his lessons and his teaching methods had been. Because he knew him so well, he had given him the richest district, that of Don Remigio, which had the most men.

Don Severo could not act quite as brutally as he might have wished simply because he was now proprietor and president of the company that was being founded. As a capitalist, president of the new company, and chief negotiator with the American and British companies that bought caoba, he must maintain a clean name, not stained or tainted by reports of cruelty to the Indian workers who moldered in the company's work areas in the jungles, worse off than animals. By some means or other it might become known, might even be written about in American and British papers, by what inhuman methods the caoba was obtained. That could happen less through the love of sensation of reporters who got to know about the conditions than, much more readily and certainly, through the rivalry of different companies which also produced and sold. Every company was out to destroy the others, or at any rate to damage them. To damage a company's reputation, to accuse it before the whole civilized world of cruelty to defenseless Indian workers and cite examples of it, was more effective than destroying the company by cutting prices. Cutting prices was expensive and could easily become a weapon that dealt a death blow to the attacking company.

For all those reasons Don Severo and his two brothers, as proprietors and directors of the company, had to work more carefully than they had in the time when they were contratistas. A company was not responsible for what its contratistas did. Even if it had full knowledge of them, it could maintain that it had no influence on the contratistas' working methods because the contratistas were independent, unconnected firms working for their own profit and on their own responsibility. So if it came to a public scandal, the company had nothing more to do than to dismiss the offending contratistas and declare that the contratistas no longer had any connection with the company. In so doing the company made it clear to the whole world that it could not stand cruelty and that it had removed from the company's territory all men who were guilty of such cruelty, with substantial financial loss to the company. By that declaration the name of the company was purged. It was widely praised by all the philanthropists, including the socialist representatives, for the swiftness and thoroughness with which it had cleared up the evil, and the hundreds of thousands of tons of caoba which had been procured by such methods could now comfortably be sold at the highest market price, and even above market price. The company used it as a brilliant advertisement; and it sold its piles of caoba more easily and more quickly, and on more favorable terms, than all the other companies, where the press did not know whether all the reported cruelties were not still practiced uninterrupted. Don Severo, knowing all this well and calculating wisely, had worked out a new plan which he now applied.

No company had ever before been managed so ingeniously as he would do now. He ensured that everything went as calmly and humanely as is ever possible in a montería. But he had taken on the smallest district, with the fewest men working in it, and selected men moreover who because of their physical constitution were not able to achieve much, whether or not they were tortured. He transferred all the strong men to other districts. His district was simply the decorated façade of the building. No one could hold him responsible for all the contratistas did. He was not there; no one expected him to be ubiquitous. Nothing terrible had been published so far. If anything shameful got into the press, the mayordomos were sacked in disgrace, and if necessary he handed them over in person to the authorities. He took good care that nothing happened to them; and if they should say more to the authorities than he expected of them, he simply abandoned them, or they committed suicide in their cell, tormented by their conscience. To arouse a conscience whose torments led to suicide was not so difficult. All you had to do was to slip a hundred pesos in the right pocket. It was just as it is in all dictatorships. The dictator is always innocent. He is always surrounded with clouds of glory. It is always the mayordomos, the capataces, the prison warders, the policemen, the sergeants, the secret agents, who practice brutalities and injustices.

Don Severo also explained his clever plan to Don Acacio, who managed the two smaller monterías. Don Acacio also ran only one insignificant district with few muchachos. And he ran it in such a way that even the Archangel Gabriel could have said to him: "Mortal man, your earthly deeds are without sin and error, and you are sure to go to the kingdom of heaven. Amen."

3

The boyeros, the ox-drivers, slept in a miserable palm hut, put up quickly near the pasture where the oxen were. A new hut had to be put up almost every week because the production sites changed. Pastures for the oxen were never near. If they were too far from the areas where production was proceeding, the macheteros had to cut fodder from the trees. Only a few trees' leaves were suitable as fodder for the oxen. The oxen needed not only green fodder. Their work was too hard for them to subsist on that. Maize was therefore grown in all the districts. It ripened in ten to twelve weeks, often even more quickly. And every morning the oxen received a good ration of maize which was issued from the headquarters of each district and collected by the boyeros or the ox-boys. Strong mules were provided for its transport.

The districts were so big that the working sites were often two, three, or even five hours from the Oficina, while that was a further one or two days' ride from the headquarters of the montería.

4

It was midnight when El Gusano came to wake up the boyeros for work.

He owned a watch, which he left behind in the Oficina for

fear of losing it, so he could not say whether it was one o'clock at night or two o'clock.

El Pícaro, mayordomo of the district, likewise had a pocket watch. He also had an alarm clock in the Oficina, where he was now in charge as if he were an independent contratista. Most days, pretty well every other day, he forgot to wind up one or the other. Often both clocks stopped. And because the time could then never be told exactly, everyone there got into the habit of telling the time by the sun in daytime and the stars at night. It must of course be said that El Pícaro did occasionally wind the clocks and set the hands according to his own reckoning. And it must further be said that El Pícaro, when he came back to the Administration after maybe four or six months working in the jungle, could find that his watch was seldom more than twenty or twenty-five minutes wrong by the clocks he found there. What cannot be said, of course, is that the clocks in the Administration always agreed with the right time, say that of the railroads or the post offices; for even in the central Oficinas it happened that everyone sometimes forgot to wind their clocks. All clocks suffered considerably because of the endless hot damp that ruled in the jungle, so that they either rusted or became unreliable in some other way, even if they were wound regularly. But whether the clocks went or didn't go had no kind of meaning anyway, because time there lost all meaning. Dividing the day or the night into definite periods, something that was often necessary when riding so as to be able to get to a certain place before nightfall, for that everyone relied mainly on the sun and the stars, which were only unreliable if the sky was clouded for a long time. The Indian muchachos nevertheless possessed an instinctive time, even under cloudy skies, which was quite enough for them for the tasks they had to do.

When El Gusano bawled at the sleeping boyeros that it was nearly sunrise, while in fact it was only midnight, he did so with the same urge to exaggerate that everyone feels when they have to get up earlier because they have to wake others who could well sleep two minutes longer. As soon as he was sure they were all up and at work, he rolled himself up in his blanket until nearly three o'clock, going by instinctive time, to go on sleeping and then to wake the hacheros, who went off to their work sites at four o'clock.

El Gusano emphasized his alarm with the heels of his boots, which he kicked hard into the ribs of the sleepers, so hard that they woke up with a startled groan and then sat up rubbing their hurt ribs with their hands. But if they weren't up then within the next three seconds, El Gusano kicked them with the whole of his foot in the stomach or the thigh or whatever he could reach. Goddam and blast it all, Indian jungle workers aren't feeble degenerate soldiers who are allowed to enjoy another five minutes of the tuneful signals of the trumpet that somebody plays for them for their entertainment before they get up.

"Filthy swine, I'll kick you right in your stinking face if you're not up this instant!"

It was Santiago who called to El Gusano. Santiago was up. He was already busy folding his blankets and mosquito net and rolling up his palm mat.

"Pero, jefe, I just want to roll up my two little cloths so they don't get full of spiders and ants and ticks, and maybe wet as well if it rains."

"Who's that still talking? You miserable bugger of a lousy Chamula, you shut your mouth when I give orders," roared El Gusano in a rage, and with the whip that he had already un-strapped as he woke the muchachos, he gave Santiago a hard blow right in the face. He couldn't see exactly where Santiago was, for it was pitch dark all round. But one of the ox-drivers had already lit a lantern and was outside the palm hut. That gave a faint beam of light in the corner where Santiago was arranging his things. And that feeble glow was enough for El Gusano to be able to aim at Santiago's face.

"You swine, I'll soon teach you to talk back at me and show you what work means!" With that the short whip whistled across the back of the neck of another man, who had just bent down to pick up his lantern, pull out the thick wick, and light it.

"You've got to know who I am, you stinking idle mulas!"

5

He had hardly said that, just as he had drawn the whip back again to give another violent blow, when out of the pitch-dark thicket, only about twenty meters away, came the sound of a man singing. It was not a very tuneful song. Clearly the notes had been put together by the singer himself, or taken from liturgies that the man had probably heard, and fitted to the words of the song. Even if the song was not tuneful, it was rhythmical and lively. The singer's voice was strong and firm; every single word of his song could be heard clearly and rang brightly through the dark night: "Gusano, Gusano, tu hijo, ay, de un cabrón; e hijo d'una puta perra; tu alma es de chapapote; tu corazón un hueso del infierno; el diablo ya te espera; y pronto él feliz será; que se muere El Gusano, que se mueren los gusanos los malditos y que viven los Inditos!" "El Gusano, El Gusano, you son of a whoremonger and son of a bitch, your soul is pitch, your heart a bone out of hell; the devil is waiting for you and soon he will enjoy you; El Gusano must die, the cursed one, and long live the Indians!"

El Gusano stopped as if petrified when he heard the words. But by the time the last two lines rang out, he had pulled himself together. With a swift, jerky movement he drew his revolver and fired three times in the direction from which the song had come. But in the echo of the last shot, it was not despondent laughter that resounded from the thicket, it was the healthy, even shrill laughter of a man who knew what he wanted and why he wanted it.

El Gusano snatched a lantern from the hand of one of the boyeros standing near him and rushed over to the place where he thought the singer must be. But the undergrowth was so thick that he could see no farther. He called for a machete. When a muchacho finally brought him one, with which he thought he could clear a way for himself, he felt that he would only make himself ridiculous if he tried to find the singer.

His next idea was to fire more shots into the thicket in the hope of hitting the man and capturing him. But he quickly gave up that idea. It would have been crazy to fire more ammunition when he was still not sure where the singer actually was. In the jungle ammunition was too valuable to waste.

He turned round to go back to the hut. Then he had another idea. Revolver in hand, in two long strides he forced his way into the middle of the muchachos who were gathered by the hut. With rapid gestures he swung the lantern round and counted the men. They were all there. So it couldn't have been one of the men who worked with the oxen. For a moment he looked suspiciously at Santiago. But he knew very well that Santiago couldn't in any circumstances have been the singer. He would still have been in the corner of the hut rolling up his petate when the singing began. Thinking slowly about the song, El Gusano came to the conclusion that it couldn't possibly have been one of the boyeros; none of them had a voice that sounded like the singer's.

"Off to work!" he ordered. But he said it in a much quieter voice than he had used before the song.

6

The muchachos moved off to their work, and El Gusano turned round with the intention of going back to the camp, where he had his lodgings in the same rickety building that El Pícaro lived in. It was El Gusano's job to wake all the muchachos in the morning and see that they were all at work by the time laid down. El Pícaro always slept a bit longer and didn't appear until the whole semaneo for which he was responsible was fully active. He did that not so much out of laziness but rather with the well-considered object of making it clear that he was the absolute ruler and dictator who had no fixed hours of work but could come and go as he pleased.

El Gusano had gone about ten paces when he stopped, paused for a couple of seconds, then went back to the hut and shouted: "Valentín, come here and bring your machete with you!"

Valentín was zacatero in the boyeros' gang, the boy responsible for feeding and looking after the oxen, who, if the grazing is poor, or there is no grazing in the neighborhood, helps the macheteros to collect leaves from the trees and bushes for fodder.

"Come to the camp with me," said El Gusano to Valentín.

El Gusano had suddenly become afraid to go back to the camp through the dark jungle by himself. The uncomfortable feeling came over him that the singer might still be hidden somewhere in the thicket and was waiting, as it had said clearly enough in the song, to send him to the devil, to give them some fun in hell.

El Gusano could see by the light of the boys' lanterns that they were waiting, and he saw, if not clearly, by the light of their lanterns from where he stood that the lads were all talking to one another. He imagined, and he was not far wrong, what the muchachos would be saying to each other, even if he could not hear it.

So he pulled himself together, and instead of telling the zacatero to accompany him, he just said: "Come to the camp early this afternoon and pick up more maize for the oxen. They must have more maize, they're losing too much weight."

"Si, jefe, vengo, I'll come early this afternoon. I think you're right, the bueyes are very thin and ill fed, the grazing we have round here is no good," answered Valentín.

In a louder voice El Gusano shouted to the muchachos who were still standing there with their lanterns, waiting: "Damned idle, stinking rabble, what's holding you up there, staring like a lot of slaughtered donkeys! I'll teach you to dance if you don't get a move on. The sun will be up soon. Filthy riffraff you are!" El Gusano unloosened his revolver. "Run off, and quick," he said to Valentín, "give the muchachos a hand with the yoking."

"I always do, jefe," the lad defended himself.

"Good, off you go then, off to the others!" El Gusano turned round, held his lantern up to light his path, and went off to the camp.

"What did he want you for?" asked Pedro, one of the boyeros, as Valentín joined them.

"More maize for the oxen. I have to go to the camp this afternoon to fetch more maize."

"All twaddle," commented Andrés, the head boyero, "nothing more than absolute rubbish, all that about maize. He was shitting in his pants, that's what's the matter with him, and because he saw us standing here he got it even worse, thinking we should be laughing at him when he dragged you off with him to keep him company on the way."

"Damn it, muchachos, that canción, that song, I reckon it's really given him a bellyache. Now he's got his arse all wet and full of mud, the goddam swine." Pedro croaked, deep down in his throat, then spat all round him. As the lads tramped on through the dark jungle to get to their place of work, Fidel, another of the boyeros, said: "How did that song go, anyway? I couldn't take it all in. It was right enough, what the singer sang. Every word was as right as if it had been written down. If only I knew how it went."

"Let's just see how it went," repeated Andrés. "It was something like: Los gusanos, los gusanos, ay, they creep through the mud; eat shit and drink piss and bore through stinking fat; they can eat dead bodies and creep up mulas' arseholes."

"No, it wasn't quite like that," said Pedro.

"If you know it better," replied Andrés with a laugh, "then out with it."

"You, Andrés," Matías joined in, "the way you say it, it's still absolutely great, maybe even better than what the singer sang. Where did you pick that up? It sounded like a real church song."

"That guy, that Andrés?" said Fidel. "You don't have to be surprised over him. He can read and write, a lot better than the cura, the fat priest. He got it out of his book."

"Maybe. Maybe I just thought it up by myself," said Andrés casually.

"Nobody on earth can make up that sort of thing by himself. You can only read it in a book, or a paper, if you asses had only learned to read." Fidel had not been looking where he was going and had fallen into a hole.

7

The lads had reached the pasture where the bueyes were resting. Some of the oxen stood up slowly by themselves when they saw the muchachos with their lanterns; they had enough experience to know that if they took too long to get up they would be kicked in the hindquarters, just as the muchachos had been kicked on the bottom when they did not get up quickly enough when El Gusano woke them.

Santiago, holding his lantern high, looked around and counted the oxen. Then he called out: "Que chingan todos sus madres, there are six missing. Come on, everyone! Let's have some help! They're stuck in the thicket, looking for fodder from the bushes." Andrés stayed in the pasture and with Valentín's help began to drive the oxen toward the sleeping hut where the maize was stored which the oxen would get before they started work.

When this first herd reached the hut three of the missing oxen were already standing there; they had come of their own accord because they knew where the maize was.

Valentín ran back to the pasture and called the search party out of the thicket. They had found the other three but didn't know about the three by the hut.

While the oxen were chewing their maize the muchachos squatted down round a fire where they boiled coffee and warmed up their frijoles and tortillas. The black beans were given more flavor with wild pepper, and the tortillas, which were very tough, tasted better with certain spicy leaves and herbs from the jungle crushed over them. Many of those herbs had a flavor reminiscent of peppermint, others of celery, others again of strong leeks, others of bitter parsley. The coffee stood over the fire in tin cans which looked like small, thin barrels standing upright. Each muchacho had his own can, his own coffee, and a piece of brown sugar cane.

Matías said: "We must go hunting again and catch a pair of good fat snakes to give us some meat with our frijoles."

"Or better, get another pescuintle out of a tree trunk," advised Pedro. "That would really give me an appetite, a fat pescuintle."

"Why not some pig's meat, too?" said Santiago.

"Yes, why not some pig's meat?" agreed Matías. "The whole jungle here is thick with pigs. You need only stick your hand out."

"Have you got a gun, maybe? How can you get a wild pig without a gun? Just tell me that," demanded Santiago.

"I once caught two puercos silvestres with one swing of a machete," said Matías, boasting of his great skill at hunting.

But no one there believed him for they were remarkable hunters, not as an entertainment but out of poverty and hunger; they could take turkeys, wild pigeons, jaguars, and snakes with a stone and sling, a bow and arrow, or a primitive spear.

"You? Two wild puercos with a machete? Huh, that's a hell of a laugh." Santiago looked at Matías as crossly as if Matías's boasting had been a personal insult to him. "You killed two puercos with a machete? Not even one, you didn't. Not even one just newborn. You can't even hit one lame leg of a wild puerco with a machete. I know you well enough, the way you handle a machete. And I know what sort of a hunter you are, too. You killed two wild puercos at once with a machete? Maybe at home in your village, two tame and lame ones that had been cooped up and couldn't run away, so old and ill that they collapsed with fright when a five-year-old boy rattled the posts round their cage."

"So you mean I'm a common bloody cheat and a cabrón and a stinking son of a whore? Is that maybe what you mean? Then get up and you'll see how I can deal with you right enough. Three like you and two more into the bargain, and afterward I'll lie down with two great girls on the petate and give both of them a kid," said Matías, rolling his beans in a hot tortilla and biting off a piece with a violent gesture as if he were biting off the head of one of his battered enemies.

"Each of those two great girls, only one kid each?" Andrés joined in, helping to make fun of Matías, who was well known for his boasting. "Only one kid for each muchacha you're lying on the petate with? What sort of a wretch are you, then? Why don't you give them triplets at least, while you're on the job?"

"Maybe you think I can't do that? I could bring you proof that will stretch your eyes wide and stick them wide open. I can, too. Do you know how many I could have had if I'd only wanted?"

"Oh yes, we know, two hundred and thirty, if they'd all gone right and you weren't too dumb to have it off with one great girl on a petate so that she gets real fun out of it," said Cirilo, while everyone around laughed and went on laughing until even Matías began to laugh, and then the breakfast program came to an end as he said: "You don't know me, little brothers, that's the reason. That's the only reason. And I'll show you, whether it's here or anywhere else, that I know damn well what I can do and what I can't."

"We all know what you can't do, just show us what you can," said Pedro, who shook the coffee grounds out of the can he had drained, and stood up.

"Hey, Valentín," called Andrés, "have the oxen done feeding?"

"They're still chewing."

"If we want to wait till they've stopped chewing we shall be sitting here until next Candelaria. Come on, quick, quick! If El Gusano catches us still sitting here he'll take us on one of his fiestas and then we can pick the maggots out of our battered backs."

At that the muchachos became very active. In less than two minutes they had hung up their cooking gear and the rest of their food from the crossbeam in the hut, rolled cigarettes for themselves and lit them, and then driven the oxen off to get down to work.

By now it might have been half past one in the morning. The air began to get misty and hung in wisps round the low bushes of the jungle.

10

Andrés called Vicente over.

Vicente was a small, thin Indian boy barely ten years old. His mother had had to incur debts of thirty pesos when his father had been kicked by a refractory mule and died. She did not want her husband, who had given her eight children, to be buried like a dog. She bought a simple coffin and asked the cura to lay the father of her children in the earth in Christian fashion.

The priest could not do that for nothing, for since God had presumably endowed him with intelligence but also with a healthy stomach which had to be filled every day so as not to let the intelligence get rusty, and a body that must be clothed in order not to cause offense, there was nothing left for the cura but to let himself be paid for God's blessing in the coin of the realm when he administered it. That is not a sin in itself, and it is just as respectable a business as cutting shafts for wagons or forging horseshoes. The sin in this holy career appears only in that the curas persuade people that bodies must unconditionally be laid in the earth in the Christian manner; and the Christian manner of course means with the help of a cura, with the tolling of bells and the sprinkling of water, and if bodies are buried without that special blessing, which only an anointed cura can give, then it all goes wrong with the poor souls, for they are burnt and can know only weeping and gnashing of teeth instead of the singing of holy songs and the playing of harps. Thus the people, whether poor or rich, are convinced that God's blessing is essential and that they must take the trouble to acquire, or, to put it plainly, to buy that blessing for themselves or for the souls of their departed.

The cura had a price list for the various kinds and grades of blessings that he sold in his shop. A quiet prayer in the church, which he recited so quietly that nobody heard it, cost one peso twenty-five. If he prayed aloud so that his murmuring could be heard, without what he said being understood, that cost two pesos fifty. If a given number of candles were to burn at the service, to make the prayer more solemn, then it cost five pesos. With choirboys singing, nine pesos. With the tolling of bells, twelve pesos. The prices went up as high as two hundred and fifty pesos, for which everything in the repertoire was performed—special mass, full illumination of the church, music and singing by the grave, and all sorts of toys and trivialities, little speeches and songs, incense and holy water, Latin litanies and genuflection. Those luxuries, of course, were only for the rich finqueros, owners of the big estates, generals, the newly rich diputados and jefe políticos, contratistas and recruiting agents for the monterías.

Vicente's mother, the wife of a poor Indian peon, although she wanted to show all conceivable honor to her late husband, could spend no more than thirty pesos for him all included— coffin, burial, funeral service, God's blessing, aguardiente for the bereaved men and aniseed brandy and some very cheap little cakes for the women. Of course the poor woman did not have thirty pesos. All she had in the house was thirty-four centavos. So she went to the finquero, the head of the estate where her husband had worked and had, in the course of his work and due to his work, been killed. After long bargaining and talking, many tears and prayers, the finquero was so touched by the fate of the woman, now left with eight children, that he felt prepared to lend the woman the thirty pesos.

"But you do know, Chabela," said the finquero in a businesslike way, "that I can't give anything away. Least of all thirty pesos."

"I know that well, patroncito. Nobody on earth can give anything away."

"Right, Chabela, and good that you realize it. Elpidio, your husband, God bless his poor soul, left a debt to me of ninety-two pesos and sixty-five centavos for goods at the tienda which he didn't pay for and which I had to enter on his account."

"I know, patroncito."

"How many children do you have, Chabela?"

"Eight, patroncito. Five varones and three hembras."

"That's very good for you, having five boys; the girls aren't worth much."

"Of course not, patroncito. And I often prayed to the Santísima, and lit candles for her, that she would give me only machos and no hembras. But the Madre Santísima, I suppose because she is a muchacha herself, even if she is a saint, has now sent me three muchachas."

"Well, we can do nothing about that, Chabela. That is the will of Nuestro Señor, our Lord in heaven, and we have to obey his will."

"Sí, patroncito."

"How old is your eldest muchacho?"

"Vicente? He is now—he would have been born in the same year as Don Eulalio's cantina was burnt down during the Candelaria festival."

"Then Vicente is ten years old now. Good, I'll lend you the thirty pesos, Chabela, but Vicente also has to pay. I'll speak to

Don Gabriel when he comes this way and get him to take him on
for the monterías, and Don Gabriel will give me the money back."

"But Vicente won't be able to stand the monterías, patroncito.
He's still very young and weak."

"Do you want thirty pesos for the funeral, or not?"

"Of course, patroncito. I can't let my good Elpidio be buried
like a dead dog."

"Then Vicente goes to the monterías."

"Sí, patroncito, then Vicente goes to the monterías."

"The three eldest boys that you have, Chabela, come over to
work in the house, also the eldest girl. The ninety-two pesos that
Elpidio owes me must be worked off. You know that, don't you?"

"Sí, patroncito." The woman sighed. She sighed now for the
first time during the long interview.

"You'll stay on the finca, of course, with all your children, and
work just the same as before. Your children will grow up in the
meantime and become efficient peons. If you need anything
from the tienda, then come after the funeral. I'll open an
account for you, Chabela."

"Muchas gracias, patroncito."

"And, right, I'll pay you the thirty pesos that you have to have
now. Send Vicente to the tienda to fetch everything you need
immediately for the entierro, the funeral, I mean."

"Muchas, muchísimas, mil gracias, patroncito," said the
woman. During the interview she had been standing in front of
the finquero, who was swinging in a hammock in the portico of
the house. Now she went up close to him, bowed deeply, seized
his hand, and kissed it reverently.

The finquero patted the woman's uncombed, shaggy hair
with his hand, and said: "Que vaya con Dios, hija; go with God,
daughter."

2

Vicente had taken twenty-five pesos advance from the enganchador, Don Gabriel, when he had let himself be recruited for

the montería, as arranged by the finquero for the thirty pesos' cost of his father's funeral. Of the twenty-five pesos the boy gave twenty to his mother, to buy shirts and pants for his younger brothers and sisters, in order not to incur unnecessarily high debts with the finquero. He had to keep five pesos for himself because he needed a cobija, a blanket, a petate, a tin can for coffee, and two little pots, to be able to cook beans and maybe a little scrap of meat when he was on the long, difficult way through the jungle, being taken to the monterías with the other men recruited for caoba work. The blanket was as good as worthless; he didn't have enough money to buy a good one.

So now he had twenty-five pesos on his account. Added to that was the twenty-five pesos cost of the stamps of the president of the municipalidad in Hucutsin for the statutory confirmation of his work contract.

Don Gabriel, the agent, paid the thirty pesos back to the finquero when the boy was handed over to him for the contract. Don Gabriel, to whom surely no one could impute a soft heart, felt in this case, maybe for the first time in his life, a little sympathy for the puny boy. He therefore charged him only twenty-five pesos recruitment commission. He also took pains to sell the boy to that montería where he knew things were not as hard as in most of the others.

That was the La Armonía montería, where Don Leobardo Chavero was administrator, one who, possibly more out of idleness and lack of interest, treated the workers less severely and who, if they came to him with complaints of cruel treatment which they said they had suffered from the contratistas or their capataces, held the affair over, saying that he would see it was settled justly. He forgot it completely after half an hour, but the workers had at least enjoyed the splendid feeling that there was somebody in the world who listened to their complaints and made a dozen promises to them that sounded fine when they were pronounced. In nearly all cases it was quite enough if workers were made a whole lot of promises by their employers or their rulers or their own leaders. No one expected such promises to be kept. Only during a revolution do the workers remember them, while those who made the promises then declare that the promises were not meant in the way they were interpreted by the workers but so as to promote the public welfare. And that public welfare is always against the workers, because if it favored the workers it would not be necessary to talk about the public welfare or the good of the people but simply about far more ordinary, unadorned justice.

3

Having arrived at the montería, Vicente had to buy all sorts of things in the tienda which were indispensable: a mosquito net, a better blanket, a pair of sandals, a pair of pants. With all that his account, which began with the thirty pesos for his father's funeral, had grown to a hundred and forty pesos without his having earned a single centavo. In other words, the original thirty pesos had increased nearly five times.

The boy was paid two reales, twenty-five centavos, daily for a work time that was seldom under sixteen hours. Just to work off the hundred and forty pesos he would have to work hard for five hundred and sixty days. But since there was also a small amount taken from those two reales for his food, since later in the course of the month more purchases of pants, sandals, shirts, and other items were unavoidable, it was pretty correct when it was declared: Vicente will have to work in the montería for ten thousand years before he will have worked off the original thirty pesos funeral expenses for his father. It might be that only eight thousand years would be needed, but one or two thousand years more or less didn't really matter.

Justice ruled in the monterías. That must be said lest any mistakes should arise. There were no exceptions made among the workers. Everybody in the monterías was bound in the same way as Vicente. The hard workers, the fellers and boyeros, earned rather more, four or five reales a day, but for that they also had higher advances and debts, and moreover higher deductions for inadequate production and higher payment to the kitchen. It was all so fair, every one of them needed between six thousand and ten thousand years to be absolved of his debts through his work.

4

Maybe on account of the touching look in his sad eyes, Vicente aroused sympathy even in Don Leobardo. He saw that the boy could not last long in the jungle. So he gave him an easier job as mozo, the boy who cleans the staff members' bungalows and keeps them tidy. In that way life was quite tolerable for Vicente. He got a few slaps now and then from Don Leobardo or one of the others of the staff when they were tipsy or annoyed. But those same staff members, or the girls who lived with them, made up for it when they slipped the boy all sorts of things that he would never have been able to have if he had worked in the equipment store or with the manual workers. He was allowed to finish off the remains of open sardine tins or lick the juice from cans of preserved fruit; here he got a piece of pineapple tart that had been left on the table, there a bar of chocolate that had only been bitten, good half-smoked cigarettes, a drink of wine or comiteco, and sometimes even a shirt that may have been too big for him but was fit for use after he had sewn up the parts that were too roomy with a few stitches of thread.

If he hadn't missed his mother and his brothers and sisters so much he would possibly have felt happy there; he would never have found it so easy and pleasant on the finca, where the work in the fields was far from easy and people were beaten more, and beaten harder, than they were in the montería. Since the finqueros could not afford to lose workers by sticking disobedient or lazy peons in the calabozo, the finca's prison, for any offense they had committed against the interests of the finqueros the men were severely beaten by the mayordomo, and always in the evening so that they could appear fit for work the next morning.

All things considered, Vicente could rightly say that he was well off in the montería. But that he had not only been well off in the montería until then, but indeed had lived as if in heaven, he learned on the very day that Don Leobardo left and the Montellanos took over the montería. Human sympathy or consideration of a worker's physical capabilities were quite foreign to the Montellanos. They knew only soldiers, subordinates, who had no other task in life to fulfill than to promote the prosperity of the Montellanos. The workers were just figures which could be shoved here and there at the will of Don Severo, the local dictator, without having the least right to say yes or no or even to express any sort of wish. If anyone uttered a single word against any order he got a hefty kick on the behind or in the belly, and that was the mildest kind of punishment. After those kicks they got from their masters, the Indians called the Spaniards gachupines, as they called the German coffee planters and landowners Chinos Blancos, reflecting other virtues that were observed, and well observed, by the Indians in their German masters.

5

Don Leobardo and his caravan had hardly left when Don Severo began to hold a general inspection, beginning in the Oficinas Centrales.

"What do you do here then, muchacho?" Vicente was asked.

"Soy el mozo, patrón; I am the boy here."

"Mozo, who for?"

"For Don Leobardo and the other caballeros."

Don Severo had a look at the boy. "Can you cook?" He hoped he might be able to use the boy as cook.

"No, patrón."

Don Severo looked at the boy again, then he said: "Turn around, let me see you the other way round."

He looked at the boy from behind, then made him turn round again so as to examine him again more closely.

"You're not very big." He took him by the arms and felt his muscles. "Show me your hands."

The boy held out his hands.

"You don't seem to have done any serious work."

"I am the mozo here, jefe."

"That's not what I'm asking you. And shut up or I'll give you a good clout."

Then he began to think it over.

"Damn it all, where can I stick you in? For a mozo I'll find myself a little boy, maybe from some woman who doesn't know what to do with him and would rather have throttled him before he hatched out. He could do it all right. How much do you get here?"

"Two reales, patroncito."

"It's disgraceful how the people here chucked money around. Giving two reales to a baby still sucking at the teats! That really is something to laugh at. Two reales. With that we'll go to the dogs in four weeks and can all drink ourselves silly."

"Two reales is in my contract, patroncito." Vicente defended his wretched pay.

"Did I ask you?"

"No, jefe, perdóneme."

"Then keep your mouth shut."

The boy stood there, cowed, and shrank into himself timidly so that he looked much smaller and weaker than he really was.

"Nobody wastes time here," said Don Severo, "here every-body works. What you're doing here is no work for a big, strong boy like you. All right, you'll still get your two reales, because that's what's in your contract. Now you'll go to the bodega, the equipment store, and work with Don Félix until I find something else for you. And make yourself useful and get down to it, or you'll get a good thrashing."

"Sí, patroncito."

Vicente went to the bodega and worked with Don Félix. In the first half-hour he was slapped in the face four times, and during the next half-hour he got two blows with the bar of a yoke and a stick smashed on his head so that his scalp was gashed and the blood flowed.

"You work here, you don't sleep!" Don Félix accompanied every slap, every blow with a stick or a climbing iron, with those words. It was of course a formula he had adopted from the vocabulary of his brother Don Severo. But he could strictly apply it all the time. In plain words he applied it all the time because he always made it fit with what he had in mind if he didn't know what else to say.

6

When, five weeks later, Don Severo went to the Oficinas Centrales with the intention of once more carrying out a general inspection, because he needed more men to work on the trees, he came across Vicente.

"Where are you working now?"

"In the bodega, patroncito."

"That's no work for a strong boy like you. You look pale. I'll take you to work with me in the semaneo. There's good fresh air there. It will do you good."

"Sí, jefecito."

"How much are you paid, now?"

"Two reales, jefe."

"That's a sin, God knows, to give twenty-five centavos pay a day to a pathetic bit of a boy like you. It's money thrown away.

You're coming with me. You can work with the boyeros. You'll earn your two reales there. Here in the bodega you don't even earn a quinto. It's work that a younger boy could do. One from those whores who only have kids and drink like fishes. I'll make an efficient hachero out of you. Let me feel your arms. Not yet, then, but in a couple of weeks. Then you can earn three reales. And if you manage your two tons, I'll even give you four reales."

"Muchas gracias, patroncito." His voice sounded scared.

"Four reales if you manage your two tons. I don't rob a poor Indian. I don't cheat anybody over his pay. Get what you need in the tienda."

"Yes, patroncito, I'm going. There must be things I shall want from the tienda if I'm going off into the semaneo."

"I'll attach you to Andrés. He's a smart boyero. He can teach you all right."

"A sus órdenes, patroncito."

Although Vicente had certainly had nothing to laugh at in the first week of his work in the bodega, he had soon got used to it; and Don Félix, because he was more occupied with other jobs in his oficina, didn't very often go to the bodega, where Vicente in the past three weeks had carried out all the work that formerly, under Don Leobardo as administrator, had been done by Don Mariano Tello as the well-paid manager. There was of course less to do just now in the bodega than under Don Mariano, since no new groups of workers had arrived during that time. But the work was still important enough even in quiet times to require an intelligent adult man. The intelligence and the adulthood were of course contributed by Don Félix, who gave Vicente all the instructions; and if they were not followed exactly, he gave Vicente half a dozen good blows on the bottom or the mule whip over his neck.

All the same, compared with the cruelly hard work in the jungle and the five hundred dangers that lay in wait for every man there, the jobs in the bodega were just about tolerable for a delicate boy like Vicente. When he realized he would now be sent to the semaneo, he felt the very last bit of what had held him bound to paradise had been cut. It was not dread of the work in the jungle that made him miserable. It was the final cutting off from the life he had led under Don Leobardo that aroused a deep homesickness in him, a pining for the rest and security he had known on the finca with his mother and his brothers and sisters. He was not a man yet, although Don Félix had forced on him, had beaten out of him, the work of a full-grown man. He was not even a young man. He was a child. And never before in his life had he felt himself more of a child, a little one needing protection and crying for his mother, than when Don Severo with cold words ordered him to the jungle. Maybe it would have been better if he could have sat down under a tree and, unseen by anyone, cried his heart out. That would have eased his mind and the feelings of injury that he felt. But for that he had neither time nor opportunity. He had hardly bought his things in the tienda when Don Severo shouted angrily at him: "Hey, you lazy devil, you sickly little brute of a kid, where do you think you're off to? Saddle my horse and help the arrieros pack the mules that we're taking to the semaneo. Get moving, goddam it! I'm the one who pays you. I haven't got money to give away to lazy Indian trash."

Before Vicente had really become aware of what was going on all round him, he was already on the march with a heavy pack on his back. He trotted behind the pack mules, going at the same pace as they did. Like the pack mules, he too kept sinking deep in the clinging jungle mire; and like the mules he found it hard to free his legs from the mire. Like the mules he stumbled and staggered up and down the stony slopes; sometimes, when they rose too steeply, he moaned and groaned as the mules did. Then he had to breathe the buzzing and squeaking farts of the pack animals loping in front of him. For he was afraid to stay too far behind the train and be taken by a jaguar, or lose the way.

And if he didn't stay close enough, he lost the assistance that the last mule in the train readily gave him on the hard parts of the road, not kicking him when he helped himself forward holding the animal's tail. The mule had more sympathy for him than Don Severo. All the same, it should not be forgotten that it wasn't the mule that paid his wages. Maybe the animal felt, and quite rightly, that the boy was nearer to him than anyone else. For the two jogged along as links in the same chain. And the truest comradeship develops between those who are forged in the same chain and so have to suffer the same pains.

7

That morning, when he went to wake the boyeros, El Gusano had brought Vicente with him and handed him over to Andrés. Andrés was to teach him so that he would become a stronger man, superfluous to the boyeros, and could be sent to the fellers. "What can I do with this little mosco? He can't even lift a yoke and isn't big enough to strap it up. Even now there aren't enough strong men among the tiros."

"You do what El Pícaro tells you, understand! And no answering back. I can give you a second anointing like that first one. Or have you forgotten that already?"

"Don't worry, I'll never forget what you did then."

"Don't talk to me in that familiar way! I haven't slept on the same petate with you yet. And: a sus órdenes, jefe! Do you understand?"

"Sure, I must be polite. You're the one with the revolver."

"I'll get you for the fiesta again, a second and a third time. And I'll deal with you first, while I still have my full strength in my arms and can take a good swing."

El Gusano grinned so that not only his short teeth could be seen but also the thick purple gums that protruded as soon as his lips were opened wide in a grin. Whenever he grinned his purple gums stuck out so far from his open mouth that his short teeth were completely forgotten and his teeth looked as unimportant as if they were only a yellowish white crust that had no other purpose but to prevent his gums from protruding still further.

"But first, teach this kid here," he added, "and when you've done and have half an hour to spare, I'll crush your obstreperous flesh onto your rebellious bones."

"I know, Gusano."

"Jefe!"

"Muy bien, all right, jefe," said Andrés, shrugging his shoulders. "The word itself doesn't make any difference. I can say jefe or I can say emperador. The word doesn't matter. It all depends what I'm thinking when I say jefe or sir or führer or leader. And you just have to guess what it is I'm thinking. Lick-my-arse is absolutely nothing to it. A sus órdenes, jefe!"

"You talk well enough, and maybe we'll understand each other one of these days. But you won't get away with that anointing. And now come on, get busy on this boy. He's a goddam idler, and he must be christened so that he knows what we're talking about."

Vicente was standing there, terrified, while Andrés and El Gusano discussed him.

Now El Gusano looked at the boy. "Pick up your pack and take it into the choza."

Vicente bent down to pick up the heavy pack. He was going to grasp the pack with his hands when El Gusano gave him half a dozen with the mule whip on his back.

"To get the laziness out of your bones!"

Vicente screamed and fell on his pack, crying.

El Gusano hung the whip back on his belt, rolled himself a cigarette, and as he lighted it said to Andrés: "If he's not a good boy and doesn't learn, you tell me. I'll remember him in my prayers and book him for the fiesta."

"Sí, jefe."

"A sus órdenes, jefe!" El Gusano ordered Andrés to answer.

Andrés picked up one of the towing chains that had been

lying on the ground. He held it in his right hand, as if he wanted to go off to work.

"A sus órdenes, mi jefe!" repeated El Gusano emphatically, and put his hand to his belt to undo the mule whip again.

Andrés took half a swing with the chain.

El Gusano spotted the movement in the flickering, uncertain light of the lantern, left the whip untouched, and bawled at Vicente, who was just beginning to get up: "Did you hear what I've been saying to your master, your teacher, and what you can expect if you're lazy?"

"Sí, jefe," the boy said, sobbing.

"And then let him tell you what a fiesta is, so that you understand better how we work here and what rewards there are," El Gusano continued.

Then he looked at Andrés, his eyes half closed, and said: "And I shall have something to whisper to you now and again."

At that moment, from the thicket about a hundred paces from the boyeros' choza, they heard the singer again, whose ringing voice had not been heard since the morning he had so frightened El Gusano: "El Pícaro y El Gusano, los hijos de un perro y de una puta; I'll sling their flesh to the wild pigs and their bones to hungry dogs; and the same for Severo and Félix and Acacio, y ellos van a morir ya mas despacio."

That was the first time the singer had also mentioned the three Montellanos among those he promised to deal with.

El Gusano didn't waste any ammunition this time on the invisible singer. He swung round, picked up his lantern, and ran to the semaneo bungalow as fast as the jungle allowed him.

8

He was out of breath when he arrived. He didn't waste time running to the Oficina first, to talk to El Pícaro. As if he'd gone mad he ran over to the jacalitos in which the hacheros slept. He grabbed a lantern hanging on a post and lit it from the one he had in his hand. As he did that, he yelled: "Out, all of you out!" Gabino, one of the muchachos, answered sleepily: "But jefe, it can't be four o'clock yet, it's still only about medianoche, midnight."

"Shut up, you bitch," shouted El Gusano. "When I tell you 'Out' that means 'Out' for you stinkers, and not a sound from you."

Before he had finished the sentence he had already reached the next jacalito, to rouse the lads sleeping there too. The muchachos, all half asleep, came running onto the square in front of the Oficina and gathered there. They were totally confused, chattering to each other excitedly and wrapping their blankets tightly round themselves, for the morning mists had crept in and it was very cool. At first they thought that fire had broken out in the Oficina. Then again they thought that maybe some pumas had slunk into the camp and killed or made off with some men who had just had to go outside. That did occur and was generally discovered too late. Often it was only after days or even weeks that the lads, when they were looking for new trees, found the gnawed bones of their comrade who had been carried off, only recognizable from the ragged shreds of his pants lying all round.

It had taken El Gusano only three minutes to get all the men from the Oficinas together.

"Come here, Gregorio," he called to one of the Indians. "Take the two lanterns and follow me."

Then he made all the lads form a line. He walked along the line, and each man had to raise his feet, first one, then the other. Gregorio had to hold the lantern so close that he almost scorched their feet.

El Gusano didn't say what he was looking for or why he was inspecting their feet. But some of the lads were just as smart as he was, if not much cleverer at that sort of thing.

Gabino said to Celso: "I know what the Worm's looking for."

"Well I'm damned," answered Celso. "I'd never have believed you were such a smart guy. So what is it the mangy dog is looking for?"

"He's looking for feet that have got fresh mud on them. Probably someone's pinched a bottle of aguardiente or a can of sardines and run off with it. Since he'd have to run through the mud, his feet would actually be the best way to tell who it was."

"Well spotted, Gabi, and well worked out." Celso laughed. Then he looked down at his own feet. "My hind hooves are as dry as my ears."

"You can be glad of that, then, Celso."

"Glad, why?"

"He'd beat you to a jelly if you had wet feet."

At that moment El Gusano reached them. "Feet up!" he shouted.

Gregorio shone the lantern on them.

"Those are wet, all right," said El Gusano suspiciously and pushed Gregorio's arm with the lantern nearer to their feet.

"Naturally they're wet," grunted Celso crossly. "Why shouldn't my hooves be wet? I had to run like mad through grass wet with dew because you'd chased me off my petate. Gabi here has got wet feet too. And your boots are wet. And so has Gregorio got wet feet."

"Shut up!" growled El Gusano and went on to the next man looking for fresh mud on the naked feet.

When he had examined all the men he stood in front of them for a while, looked at them undecidedly, pushed his hat to one side, rubbed his neck with the palm of his hand, scratched himself on the hips, and finally said: "Back to your chozas. Up at four, or I'll help you to your feet. Dirty rabble."

"Stop!" he suddenly yelled as the men turned to go back. "Has any of you seen his neighbor get up for half an hour and only get back a few minutes ago? If any of you can say who that was, I'll give them a bottle of aguardiente as a reward."

Not a man stirred.

"Of course not, nobody's seen anything. Huh!" He turned to Dionisio, the lad who stood just in front of him. "Didn't you see anybody get up and stay out for half an hour?"

"No, mi jefe, dormí, I was fast asleep."

"And you?" he asked the next man.

"También dormí, mi jefe, I was asleep too."

"I'll catch him all right, don't you worry," said El Gusano, at once confidently and menacingly. Then he strolled over to the bungalow to resume his interrupted sleep.

Later in the morning, when El Gusano sat at breakfast with El Pícaro, he said: "Caray, damn it all, what an absolute ass I am!"

"Have you just noticed that, Gusano?" answered El Pícaro with a grin, as he tore off a piece of tortilla and, after fishing up some black beans with it, shoved it roughly into his wide open mouth. Chewing gluttonously, and delighting in his own wit, he asked again: "Have you really just found that out, Gusano, that you're an old ass and a silly donkey? I knew that five minutes after I first got to know you, and if you'd asked me what I thought of you I'd have said right out to your face that you were a hundred times more dumb than you look, and you look dumber than scarcely anyone can look that God has created."

"Yes, but this time I've done something really stupid."

"Well, what was that?"

"We've got an agitator here, a spy. I must find out who it is. Then I'll take him to Don Severo, to drive him into the jungle and shoot him. Even though we really need every man here for our work, spies and agitators are dangerous and must be shot. Then the rest of them can be kept more easily under control. Don Severo told me that. He has dealt with more than a dozen in that way."

"I know that better than you. I've worked with him for years and I've helped him shoot spies. Have you caught the spy?"

"Not just yet. That's why I could throttle myself. I believed he was one of the boyeros. But the boyeros were all there when I counted them. So I ran back here and counted the muchachos here. If anyone was missing, that would be the spy. But there wasn't anybody missing. Then I looked at their legs. There must be wet mud on them from running through the jungle. But however much I inspected their hooves, none of them had any wet mud on them. And of course by inspecting them I've warned the cursed bastard. In the future he'll make certain he has dry feet. I should have done it unobtrusively, so that the muchachos didn't spot what I was looking for. One night I'd have caught the son of a whore."

El Pícaro chuckled as he gulped down his coffee and, still chewing, he said with his mouth full: "Pity we don't have enough chains here. Then we could chain up all the muchachos at night so that they don't get up to anything silly. I should like to see them chained anyway, even at work. Then none of them could ever desert and we shouldn't waste time catching them."

"Don't worry, Pícaro! I'll catch him all right. I believe he disguises his voice when he squawks all that filth at night, so that you can't tell who it is from his voice. But he's dangerous. We must catch him and shoot him. Or he'll ruin the whole business here."

"I'll talk to Don Severo about it when he comes over to our camp sometime. And now, off we go, Gusano. We've got trees to mark."

11

 Andrés trudged over to the pasture with the other boyeros to fetch the oxen in and yoke them.

"Have you ever worked with bueyes, Nene?" Andrés asked Vicente kindly. "I'll call you Nene, baby. You're still only a tiny baby. What's your right name, then?—Vicente. Miserable name. Nene suits you better! Oh yes, I was asking, do you know about working with oxen?"

"No, compañero."

"I thought as much. Did you come from a finca? So did I. My father had a debt of about a hundred pesos to the boss of the finca. And when the enganchador came to our finca buying people for the monterías, the patrón sold my father for the amount of the debt, because the patrón said he must have his money and couldn't wait a hundred years for it. At that time I was carretero, driver of the ox cart with a contractor at Socton. When I heard that my poor father had been sold, and I knew he could never stand the work and the beatings here in the jungle, I went home and took over my father's account and came to the montería. You see, Nene, that's how it goes. How did you come here?"

"For the expenses of my father's funeral."

"Very nice, too. Only pull yourself together. You don't look as if your chest is very strong. If you don't eat properly and don't look after yourself, you won't last long here. Have you still got a mother?"

"Sí, también hermanos, younger brothers and sisters, too. Say, why did El Gusano whip me? I hadn't done anything," said Vicente in a pathetic voice.

"That's how it is here. You'll soon learn. El Pícaro and El Gusano, those spiteful sons of whores, give everybody who's new here a good beating, to settle them in, as they say. That is the policy of the Montellanos who own the montería. You can see what mean creatures those wretched bastards are, they whip us whenever they feel like it, and we're quite helpless. Those beasts are the most pitiless wretches you could ever think of. If I had the revolver and the whip and they hadn't, you'd soon see what sort of pathetic little beasts they are. They'd whine and beg for mercy, worse than a sick dog. Not the least drop of courage and blood in their hearts, those men who abuse the defenseless Indians and whip them. They'd never dare to go into an Indian village, even with half a hundred revolvers hung round them. You'll find that all the time, everywhere; the feeblest, most pitiful wretches are the worst torturers of the defenseless. Cowardice is the mark of the dictator!"

"Is he like that with all the new ones? Or only with me?"

"With all of them. I want to tell you something, Nene. I was sorry when he whipped you so cruelly, and you just a little kid. We were all sorry. I wanted to jump up and take the whipping myself. And Santiago wanted to as well. But then we thought it might be better for you to get to know about it. It toughens you up, and you get the right sort of anger that we need. The next time, when he wants to sort you out at the fiesta, you'll have started not taking it so hard, taking it all bravely. Only don't cry. Our revenge will come sometime. You never know. Did you hear the cancionero, the singer, singing? In the jungle. There's something in the wind here, I can tell you. And one more thing. If I, or if Santiago, had let ourselves be whipped instead of you, it wouldn't have done you any good. Believe me. He'd have got at you tomorrow or the day after. You just forget to say 'a sus órdenes, mi jefe' and then you get your flogging, four times worse than today, when he was only just tapping you, as he calls it."

"Tapping me. Fine sort of tapping. I'm sure my back is cut."

"Let's look when we come to the water. I'll rub some salt in so that it doesn't fester. If it starts to fester in the jungle, that's bad. You get worms in it. And we can only burn those out with creolene, and that hurts terribly, I can damn well tell you. And if you aren't better by the fiesta, he'll bash them all out again."

"Then it's better to drown yourself in the river."

"It is better, Nene. I know. But you've still got a mother whom you'd like to see again and who would be so unhappy if she lost you. Isn't that right?

"And you've got brothers and sisters too, all younger than you. Maybe you won't survive it here. More than half of all the muchachos never go home. They die off like flies. Many of marsh fever. Others get something in the belly from the polluted water that we drink from polluted puddles when it's too dry. The oxen won't drink it. We have to because we can't hold out as long as the oxen. Others cut themselves in the leg with an ax out of carelessness, and the leg gets gangrene, an incurable rottenness in their flesh and bones. Then you're glad if someone relieves you of your pain and sticks his machete in your heart, to do you a last favor. Others are eaten or carried off by jaguars or mountain lions. Or a falling tree kills you. Or you fall under the oxen when they're hauling and half a dozen trozas pass over you and squash your belly as flat as a tortilla. Why do you want to drown yourself in the river, then? And maybe you'll survive it all and see your mother and your family again. It's hoping for that, Nene, that teaches you to bear everything and not end it all."

"And you," asked Vicente, "have you got such a hope too?"

"We all have, me too. I've got a girl who's waiting for me. A dear little girl. Goddam it all, let's talk about something else. Damn and blast and shit! And here we are with the oxen."

Andrés lifted his lantern high and shouted: "Have you got them all together? Or have two or three of the cabrones broken out again?"

"They're all here," called one of the boyeros.

"I've got that towing chain here that we lost last night," said Andrés, letting the chain fall from his shoulders. "One of the oxen must have dropped it behind in the dark. It was lying by the jacalito."

2

The oxen were all yoked together in pairs. Each boyero took a boy with him and set off with a pair of oxen.

"So that you understand better, Nene, I'll explain a few things to you. A pair of oxen yoked together, we here call a mancuerna; five pairs of oxen, five mancuernas that is, we call a tiro. You, the boy who walks in front of the oxen and leads them, you're a gañán, and I, the one responsible for a pair of oxen, I'm the boyero. So now, off we go to work."

It was still pitch-dark, probably hardly two o'clock.

"Why do we start so early, Andrés?" asked El Nene.

"Because we have to be pretty well through our day's work by ten o'clock. It will be so unbearably hot by then that the oxen can't work anymore. And that's when the great biting flies come out too, which give the oxen hell, so that they get wild and we can hardly control them anymore. They kick all round them, try to throw off the yoke, and it's as good as impossible to work with them. You can't manage them anymore; they break away."

"But the fellers are still not working. They don't start until four and work till the evening."

"Big difference there, Nene. You'll get to know all sorts of differences. The oxen, you see, are just oxen. We, the boyeros and the hacheros, we're not oxen, we're Indians, humans; we put up with things that the oxen won't put up with. That's why the Montellanos, and most of all El Pícaro and El Gusano, can do things with us that they can't do with the oxen. Do you see the difference now, why the oxen work early and stop early, while we and the fellers have to work twice as long as the oxen? When the oxen are resting, about eleven o'clock in the morning, we boyeros and gañanes don't get much rest then. We work right on into the afternoon because we just aren't oxen."

"It seems to be much worse here than it was on our finca at home," said Vicente.

"Huh, a finca, Nene, that's heaven on earth compared with a montería. You don't know that yet, but in four weeks you will want nothing more in this life or after your death than to live on a finca as an indebted peon. Even there you still get the whip from the mayordomo now and then. But it's always perfectly just, and you've never heard of a peon who has worked himself to death on a finca. And a fiesta on a finca is a proper fiesta, with church, music, dancing, and so much good food you'd think your stomach would burst. Here a fiesta is the mass dance of the mule-whips on the backs of the caoba men, and the music here is the whimpering and groaning and howling and curses of the tormented and tortured muchachos who couldn't produce their daily tonnage and so are unmercifully whipped, or even more unmercifully hanged."

"Hanged?"

"Yes, hanged. That is the Montellanos' very own invention, to torture the hacheros, who have to produce only two tons a day under their contract, so mercilessly that they can only avoid such cruelty if they produce three tons of caoba a day."

"But, hanged? What do you mean, hanged?" asked Vicente.

"Don't think about it anymore now, Nene. You'll learn about it soon enough. We've got other things to do now. You'd better watch your foot, so that you don't take a false step and slip under the oxen. They trample you in the mud without meaning to. And before I've scraped you out, you're already suffocated. Don't think about anything else but that just now, about what I'm teaching you."

3

"Here we are at my semaneo," said Andrés. "Hold up your lantern and look for the nearest troza, and when you've found one, call me. I'll be looking for one too."

"A troza, what's that? You must tell me that if I've got to look for one."

"It's the trunk of a felled caoba, a ton of mahogany. Cut into the right lengths, stripped of bark, and hewn square, so that the trunk has a diameter of about a foot. You must make sure that you find a transportable troza, one that's ready to be hauled away. There's a whole lot of trunks lying around which cost the hacheros a lot of work but which weren't credited to them. Those will be trunks that are rotten inside, though only a bit of it is rotten and the feller can't see that before he's finished felling it. There are other trunks too that are cracked lengthwise; that's another thing the feller can't see before the trunk is lying on the ground. It won't be credited to him, and he's done that work for nothing. Trunks like that just lie here and rot. Don't bother about them. The trunk that is ready to move is cut to a point at one end. This hewn part is called chuzo. So if a trunk has no chuzo, leave it. It's either rotten or cracked, or else the feller isn't going to hew it until tomorrow because he couldn't finish it today." Vicente went off one way with his lantern and Andrés in the opposite direction. Each of them ran off on both sides of the way he was taking.

"Hey, Nene, something I must tell you, so you can find the trozas more easily," shouted Andrés after the boy. "Look for newly felled boughs and branches on the ground. Where there are fresh-cut branches lying around you'll also see the tree stump, and just by it one or two trozas. Most of the trees give just one ton, but there are a lot that give two tons. If the branches aren't fresh, they come from trees that were felled a week ago, and those trozas have been hauled away already."

"I'll look carefully."

4

What the muchachos called linternas, lanterns, had no more in common with what civilized people understand by lanterns than that the linterna also gave light. It was a tin can containing about three quarters of a liter of kerosene. A tube was stuck in and fastened, and a bit of woolen rag was stuck into the tube. That was the whole lantern. But for this kind of work it was more useful than any other kind. It was a sort of kerosene torch. A proper lantern would not have lasted an hour; all the glass would have been broken and the case so dented and bent that it would only be by long guesswork that you could figure out that you were looking at a former lantern. Although the lanterns were open they withstood the gales and even the rain to a certain extent. If they went out the boyeros had a great deal of trouble lighting them again. Not one of the men had matches. Matches were too dear to begin with, and anyway they were useless after being carried for two hours. Either they got wet from the rain or from the thick mists and the heavy dew, or—and that was the commonest cause—they were ruined by the sweat of the muchachos as they worked.

Every muchacho had a cigarette lighter, something a man working in the jungle or traveling through the jungle can always rely on. Matches were untrustworthy. But those lighters that the caoba men had, consisting of a piece of steel, a flint, and a wick, were always reliable. To light a lantern that had gone out, a little fire had to be lit, of dry leaves and thin dry twigs, of course with the help of the lighter. From that flame the lantern was lit. In windy and very rainy weather the boyeros always maintained little fires in their work areas, to be able to light their lanterns more quickly.

The light from one of those lanterns extended only a few paces. Consequently, looking for trozas was difficult and time consuming. The boyeros and the boys helping them, the gañanes like Vicente, could not just walk as they searched. They ran like devils gone wild over every bit of the bush and the undergrowth of the jungle to find the nearest troza. And they not only ran about like devils gone wild, they *looked* like devils gone wild as, wearing only dirty white rolled-up pants, their upper body naked and a ragged palm hat on their long pitch-black hair, their dark brown bodies eerily illuminated by the flickering open lights, a machete in their hand, they fought their way half bent through the thorny undergrowth with catlike speed and suppleness.

Like the hacheros, the boyeros also had their daily, or more precisely their nightly, requirement to achieve, and if they didn't reach that level they were not paid for that day, even if they had done four-fifths of their requirement. If they were behind in their work twice in one week, they were booked for the fiesta or hanged in the evening next to the fellers who, because of their poor production, were being shaken out of their laziness.

A given district, cut by the fellers the previous day, was allotted to each boyero for the night and the following morning. The work of three or four fellers went to one boyero. The Montellanos, however, had worked it out on such a wide scale that they put one boyero, with his gañán, to every six fellers for the clearance of the felled caoba. The whole area allotted to a boyero had to be cleared of all transportable trozas during his working period.

However hardworking and efficient a boyero might be, he could not manage the work by himself. That was why he had oxen to help him. Indians or other people can be compelled to achieve a certain output, just as they can also be trained, let themselves be fitted with uniforms and gas other people or shoot them down, and let themselves be cut down if so ordered. That can't be done so easily with oxen; that is why people who are not expected to know anything about the national honor are called oxen. And therefore it was not enough that a boyero was as industrious as a young bee in the springtime. If the oxen were unwilling, or tired, or were distressed by the swarms of biting flies, neither hard work nor goodwill was any help to the boyero. The oxen did not want to work, and without their help the boyero could not haul off a single troza. Since the oxen had no understanding, neither the Montellanos nor El Pícaro or El Gusano could blame them if production fell short. The boyeros were blamed, however; they were not credited with that night's work, they were whipped at the fiesta, they were hanged; for they were boyeros. They had to understand their oxen, make their oxen work, train their oxen so that they learned to understand that the world knew only one objective, had only one aim, and that was to make the Montellanos millionaires in three years so that their relatives and friends in Spain could say: those are really efficient people, they have made something of themselves, they have made a fortune over in America, and America is the land of infinite possibilities. How things went on in the kingdom of caoba the world did not hear about; at least those who did hear about it sat at the heavy mahogany conference table, discussed the balancing of the accounts and also considered how the outbreak of dangerous communist ideas could be successfully arrested among white and colored workers.

5

Vicente gave a loud shout which he sent echoing through the darkness, pressing his two hands against his mouth like a megaphone.

"Hold your lantern up!" Andrés called back.

"What do you say?"

"Hold your lantern up so I can see where you are," repeated Andrés.

Andrés ran over to the oxen which were nearer to him than to Vicente. He drove the oxen up to the light that Vicente was holding up. When he reached the troza that Vicente had found, he said: "Stick your nose up high in the air, Nene, so that you catch the smell. Where there's a freshly felled troza lying, it smells different from the other parts of the selva. Do you smell it?"

"Yes, it smells fresher and greener. Juicier."

"That's it, Nene. When you've really picked up the smell properly, that's half the job. And if the wind is really blowing toward you, you go to a fresh troza like a dog to a newly roasted joint. It's well worth it to follow your nose. Often your lantern goes out and you have to search with your nose if you want to find a troza. It's not always such good weather as we're having now in the dry season."

"Dry season? But it rains practically every other day."

"It's different here from the open country and on the fincas and in the villages. The way it is now we call bone-dry. Actually it's never really dry here. The crown of the trees is too dense. No sunlight comes through to the ground. And down below it's all thick bush. Everything is always wet and muddy. That's why we always have that thick, heavy mist in the second half of the night and dew so thick that you think it must have rained all night. But once we begin the rainy season, boy, then you really will see something. Then you swim four times a day and four times in the night. But we shan't be working here then, we're at the barrancas, the ditches, and at the river, where we float. With that you can easily get both legs or both arms or your head crushed. It's all over in a flash, and off goes your head as if it had been nipped off. I'd better not tell you everything while you're still new. But maybe it's only fair that I should tell you everything right now. Better that I should tell you than the others, who exaggerate ten times to make the most of their fear."

"Just next to that is another troza, and twenty paces further on there are two more that I've seen already."

"That's good. Very good, Nene. Now we needn't look in the dark anymore. It will be morning before we've hauled those four away, and we'll find the trozas more quickly because we can see better than with these goddam linternas, which aren't worth anything. But now, down to work. I've been talking so much that we've lost nearly half an hour. Help me lead the oxen back so that we can hook the chain on."

The towing chain was slung over the back of one of the oxen so that it would not drag behind and get caught in the undergrowth when the oxen were being led.

"Now we knock the towing hooks into the troza, one each side. See, like that. The hooks will dig deeper into the wood when the oxen really start to pull. And now we pull the end of the chain through the two hooks and fasten it with the catch."

"Have you been working long with the oxen in the caoba, Andrésillo?"

"No. Only about four months. It might even be eight. You forget time here, and it's only when the heavy rainy season begins that you know that another year has passed, and since we haven't had any heavy rains yet, I know I haven't been here a full year."

"Then you've learned very well."

"But, man, I know how to handle oxen. It's my job, as I told you. I was actually carretero. More, I was encargado, leader of a caravan. Oxen can't say anything to me without my knowing what's the matter with them. I can talk to oxen better than I can talk to you, Nene; and the oxen talk to me better than you do."

Vicente laughed out loud in his boyish way. "Don't tell me such exaggerated stories, Andito. How can oxen talk?"

"Adelante, Moreno! No, not you, Rojo, Moreno, adelante!" shouted Andrés to the oxen. Then he said: "Do you see how only the brown one is pulling now, and the red one has stopped?"

"Good heavens, Andrés, you're a gran maestro, a great master," said Vicente with admiration, in a voice that sounded as if he had almost lost his breath with excitement.

"To be able to manage the oxen so that only one tows and the other stays still, that's necessary, you'll soon see that. The troza buries itself deep in a bog, and then if they both tow it just buries itself deeper. You can only drag it out of the really sticky mud if one ox pulls and drags the troza to the side to get it moving again."

"Adelante!" Andrés shouted now to the two oxen, and they pulled.

"You go with the oxen, Nene, with your lantern, and you can prick them with the goad to make them run smartly. Off you go!"

The towing began. They didn't get ahead all that smartly, because oxen are not horses. Their pace is leisurely and deliberate, but steady.

The ground was firm there, and progress was hardly stalled. "Wait, Nene," called Andrés. "When you're leading you must take care the troza doesn't get into thick bush, where we should have a lot of trouble getting it out with the machete. Off you go!"

Andrés ran up behind the troza. He had a machete in a leather sheath at his belt. Vicente also carried a machete. Andrés had his lantern in one hand; in the other, his right hand, he held a strong iron hook. With that hook he continually worked on the troza, dragged it this way and that so as to guide it well, lifted it if it wanted to bury itself in the ground, and shook it violently if it looked like it was sticking in the undergrowth.

After about thirty minutes the troza had been towed for a kilometer.

"Stop!" ordered Andrés. But the oxen had already stopped before Andrés called. He ordered "Stop, Vicente" then, because when the oxen stood still the boy hastened to drive them on energetically because he thought they were being lazy.

"Now you can see, Nene, that the oxen understand more than you. They know that we've now reached the callejón, the trail, and that they must stop here. We unhook here and go back and bring the other trozas as far as this callejón, one after the other. When we have all that we've got to haul here, at this path, then we tow each one on, about a kilometer. If we were to haul each troza all the way to the dump, we should manage to deliver only half of them. The oxen have to recover, they have to rest, and they can only do that if they work hard only for short periods and then are led back again, when they go unloaded at an easy pace, and gain new strength."

"But the work wasn't so hard that they have to recover from it already," answered Vicente.

"Don't be too sure, baby. I've told you already, the ground here is firm, that's the first thing, of course. Just you wait until we're hauling in the callejón. You'll really see something. You can be glad then if we don't need four tiros, twenty pairs of oxen, to haul every single troza. Then we work thirty-six hours without a break to haul the trozas felled in a single day. That won't happen now, not today. It doesn't look like rain. But we're coming to a place, close before the tumbo, where we bring up the rest of them and have to have five mancuernas, five pairs of oxen, for each troza."

"What's a tumbo, then?" asked Vicente.

"That's the place where the trozas are piled up and wait until the rainy season starts and the dry ditch—the arroyo, you'll understand that better—fills with flood water, and then they can be floated as far as the little stream and then on to the big river."

The two lads went back to the team of oxen to haul the next troza to the callejón.

Suddenly Andrés stopped, shone the light nearer, and said: "Listen, Nene, didn't you see this troza here? It was right in your path when we were looking for trozas."

"Of course I saw it. I haven't got gum in my eyes," the boy defended himself.

"Doesn't look like that to me. Why didn't you count it? It's nearer to the callejón."

"I thought it didn't count. It's not ready. Not cut off to a point."

"But that one is a rollete, which doesn't get squared off."

"Why isn't a rollete hewn square along its whole length?"

"That's a long story. And since I've got to teach you, I can tell you all of it now. In any case I'm sure I'm not reaching my deber, my requirement. We'll both lose a day and maybe El Gusano will give me an anointing on top of it. He promised me another, as you heard. Because I was too unruly."

"How are you unruly, Andrésillo? You're the finest boyero in the whole world," said Vicente devotedly.

"In your opinion, Nene. Pity your opinion doesn't count here. What counts here is the opinion of El Pícaro and El Gusano, and if you tell them your opinion they'll just give you a dozen on your back, and you can think yourself lucky if a couple of the dozen don't rattle over your head and ears. Come on, send the oxen round here and throw the chain down to me so I can hook up."

The second troza was hauled to the trail.

As the two of them went back again without a load, Vicente said: "You were going to tell me why a rollete isn't hewn square but only stripped of bark and left round."

"Right. It's really all the same to us, especially to you,

whether the trozas are left round or square. For the fellers, of course, a rollete means less work; they don't need to spend so much time hewing it and can go on to the next tree. The Montellanos are very clever businessmen. So as not to miss any purchasers they produce square trozas as well as rolletes. In America and England the people are so keen on caoba that they saw the wood into quite thin sheets and then glue those thin sheets onto ordinary wood and give them a good polish. Naturally that's a fraud. The people who buy mahogany furniture think it's mahogany all the way through, as if it were all made of mahogany. That's the reason many purchasers prefer the round trunks, because from the middle of the round trunks you can saw thin sheets that are a few centimeters wider than the sheets that can be sawed out of the square ones."

"Then couldn't all the trozas be left round?" asked Vicente.

"They could be, but it isn't done. The rolletes also have their disadvantages. They split more easily lengthwise, and that makes them half or even absolutely worthless. The trozas that are hewn square don't so often split, and the purchaser can see more quickly with them whether the trunk may be cracked, something that is harder with the rolletes, where often it can't be seen and is only noticed when the purchaser has the troza under the saw."

"Who told you all this so clearly, Andrés?"

"One of the fellers. He's a Chamula, called Celso. He is El Tate in our camp, the reverend father. He's already been here for years and knows more than the contratistas. El Pícaro and El Gusano both shit in their pants over him, they're so scared of him."

"Doesn't he ever get a fiesta?"

"I don't think so. Cirilo told me that a year ago our last contratista, Don Remigio, booked Celso for the fiesta because Celso had been rude to him. When Celso's whipping was over, he just lay down and didn't do a stroke of work for a week. He's the best feller who ever worked in a selva, the only one who can produce five tons in a day if he wants to. But he doesn't. Don Remigio couldn't get on without Celso. He sent for him, but Celso didn't come. So the great contratista had to go over and speak to Celso. Don Remigio said he'd soon break him. So Celso said yes, he could do that, but the more he was whipped the less he would work, and it meant nothing to him anyway whether he was shot to death or beaten to death. It was just the same to him. And then he said that in the future for every blow he was given he would not work for a whole week, and if he got fifty, he wouldn't work for a whole year. Don Remigio spoke to him better then, and Celso got up and went off to work. Since then he's never been whipped again. But it's a fact that neither El Pícaro nor El Gusano dares go near him. He's dangerous. And Don Severo too has told them to leave Celso alone because his work is more important to him than the work of the two overseers."

"Why doesn't he run away?" asked Vicente.

"That's not so easy, not even for him. And now, that's enough, we must get down to it and clear the field of trozas. It won't be too long before El Gusano comes riding up, and if we haven't got all the trozas in the callejón by then there will be hell for both of us. I can stand it. Whether you can stand it I don't know, and I don't believe you can. And if you get into trouble, you put the blame on me. The best I can do for you here, as long as you and I are working together, is to do everything possible to prevent El Gusano from booking us both; for then you'll come off worst, poor kid. So let's really get down to it thoroughly."

6

The sun rose when all the trozas were on the trail ready to be hauled on.

"Now we'll have breakfast," said Andrés.

During the night they had brought some maize in a sack, some of which was now given to each of the oxen; then, when they came to the place where they were working, the sack was hung on a tree to prevent the wild pigs from finishing it off.

"Spread the maize in front of the oxen," said Andrés. "Be careful that it lies on flat ground."

"Shall I unyoke?" asked Vicente.

"No. It makes too much work yoking them up again."

Both lads had brought the breakfast issued to them, the morrales, in a little bast bag, and had hung the bag next to the maize, on the same tree.

In a few moments Andrés had a fire burning. Vicente ran down to a muddy stream and filled the metal cans with water, and at the same time filled the pumpkin-skin bottles which had been drunk dry during the night. They put the ground coffee and a piece of brown sugar cane into the cans and put them over the fire.

They had boiled black beans rolled up in big green leaves, some salt in dry maize leaves, and to go with that a dozen big tortillas. They laid the tortillas in hot ashes taken from the fire, and the beans were in a little earthenware dish and were put on the fire to warm them. Then they cut green pepper pods into little pieces and mixed them with the beans. Each of them had a little bunch of green herbs of various kinds which grew in the jungle. When the beans were hot they were wrapped in pieces of hot tortilla and put into the mouth all rolled up. They took the salt between their fingers and had some after each bite. Their little green herbs were put in afterward. Meanwhile the coffee had boiled and they drank it from a fruit shell which served them both as a cup and also as a little bowl in which the pozol was kneaded during pauses in their work. As they drank their coffee they took out some raw tobacco and rolled cigarettes for themselves. Vicente, although he was a boy, managed to roll himself a cigarette well and smoked it with the same enjoyment as Andrés. Their cigarettes were hardly half smoked when El Gusano rode up. He stayed on his horse and without saying "Buenos días! Good morning!" shouted out: "All the trozas found and on the callejón?"

"Sí, todas, all out," answered Andrés, still sitting by the fire and continuing to smoke comfortably.

"Off with you and arrastrando al tumbo, haul them down to the dump. And not so much sitting here idly and smoking cigarettes. You've got the evening for smoking." El Gusano looked down the trail.

"The oxen must have their maize first," Andrés defended himself.

"I can see that myself, you don't have to tell me," grunted El Gusano, less to give credit to Andrés than to agree that there was nothing the two lads could do at that moment, so they could just as well smoke peacefully until the oxen had chewed their maize.

"What is the bajada like, the part of the trail leading down to the ditch?" asked El Gusano. "Mucho lodo, lot of mud and mire?"

"Yesterday we sank up to our hips, and it won't be any better today," said Andrés.

"How many tiros will you need then for the subida and the bajado, for the hill before the dump?"

"Maybe I can manage with two tiros, ten span of oxen. Last week we had to have twenty pairs of oxen on four days. We were sitting up to our arms in mud with our trozas," Andrés told him.

"I know. All right, I'll send you two tiros, two pairs. Cirilo and Fidel will have them there about nine o'clock. With your mancuerna that makes eleven span we shall have then. And now, not so long sitting there and smoking. Tomorrow you go to the other side of the arroyo, where they've already been felling for three days and they've got a good output that has to be towed away."

El Gusano gave his horse a blow and trotted off to inspect other boyeros.

"How far do we have to haul from here to the tumbo?" asked Vicente when the two were alone again.

"About two leagues, say eight kilometers."

"And every troza has to be hauled two leagues?"

"The trozas we've brought here to the trail today must all be hauled two leagues," said Andrés. "That's nothing at all; two months ago we had fully five leagues from the felling area to the tumbo. On such a long haul you often meet a dozen ditches, arroyos. But they can all be arroyos that don't lead to the main stream but run dry after a few miles or lead to a lake, and the lakes have no direct connection with the river. And then some of the ditches do lead to the river but get wider at certain places and pass over wide stretches of gravel, and then the trozas sink so deep there's not enough water for them to float. You can believe, and Celso told me, it's not so easy to find a montería and then establish it. There may be plenty of wood there for felling, but if there are no ditches there, or the ditches don't run the right way to let the trozas be floated to the river, then the montería is pretty well worthless, however fine the caoba is there. If every troza starts by having to be hauled more than twenty kilometers, or even further, then it's not worth it. Then you're hauling three or four days for every troza and maybe with as many as twenty span. The contratistas' work is not as easy as you may think. They often spend a whole week, even two or three weeks, looking for arroyos that will definitely lead to the river when they have deep water in them. The contratistas then have to walk along the whole ditch with a pair of muchachos with machetes, to make sure where it leads. Often the ditches are fifty, maybe a hundred kilometers long before they flow into the river. And maybe the men spend three or four days in the jungle, going along the ditch all the time, only to find out after all that trouble that the ditch can't be used for floating. And then the ditches have to be cleared of trees and brushwood so that the trozas aren't held up as they float. That's what we have macheteros for. That's why the monterías are so dear and only people with a lot of money can buy them, because a good montería has broad, deep ditches for floating, and all the ditches are explored and recorded to show whether or not they can be used. That work alone, exploring and recording all the ditches, that takes months, and it's work that has got to be done even though not one troza is taken along it."

"Andrésillo, you're the cleverest muchacho I've ever met in my life," said Vicente admiringly. "I'm so glad I was made your gañán."

"I'm not as clever as you think. I just use my eyes and keep my ears open when other people are talking to each other who know more than I do, especially the contratistas and the people in the office. First you must learn good Spanish, then you'll learn to understand better what other people are saying. Your Indian dialect won't help you much in life, Nene. And now let's haul the trozas along the trail. Bring the bueyes over and fix the chain on the yoke."

Andrés threw the rest of his cigarette into the fire, stamped the fire out, and then hung their little bags of food on the tree again.

12

 Meanwhile day had fully broken, but the sun came only in thin streaks through the thick foliage of the trees. The heavy morning dew of the tropical jungle made the trees, the bushes, and the undergrowth look as if it had been raining hard during the last hours of the night. If the lads or the oxen collided with a bush or one of the smaller trees, the water fell on them so that after a few steps they were soaking wet.

Although the gleaming sun was hardly visible down on the trail, it was already beginning to weigh on the crown of the trees. The boiling heat beneath the trees became more and more suffocating, and breathing grew harder and harder for men and animals the higher the sun rose. It was as if the lads were in a steambath, for the water that lay so heavily on the leaves of the bushes was beginning to evaporate. But the hot, wet vapor could not escape. It rose up to the crown of the trees and was imprisoned there, hanging and making the air hotter, denser, and more stifling.

The troza was being hauled along the trail.

Andrés labored, swearing, shouting at the oxen, calling out continual instructions to Vicente.

As he went he remembered, ten times a day, his earlier work as carretero. There too the carretas, the carts, were dragged by oxen over miserable roads, now rocky and stony, now collapsed and marshy. There too it was hard work to keep the carretas moving, not to let them sink or slip off the road and plunge into the ravine. But hard and distressing as that work had been, compared with hauling trozas the leading of a carreta was a Sunday afternoon outing.

What was called callejón here, the trail, had only one thing in common with a road, that trozas were hauled along it. Some tree trunks and thick bushes that caused an obstruction were cut down, and that was all that could be done to improve the trail.

The oxen plodded on unhurried, driven on by Vicente with shouts or with the goad, chewing, sometimes lowing, thrashing their tails round them to ward off the biting flies that attacked them. Their mouths almost touched the ground, for only when they held their heads very low could they get the full strength from their necks that they needed to haul the troza. The heavy, roughly worked, long yoke was fixed to a long bar over their heads. It was fastened with straps which had been pulled through holes bored in their horns, and did not allow one of them to move its head alone, independently of the other. If one animal was troubled by one of the great insects and stung, and shook its big head awkwardly, the whole bar was shaken and the other animal made to shake its head in the same way. The thicker the biting flies swarmed, the more furiously the dis-tressed animals shook their heads to defend themselves. Their big round eyes protruded from their sockets and turned red from the pain they had to bear. How easily could a sympathetic and loving God have lessened, even eliminated, the agonies of those innocent, hard-working beasts if it had pleased him to create no biting flies, no mosquitoes, no worms that bored into every hurt place on a living animal and bred there, to create no morasses too deep to be of use to any creature and simply acting as breeding places for all sorts of parasitic insects.

Swarms of tiny flies crawled into the ears and eyes of the animals and of the people working with them. Ticks waited in the leaves of the bushes, dropped onto the animals and men as soon as the bush was touched, and ate into the skin, digging in their heads and clinging so firmly that it was painful to pull them off, and the skin became inflamed, even more painful if the head broke off and stuck in the flesh when they were pulled off.

Two hours after sunrise there was blood flowing from the bodies of the oxen and of the two lads in hundreds of places. The finger-sized biting flies of the jungle, in their hunger for fresh blood, on which they could so seldom satisfy themselves, not only sucked the blood but were so wild and hungry that they spent little time in peaceful sucking but tore whole pieces of flesh from the bodies of their victims. And the little pica-huyas, which were not even noticed by the animals or the men when they settled on them and stung them, and whose sting could not be felt until the insect had already flown away, left blood blisters in hundreds of places. For a whole week those blisters irritated the spot that had been stung so much that the victims scratched them deeply with their fingernails in the hope of getting a little relief from the agony for a few minutes, though they knew that the relief was deceptive and that new and painful itching was sure to follow.

Leading a carreta was no work compared with hauling a troza. The carretero walked beside his carreta laughing, chattering, whistling, and singing. If the road was dry and not too difficult, he even sat in the carreta and left it to his experienced and trained oxen to find the best way. Now and then there came a stretch of road where stones had to be cleared out of the way, where he had to grip the spokes firmly to help the carreta through the mud, or where he had to find stones to fill in holes in the road so as not to let the tall wheels sink in or the axles break.

A troza, in contrast, however tiny, however innocent, however insignificant a tree trunk like that might seem compared with a carreta, created work so heavy, so demanding, so exhausting, so full of tricks and needing so much expert knowledge that you could easily have led ten carretas with the same amount of work without suffering any particular mishap.

At first sight it looked uncommonly simple, with the help of two strong, well-fed oxen, to haul a caoba trunk through the jungle. But even on a dry, paved road it would have been trouble. It was more trouble on flat, dry earth where there was no obstacle of any sort to make the hauling difficult. But on a jungle trail it demanded every effort that a pair of strong oxen and two men could achieve.

In the caoba trade a troza was called a ton. Caoba is an uncommonly hard and extraordinarily heavy wood. Consequently a troza is not a ton, not a thousand kilograms reckoned by weight. It is nearer to a freight ton, a tonelada.

When Vicente asked Andrés how much a fresh troza would weigh, Andrés said that, by his estimate, a troza could probably be fourteen arrobas in weight, that is, something like a hundred and fifty or a hundred and sixty kilograms, he didn't know exactly, and it depended on whether the troza was very fresh or dry. To handle a trunk that weighed that much certainly required great strength. Four arrobas were reckoned to be a considerable load for a pack mule. And a troza of caoba weighed pretty well four times as much as was loaded on a mule on good roads. You could only load two quintales, eight arrobas, onto a mule if the loads lay well and smoothly, like sacks of raw coffee, or if the animal had only a short way to go, on roads where there was no mud and not many steep slopes. Of course the oxen don't have to carry the troza on their backs, but whether the load gave less trouble hauled along the ground you could judge only from the fact that four mules could hardly drag a troza forward. Not here, anyway, and ten times less so in those parts of the trail farther down, nearer the dump.

2

The oxen hauled, and the troza began to move. An important job for the boyero, as Andrés told Vicente, was to make sure the chain always lay under the troza where it was attached with the hooks. If the troza turned so that the chain came up to the top, the troza must be turned again with the next haul so that the chain was underneath again. For it was only when the chain was below the chuzo that the chuzo, the point, rose, otherwise it bored into the ground. The boyero couldn't simply stroll along beside it as he could with a carreta. The troza had to be lifted every time with the iron hook that Andrés carried in his hand. The point got caught in tree roots, which stretched all over the trail. Then it had to be stopped. If the roots were not too thick they were cut, but if they were too strong and it took too long to cut them, the towing hooks had to be taken out. The oxen were turned round, the hooks inserted again at the other end of the troza, and the oxen pulled the troza out of the roots backward. Once that was managed, the hooks were pulled out again and put back at the front, by the chuzo, and the troza was lifted so that now it could be hauled over the roots and a second snarl-up with the roots avoided.

Then there were furrows in the trail and the troza had to be lifted to prevent it digging itself in. The oxen pulled with all their strength, and if the point was not lifted over the obstruction at the right half-second it bored itself half a meter into the ground. And once again the hooks had to be taken out and fitted at the other end. The oxen were turned round and the troza once more pulled out backward. This turning and reverse hauling could happen five times in a path of a hundred meters.

Then there were stones in the way, branches, trunks, all sorts of things in which the troza got caught if it was badly handled. And every stop meant lost time and twice the work.

So it was no wonder that Andrés was absolutely bathed in sweat and so out of breath that you would think he must collapse if a troza were hauled another kilometer and the oxen were led back to haul the next troza on for a kilometer. Only a practiced and strong young man could do it, in tropical heat, enveloped in hot, moist air, with no fresh breeze to cool him down, running along by a troza, continually having to lift the heavy weight and guide it along the right path. With one wrong pull by the oxen the troza could fall onto Andrés's or Vicente's naked feet, and if the lads weren't careful the troza scraped against their legs and took the skin off. That did happen sometimes, and the only words of consolation the victim got were: "You should have kept your eyes open. Days when you don't work won't be credited to you, of course. On your feet in three days or we'll hang you for four hours to teach you to look after your bones. We've paid good money for those bones, and don't let us be cheated over them, is that clear, you stinking Chamula?"

A number of the boyeros or of the ox-boys who drove the oxen as gañanes certainly did not need to swallow that well-intentioned consolation. If he fell under a troza when it was being hauled over hard roots or over stones and rocks, by the time the oxen were finally stopped the boy, or just as often the boyero, was found so crushed and mangled that there was not much left of him to waste comfort on. And if El Pícaro had really wanted to hang him the bits would have fallen apart, and what was still left hanging on the rope would maybe not even be worth burying. The soul had long since been expelled, and if it had wanted to go on living, at that moment it was hovering around somewhere and was certainly in a land where lazy or unruly caoba workers were not hanged or whipped.

"Now we've got to do the last half-league with the trozas,"

said Andrés, as he unchained the last troza next to the ones that had already been hauled down.

"The oxen must have another rest now, because it goes on like this from here on. That gives us a chance to sit down for a moment and roll a cigarette and smoke it." On the last haul the lads' little bags, the morrales, had been brought with them, to keep them near.

The oxen were as thoroughly soaked in sweat as the two lads. Their heads were still strapped together under the bar of the yoke lying on them, and they moved them in a remarkable, regular rhythm to fill their lungs with air. Their flanks pumped in and out. Their great eyes seemed to protrude even more from their sockets. There was hardly a spot on their bodies that was not red with flowing blood.

"Poor bestias," said Vicente, going over to the oxen and driving off their bodies some of the biting flies that had bitten themselves in. Thick fresh blood spurted out of the insects, filled with the blood they had drunk, so fiercely that it hit Vicente in the face.

3

Every now and then, in the richer companies, there has been an administrator who said a hundred times: "Las pobres bestias! Those poor, pitiful animals!" And often some sympathy was also shown for the Indian peons and other workers who were sacrificing their health, life, and personal happiness so that the world could have mahogany bookcases. The humane managers and directors had tried more than once over the last hundred years to reduce the suffering of the workers and the oxen. Many an administrator, in the first days after his arrival, found it so hard to accept what he saw there that he sat down at once and wrote a long report to the company declaring that he could not bear to see such suffering and that the company should send another man or should introduce some changes. But the post rider did not ride on that day, not for another five weeks. Meanwhile the newly arrived administrator had grown used to all the things he saw and suffered. He read through his report again, couldn't think how he could ever have written it, and tore it up. But in the meantime he had learned, if only to a slight extent, to endure the same ordeals that all the other people there had to endure. He was tormented by biting flies, ticks, mosquitoes like everyone else. He had to ride to the camps, got stuck with his mule and had to help it out of the mire, maybe didn't reach the camp before dark because he had lost his way and had to pass the night in the jungle, wherever he was when it got dark. Then came firm letters from the company making him responsible for a regular and full delivery. So after barely three months the administrator no longer noticed one of the torments that, in the first days of his labors, he had believed he wouldn't be able to look at without losing his senses.

Every new administrator felt in the first weeks after his arrival the most earnest wish to reduce the pain and suffering of man and animals. That wish was due less often to love for man and animals; it grew much more often from the effort to increase production. The administrator said to himself, the easier he could make the work for the men, the more they could produce. And every new manager brought with him a new system which he wanted to try out and which he believed to be infallible.

One of them had come with the magnificent idea of building a kind of wagon, running on strong, broad, very low wheels, more like rollers than wheels. He thought that with the help of those little carts the trozas could be hauled away as if they were greased and that it would even be possible, on very dry trails, to carry three or four trozas at once.

The idea was splendid in theory. But in practice it turned out that with the aid of the little carts the boyeros could produce only a third as much in a week as they had managed by the earlier, allegedly more awkward methods. The carts rammed deeper and more hopelessly into the mire than the simple trozas. When a cart first got caught in strong roots it took endless trouble to hook it out without its getting broken.

Another manager had the good and very reasonable idea that it would be possible to bring in traction engines and then haul the trozas with strong wire cables. But when he arrived at the montería and had got to know and experience the tracks on which he had ridden, how often and how deep he had got stuck with his mule in the sticky jungle clay and in the mire, how often he had to dismount and how many kilometers he had to walk because the mule with his baggage on its back had sunk up to the saddle, then he knew that his idea was impractical, for a traction engine couldn't be transported over such tracks even in sections. And what horsepower a traction engine would have to have to haul trozas over roots and through marshes, that was something he had forgotten to work out.

Another one again wondered why earlier administrators had not hit on the simple idea of coming up the main river and then the minor streams by motorboat, bringing machines in those boats. That idea also looked good in San Juan Bautista, in the town that could be reached by motorboat from the harbor. But when he was once in the motorboat and had passed through parts of the river and the streams with highly skillful and experienced cayuqueros in canoes, he knew that a motorboat would get there only if it was a flying boat, and even one of those would have had difficulties in making its way without constantly running into the danger of getting lost.

If the caobas grew as quickly as automobiles are turned out in a factory, it would be worthwhile building railroads and automobile roads. But if the railroad doesn't pass right next to the place where the caoba is felled, it would work out just the same; for then, as before and over hundreds of years, the trozas would have to be hauled by oxen right up to the line, and the trail on which the troza is hauled would be the same as it is today—marshy, muddy, stony, covered with thousands of strong roots and weak roots that are as resistant as wire cables. For it is only where all the conditions that produce such tracks are to be found that the conditions are also to be found under which caoba will grow.

When proposals are made in offices, whatever ideas are offered, it always turns out that the methods by which the trozas are now felled, hauled, and floated are the only ones by which caoba can be produced and made available to the world.

All the difficulties, all the sufferings, even most of the apparently unnecessary cruelties were brought about by conditions against which man is clearly powerless. Another economic system would probably in such circumstances have completely done without mahogany, or tried to grow caoba in special plantations, so well organized that every troza grew immediately beside the asphalted automobile road and could be loaded on a truck with a motor crane. Then a ton of caoba would probably cost ten thousand dollars; but at least no more Indians would be sold into slavery for their debts, no more mercilessly whipped or pitilessly hanged. No war can be waged without people being enslaved, dressed in uniforms, and degraded into dumb creatures incapable of resistance by foolish or brutal superiors. There cannot be war and freedom at the same time, just as one cannot have caoba and humaneness and mercy toward mankind and animals in the jungle at the same time. For even if the contratistas and the capataces conducted themselves like saints toward the Indians, there would still be the biting flies, the mosquitoes, the ticks, the marshes, the roots, the pumas, the snakes, the pitiless glare of the tropical sun. And it is safe to assume that the biting flies, the mosquitoes, the marshes, the steely roots, and the tropical heat have an important part to play in the growth of the caoba. You can't have one without the other.

4

Andrés and Vicente poured water out of their pumpkin-shell bottles into their drinking bowls. Then each of them pinched off a piece of their pozol which was wrapped up in thick green leaves and remained fresh in those leaves. The piece of pozol was stirred in the water into the jicaritas and then dissolved, so that the water looked like a yellowish white paste. The paste was then stirred up well with the fingers to dissolve the last remains of the dough. Then the boys put a pinch of raw salt in their mouth and drank the paste in small sips, in peace and comfort.

They were sitting on a troza. They had nothing on but ragged white cotton pants, rolled up to the knees. Their bronze bodies were naked from the waist up, their feet without sandals. Although they often had to tread on thorns and sandals, the so-called huaraches, would have been useful to them, especially as protection from scorpions, it was not only too expensive to wear sandals but it was also much too awkward. If they got swallowed in the clinging jungle mud up to the waist and tried to drag their feet out, the few little straps which held the huaraches onto their feet were torn off, and the sandals remained stuck deep in the mire. It took time to dig them out, and often it was unsuccessful. The mire fell back into itself like thick soup; as soon as the leg was pulled out, the mud closed up, as clinging as before, and the sandals couldn't be found. Once the foot was dragged out, the exact place where it had entered could not be found again, and the sandals might well be half a meter from where they were looking. So it was best simply to have nothing on their feet.

Although the muchachos had now been sitting still for a while, conscientiously swallowing their pozol, they were still panting heavily from the strain of their work. Their hands and legs trembled, and now and then they opened their mouths absurdly wide to breathe in the air. Their hair was soaked with sweat, and their pants looked like rags dragged out of the water.

"Did you have pozol at your finca?" asked Andrés.

"Of course," answered Vicente. "But we take pozol with us when we go to market or if we work in the fields all day and come home only late in the evening."

"Pozol is a very good thing, Nene. Here, more than on the finca. When I was with the carretas we never had pozol. They didn't know about it in those parts. Often we traveled at night and slept during the day. And I want to say this to you just now, Nene, don't drink so much water. You've been drinking at every ditch. There's fever in many of those mud holes. The water in the camp is better. But where you don't know it, do be careful. A belly pumped full of water is dangerous. You quench your thirst better with pozol than with water. Pozol soaked in water isn't dangerous. The pozol takes up a lot of room in your belly, so you don't have the same longing to fill your whole belly with water. If you haven't got any pozol, then just rinse your mouth out with water, but don't drink a lot of it. And always swallow a bit of salt with it. You know, Nene, in the months that I've worked here we've buried eight people from our camp alone who died of swamp fever. It comes on you all suddenly, you know. You suddenly begin to shake, then you get terribly hot and icy cold immediately after, and that keeps on happening. Then you talk a whole lot of silly nonsense and you get frightened of—the devil only knows what you see in your delirium, but it must be dreadful. Then you double up and hit out all round you. And all at once you're finished, like a swatted fly. And then they bury you. A kilometer behind the Oficinas, where El Pícaro lives with that swine El Gusano, that's where the campo santo, the burial ground, is. The wild pigs come in at night and dig up the graves and eat the bodies. There are a few crosses, but there isn't a soul underneath, under the crosses. The pigs don't let anything lie there."

Vicente opened his big childish eyes wide as Andrés told him all that. But then he laughed: "You're teasing me, you're just trying to make fun of me."

"Not teasing at all," said Andrés seriously. "It's just as I said. And if you don't want to be eaten by the pigs, you'd better not drink so much water. And if you must drink, then only with pozol and salt."

Then the two lads smoked a short, thick cigar.

"And now, off we go again, so we can get the trozas all the way at last. El Gusano will be at the tumbo at midday to see whether we've brought them all down. He inspects the trozas then, to see whether the muchachos have cut the right marks on them so that the Montellanos know their wood when it reaches the harbor. They make absolutely sure, El Pícaro and El Gusano, that they have their own marks on every troza, so that the Montellanos can count them. Do you know, they get bonuses for every troza. If they float off a troza on which the muchacho who felled it has forgotten to cut his mark on it, they give him fifty lashes, because that is their money. The cabrones, the damned swine. Come on, lead those oxen over here!"

5

The troza was chained on and the journey began.

"Let me try your work for once, Andrésillo," said Vicente.

"Sure. I'll do your work with pleasure."

Andrés went to the heads of the oxen, a little to the right. Vicente took the hook and started to guide the troza. They had gone only ten meters when the chuzo of the troza caught under a root and the oxen stopped dead.

"Now, Nene, you must pay attention! You must bloody well watch that the point of the troza doesn't dig into the earth or under a root. That's what you've got that hook for, so that you can guide the troza properly and raise it well before it gets stuck."

"That's what I am doing, but the troza's too heavy. I can't lift it by myself. I can't even turn it so that the chain doesn't come up on top and the chuzo drops down too far."

Andrés laughed. "That's just what I wanted to know, what I wanted to see, you little baby. El Gusano told me this morning that I must train you in a week and then you'd be a boyero by yourself, with a boy he'd get from the Oficinas. I knew already that you weren't strong enough to lift a troza. And if you aren't lifting it all the time so that you can stop it digging into the ground or in the mud or under the roots lying across the trail, then you'll never get a single troza as much as half a kilometer."

Vicente nodded and looked at Andrés in astonishment. "I didn't know, Andrésito, that you were so terrifically strong."

"I've been just as weak and rickety on my legs as you are, Nene, but that was a good time ago, when I had to help in the shop in Tenejape. You take over the oxen now, and I'll guide the trozas. El Gusano will certainly breathe poison when I tell him you can't be a boyero for the next six months, maybe ten months, even if he has you hanged for two hours every evening to ripen you."

The trozas were then hauled one after another to the Arroyo Ciego, the Blind Ditch.

13

   When the two muchachos arrived with their first troza they saw that other boyeros had got there before them and dumped their trozas on the bank of the ditch. A number of boyeros who had been hauling trozas from various points had gathered at this spot. The longer track to the tumbo was so difficult that from there on all the yokes of oxen would have to work together. Not only that, some pairs of oxen would be sent from the camp, as El Gusano had promised Andrés in the morning.

The two muchachos drove their oxen back unloaded to fetch the next troza.

"Why is that ditch called Arroyo Ciego, Andrés?" asked Vicente. "A ditch can't very well be blind," he went on, laughing as boys do when they don't feel certain whether a grown-up has lied to them or whether it can really be as the grown-up, the one with experience, has said.

"This arroyo," Andrés explained, as the two of them strolled back side by side, driving the oxen on in front of them, "this ditch has a really pretty story, with a lot of humor. It's a good story for those who didn't lose money over it. You may have noticed that the ditch falls in the direction of the river. When we have the rainy season, the water in this ditch flows into the river, so if we stack the trozas here and the currents begin to flow and the ditch is full of water, they can be floated off really well from here. When there was felling here last year, farther up the ditch, Don Remigio examined the ditch. But he didn't go all the way to the end, because he could see perfectly well that the ditch flowed into the river. So about two hundred tons of caoba were stacked by this ditch, about five kilometers farther up, ready to be floated. The rains came, the deep water filled the ditch, and the muchachos heartily and cheerfully heaved the trozas into the ditch. The trozas floated away wonderfully, without making too much work keeping them from piling up. But at the main control point on the river, the Oficinas, where the trozas were collected for booking and costing, there was a shortage of two hundred tons, which Don Remigio knew for certain had been floated off. He had his mark on all the trozas, and he was short two hundred tons. The trozas must be found. It was no easy job for Don Remigio and the muchachos to make their way along the whole ditch. Every step had to be cut clear of jungle to let them follow the ditch exactly. And what do you think had happened?"

"I can't guess," said Vicente.

"I'm sure you can't, Nene. The trozas were all found in a swamp. The ditch made a sharp curve in its course, or rather it forked. The main fork led to the swamp, and a second fork, which wasn't deep enough for trozas to be floated in it, flowed on, presumably to the river. To fish those two hundred trozas out of the swamp cost Don Remigio no end of work. He had to have balsas, rafts, made on which the muchachos could get to the trozas in the swamp to fish them out. Celso told me that hardly a hundred tons could be salvaged, the rest were stuck in the marsh and lost. So you see, the ditch is blind, I mean it has no way into the river, although it certainly looked as if it flowed the right way. But that's not our trouble. You'll learn about our trouble when we've got all the trozas beside the Blind Ditch and have to haul them over to the other side, for the main ditch which leads to the river is still half a league beyond the Blind."

2

An hour and a half later all the boyeros had their trozas on the Blind Ditch. Now their job was to haul the trozas to the other side. They started work at once.

They looked for the place by the ditch where the slope was best. Then some of the muchachos went down and hacked away all the bushes and shrubs that could have held up the trozas as they fell. The arroyo was about twenty meters deep, and the banks sloped fairly steeply. The breadth was about twelve meters.

When one bank was cleared of bush the lads crossed to the other bank. Others meanwhile were busy coupling the spans of oxen together with chains. Twelve spans of oxen were chained together in pairs to form a team. The bush was thickest at the bottom of the ditch. Eulalio, one of the boyeros, stood in this bush up to his chest and hacked right and left with his machete to clear the ditch. The ground was covered with stones which had partly fallen from higher up and had partly been washed down in the course of time. Andrés was working with his machete several meters farther up the opposite bank, cutting away the bush. The gañanes, the boyeros' boys, pulled the cut-down bush to the side so that the ditch would be really clear. Andrés stood up for a moment to shake off the sweat running into his eyes. "Hey, Nene, you must pull that bush a few steps farther, otherwise it will get in our way when we slide the trozas down." He followed Vicente with his eyes as he spoke, and as he did that his gaze fell on Eulalio, who was cutting the bush at the bottom and had just exposed the stones.

He was just about to get on with his own work when, as if by chance, he looked again at the stones on the bottom and instantly yelled: "Una culebra, Eulalio!" Eulalio had of course heard the extraordinary threatening rattle of the snake, but for a few seconds he did not become fully aware of that distinctive sound because he thought he might be mistaken and the sound could perhaps be coming from the muchachos working with the spans of oxen, who were making rustling and rattling noises with the chains. When Andrés shouted "Una culebra," Eulalio jumped back instinctively. But he tripped over a stalk that was still lying there from the bushes that had been cut down, and he finally lost his footing when he stepped on the loose stones, which shifted so that he fell. In falling he stretched out his naked foot, not deliberately, toward the snake, and the snake, infuriated by the destruction of its home, half raised its body; in the second when Andrés saw it from his position above, it was ready to strike at Eulalio like a blow with a whip. The first time it struck, its wide open fangs would probably have hit only Eulalio's rolled-up pants, and since those pants were baggy enough near the hips, the fangs would very likely only have torn the pants without wounding his body, and Eulalio could have found room to jump back farther. But now he had fallen over and stretched out his foot close to the snake, only a quarter of a meter from the rattler's fangs; the snake, seeing the outstretched foot as a weapon threatening it, instinctively struck twice, low down on Eulalio's leg, at the bottom of his calf, with full force, with all its strength, and with the second strike also hung on to the flesh for one or two seconds. After striking the snake turned and crawled into the broken bush at the bottom of the ditch with the speed and certainty of an arrow, toward where Vicente was clearing the brushwood.

"Nene, a culebra!" shouted Andrés, to warn the boy.

But Vicente had heard the first shout when Andrés was calling to Eulalio. So Vicente was already halfway up the bank of the ditch when the snake reached the spot where he had been working, pulling the brushwood to the side.

The lads working with the oxen on the bank of the ditch had also heard Andrés shouting, and they came down with their machetes to capture the snake. There were many among them who reckoned snake meat a great delicacy, all the more since the food that the cook issued to them was so monotonous that any gift that was, or could be considered as, meat meant a treat. As young and incredibly hard-working men they were always hungry, and anything that could make their meals richer was just an unexpected gift from heaven. Driven by their hunger for nourishing food, they went so far that in the afternoon, if they had time and had discovered a rich ants' nest during their work, they dug up the nest, dried the ants, and then, a few days later, cooked them in fat ready to eat them, richly seasoned with chili and wrapped in hot tortillas, with the greatest enjoyment. To have fat fried ants occasionally is better and more tolerable in any case than to have to eat, day in, day out, nothing but tortillas and black beans with green pepper at every meal.

But quickly as the lads got after the snake, it knew its surroundings better than they. Above the ditch and outside it the lads would have had little trouble. But the snake was hard to capture in the deep arroyo, thickly overgrown with thorny tropical bush, its bottom covered with loose stones, with holes, passages, and little caves dug in its walls by every possible animal that lived in this jungle. Once the snake got away, there was no point in chasing after it.

"Damn it," shouted Celso, "it was a terrific brute, I must say. I bet it was nearly two meters long and surely as thick as my arm. Pity we didn't catch it. That would have given us a good joint this evening! Snake steak. It's enough to make you cry."

"I'd never touch a single bite of a snake, even if I were starving," said Sixto, shuddering. "I like a good joint from a good big lizard or a fat iguana. That's real meat, so tender and tasty, even better than the meat of a young kid. But eating a snake! Not me, for sure."

"Then you really don't know what tastes good on this earth," Cirilo put him right. "How can a Christian eat an iguana? Iguanas are poisonous, don't you know that?"

"We've eaten enough of them at home, and nobody's died of it yet, I can tell you."

They went back to their work.

After his fall, Eulalio had jumped up quickly, and he too ran after the snake. Then he also went back and continued his work, clearing the ditch of bush.

Andrés stood up on the bank of the ditch and called to Eulalio: "I thought it had got you once, it looked just like it."

"Nothing to worry about, I got my leg away too quickly," answered Eulalio.

The ditch was cleared, and the lads pushed the trozas down on their side until they were all piled up in the ditch. Then the top troza was hooked on and the oxen began to haul it over to the opposite bank. With fewer than ten spans it would hardly come up. While the lads were still working there, more spans of oxen arrived to help, and now the whole campamento, the full team of boyeros, was gathered there. Every span had its own boy. The experienced boyeros clung to the steep wall of the ditch, hooking and shoving the troza this way and that so that it wouldn't bore too deep into the soft wall as it was pulled up. But after a few trozas had been taken across, the wall was completely torn up, and with every new troza it took more effort to drag the trunks up.

They tried taking them up sideways on, with hooks attached at each end. But then new difficulties arose. The whole width of the trunk was now pulled over the torn-up, soft wall of the ditch, and the load was too heavy, so that the oxen were no longer able to pull it. The lads undid the chains again and had the trozas hauled in the normal way, point first. A long branch was pushed under the point and four lads clambered up on each side, lifting the branch all together so as not to let the point run into the wall. But every time the oxen pulled, the lads lost their grip on the wall, fell down to the bottom with their branch, and had to climb up again to get the troza up another meter with the next pull. It was after a fall of that kind that Eulalio said to Andrés: "I can't get my breath any more, Andresillo. The ditch is so stifling." He clambered up the wall on all fours and leaned against a tree at the top, gasping for air with his mouth wide open.

After a while he seemed to have recovered, and when he saw the lads having trouble with a new troza he climbed down into the ditch again to help them. But when he wanted to move his leg he felt a tickling itch in his calf, and then it felt as if his toes had gone to sleep. But that feeling soon went away. He was making a second attempt to climb down into the ditch when he felt a bad pain in his calf. He thought the pain felt like a sting, and also like pressure, broken by a sudden jerk.

He tried to get up again and once more found that he couldn't stand firmly on his foot. He sat down on the ground and noticed that there was blood flowing from his calf, which he thought looked very dark.

He looked closely at his wound and called over Andrés, who had got to the top of the ditch and was trying with his hook to guide the troza that was being hauled up while the other lads heaved the troza from below to help the oxen drag it to the top.

"I cut myself on a thorn when I fell," Eulalio said to Andrés. "Maybe the thorn was a poisonous one. Or maybe it was a splinter from a chechen. Or a fly has stung me. And it looks as if it was poisonous. It feels hard here, and swollen."

"Let's see, Lalio," said Andrés, kneeling down beside him. He looked more closely at the wound. Then he dropped Eulalio's leg. He had a dreadful expression on his face. "Lalio, that's goddam bad. I thought it had missed you. But it got you. And properly. Here's where its fangs went in. You can see it clearly. That's not biting flies or thorns."

The muchachos were standing at the top of the ditch wall, getting their breath back, while the ox-boys led the team of oxen back to haul up the next troza.

3

"Hey, muchachos!" called Andrés. "Come here! Light a fire. That goddam brute of a chingada culebra bit Lalio. Vicente, let me look at your throat." Vicente came over willingly and opened his mouth wide. Andrés looked at the boy's lips and then asked him: "Have you been stung by a mosquito, or have you got a sore throat?"

"No, Andrés."

"Good, then lie down here next to Eulalio's leg, suck the blood out of those marks. As strong as you possibly can."

Without asking and without thinking, Vicente did what his master told him. Andrés took his machete and scratched the point of it sharp on a stone. "Spit it out, what you've got in your mouth now, Nene. You haven't swallowed any of the blood you sucked out?"

"I'm not as silly as that," laughed Vicente. "Anyway, I've done that twice on our finca, when boys were bitten by a cascabel. But only one of them got better, the other one died of it."

Andrés knelt down by Eulalio and cut his calf open with his machete, so wide that the marks left by the bite now became a wound. Then he made a deep cut across, so as to open the wound further.

He called over one of the other boys, looked at his mouth, and told him to suck the wound, which of course was now much bigger. Meanwhile there was a fire burning, and the muchachos, knowing how the bite of a culebra de cascabel has to be treated, had two machetes in the fire. When the machetes were red-hot,

Andrés burned the wound with them. Then he cut the wound open even more, scorched it again, and rubbed glowing pieces of charcoal on the stained flesh.

Eulalio's expression never changed during all that painful treatment. All the time he smoked a very thick cigar which Cirilo had rolled for him. Everything the lads did or suggested he accepted patiently, without protest, without even making any suggestions himself.

"If only we had a handful of snakeroot or a decent pinch of calomel that he could swallow, that would certainly do him good, I reckon," said Matías.

"All that doesn't help," Fidel joined in. "Nothing you're doing there does any good, Andrés. We need an old Indian from our village who knows how to treat snakebites." Santiago sat down by Eulalio, rolling a cigar. "Chew your tobacco more than you smoke it, Lalio," he advised. "And when you've chewed it properly, then mix it with hot ashes and stuff that into the wound as deep as you can."

"Good idea," said Andrés. "I never knew you were so smart. We'll do that at once."

Not only Eulalio but all the other muchachos who were smoking cigars began to bite big bits off their cigars and chew them.

4

At that moment El Gusano rode up. For a while he remained sitting on his horse. He had approached close to the edge of the ditch on the opposite bank, where he seemed to be wondering whether he should try to cross to the other side on his horse or whether it would be better to dismount and clamber over on foot. He concluded that the horse would have difficulty making its way down the one bank without a rider and then climbing up the other steep wall. It had been hard enough for the oxen, and they had been led over where it was not as steep, but now the soil of the walls had been so weakened and torn by the trozas as they were dragged across that if a horse had tried to climb across the ditch at that point it would have sunk in. And to sink into the earth up to his neck, and make himself ridiculous in front of the muchachos, didn't much appeal to him at that moment.

He therefore remained sitting on his horse and just shouted over: "You stinking golfos and layabouts, haven't you got anything to do but sit around and smoke cigars, when it's nearly midday and the trozas are all still lying around? It's another half a league to the tumbo."

"Eulalio has been bitten by a culebra," shouted Pedro, "and he can't work."

"Then you lazy buggers don't need to keep him company if he can't work." But now he got down from his horse, went slowly twenty meters further up the ditch, and climbed down.

He walked over to the group, looked at the black-smeared wound, and said: "That ought to have powder rubbed in."

"Where shall we get the powder, then?" asked Santiago.

"Or chewed tobacco," said El Gusano.

"That's just what we're doing now," said Andrés.

"Well, back to work now. That bite's been doctored enough anyway. All burnt out. You can go on working quite well, muchacho," he turned to Eulalio. "You're not here to go all soft just because you've been bitten by a culebra. I've been bitten by hundreds of culebras, and I'm still alive."

"But it was a cascabel," Pedro told him. "We saw it. It was full grown, nearly two meters long."

"Why not five meters, and why not a jaguar while you're about it?" sneered El Gusano. "And now, enough of this sitting around here. The trozas have got to get to the tumbo, or I'll have you all dealt with at eleven tonight. If I come back and find you still doing nothing, something will happen, something good, I promise you."

He turned round, scrambled over the ditch to the place where he had arrived, mounted his horse, and rode off to the fellers, to get them going properly.

The lads now mixed the chewed tobacco with hot ashes, made a thick paste of it, smeared it into the wound, and wound a dirty rag round it which Andrés had torn off his pants.

5

The last trozas were dragged out of the ditch, and then they began hauling the trozas stacked on the edge of the ditch to the tumbo.

"Now, keep your eyes wide open, Nene," said Andrés to Vicente. "Now you're really going to learn something. Up to now you haven't really been working, just going for a walk with the oxen. El Gusano knows very well why he's cleared off just now. Now it's real fun. Now we get the trail on which you can slip into the mud up to your ears; and if no one sees you at the right moment you just stick there, and the ten or twelve spans of oxen tread you so deep in the morass that even God won't be able to find you on Doomsday. Don't go too near the oxen. When they begin to pull they kick out right and left and tread anything that gets in their way under their feet."

The next five hundred meters were a real pleasure: they went downhill. The boyeros made the most of it. They coupled three or four trozas together and sent them to the steepest part of the falling terrain with a single team. That didn't last long, and then all the trozas were lined up again.

The way from there to the ditch for floating was a very wide hollow in the ground. Trees and plants had decayed there for thousands of years, and that created a soft soil. Because of the dense crowns of the great jungle giants, hardly any rays of sunshine came down which sometimes could have dried out the soft earth of this hollow. From both sides, and from the hill as well, all the moisture ran into this hollow, whether it was rain or the heavy dew that dripped from trees and bushes in the early hours of the morning. As a result, a morass was built up in the hollow that could very well have been described as a swamp. But in a swamp there is generally more water. This morass was in many ways more dangerous than a swamp, when it came to wading or riding through it or dragging through heavy tree trunks. It was easier to haul trozas through a swamp than through such morasses, which are so remarkably frequent that one gets the impression that the whole jungle consists of them. With long enough chains and a good number of spans of oxen it could be a pleasure to shift trozas, compared with hauling them through those morasses. In a swamp, if it was not too over-grown, a troza could sometimes float. But the soft earth of the morass was so sticky, so adhesive, so heavily loamy, that a troza hauled through it was grasped by the sticky, loamy, chalky mass as if by a huge monster that, once it has caught its prey, is unwilling to let it go. A troza that reached the tumbo and had passed through that morass on its last stretch was three times its natural thickness, because the sticky mud clung to the troza and was hauled along with it.

This mud was so sticky that often it could not be peeled off the troza just by hand; they had to use machetes, axes, and thick branches to help scale off the hard, sticky mud.

A couple of weeks earlier, when Don Severo and El Pícaro, with the aid of some muchachos, had reconnoitered the new area to be opened up, in order to establish the regions to be exploited and to locate and record the ditches to be used for floating, they had no doubt seen this hollow in the terrain over which all the trozas that were felled in the campo would have to be hauled. They spent a whole day trying to find another, better way to this tumbo. But it was clear that over a breadth of five kilometers every trail that led to the main ditch went through similar hollows in the ground. And since all those hollows were morasses of the same sort, it was decided simply to choose the shortest route, and that was the one before which the boyeros had now lined up the trunks.

6

Matías, Pedro, and Fidel had gone ahead to look at the trail's full length. When they came back, Matías said: "Listen now, muchachos. Let's all just sit down here for a bit and roll a cigar and smoke it in peace. And if there's anything you want to know, we can tell you all right all that we've seen and what we've learned about it. El Gusano thinks we shall have all the trozas at the tumbo by midday tomorrow. And I can tell you El Gusano and El Pícaro will be lucky if we get all the trozas to the tumbo in three days. What do you think, Pedro and Fidel? Haven't I got it right?"

"Sure," said Pedro shortly.

"It might even last a week," Fidel corrected him.

Sixto commented, as he carefully licked his freshly rolled cigar: "Then we can all look forward to a proper hanging if we don't get the trozas there in at least two days."

"And if the son of a bitch does hang the lot of us, if he hangs each of us for eight hours at night, it won't do him any good, we still shan't get the trozas over in less than three days."

Matías lit his cigar.

After taking a deep pull at it, he went on: "And if we were all good muchachos and didn't have shit in our pants, for every hour that son of a whore hangs us we'd just not work for one whole day."

"Then they'll start the fiestas again, with beatings of fifty strokes each," said Cirilo.

Matías laughed grimly. It was a bark more than a laugh. And he said: "Why should those cobardes, those whorish dogs and stinking sons of a puta, beat me, or Fidel, or you, Sixto? My back has been beaten so hard by those brutes that I'll soon have nothing but corns on my back and scars as hard as wood, just a thick shell. They could give me five hundred and I'd smoke my cigar just as peacefully and contentedly as now."

Now Andrés joined in. "They know that beating us and whipping us doesn't even change the expression on our face, that it doesn't help them anymore. That's why they invented that wonderful hanging."

"They didn't invent anything," said Prócoro, another of the boyeros. "Nothing at all. They're much too stupid to invent anything. It was the Montellanos who invented it. That's what they made all their money out of, that they were able to buy the three monterías with. Just ask the hacheros how they produce three or four tons a day for fear of hanging. And that could happen to us too, I can tell you. Now that the fellers have to turn out three or four toneladas instead of the usual two, of course we've got to cart off twice as much every day, with or without the oxen. If the oxen act up and won't work, you can take the trozas off on your backs."

"Somos los Indianos colgados, the hanged Indians," said Fidel.

"Or los Indianos ahorcados, the Indians hanged to death."

"That would be better than just colgados." Prócoro puffed thick smoke from his cigar. "Ahorcados, actually hanged to death, that's much better. Then you're free of the whole of this wretchedness. But always being only half hanged and then having to do twice the work the next day in order not to be hanged for four hours that evening—that's absolute hell. We should have killed off everybody here, not just El Pícaro and El Gusano but all the other capataces in all the campos as well, and then the three goddam Montellanos on top of it all."

"But five hundred of the best for each of them first, then cured and then pumped full of hot coffee and aguardiente for four weeks every evening until they burst, and then hanged for six hours. And when they've been hanged so long that all their limbs look like string, then tied to a tree and a fire laid round the tree. Goddam it all, if I could do all that to them one of these days I'd be glad to go to hell for it ten times!" Matías stood up, threw down the rest of his cigar hard on the ground, trod on it, and twisted his foot violently one way and another as if he were trying to bury the cigar end in the ground. "Like that," he said furiously, "just like that I should like to dig the head of that son of a bloody bitch, the infernal cursed head of El Gusano, into the ground here."

"Who wouldn't like to?" said Andrés. "But that does us no good. We'll do better to cart our trozas off."

14

    There were twelve spans of oxen hauling the troza.
Three boyeros were wading on each side, shoving the
troza here and there with their hooks and dragging it out of the
morass. The lads were up to their hips in the mud and had little
control over the troza, which was always liable to disappear in
the morass and then could only be found and fished out by
following the chain attached to it.

The boys and the other boyeros waded next to the oxen,
driving the animals with sharp sticks, with shouts and oaths.
The oxen too were wading up to their loins in the sticky morass,
and maybe they had even more trouble than the lads in moving
ahead. They never raised their legs completely out of the deep
slimy mud but dragged their legs and bodies through it.

Every five paces the whole column stopped. Boys and oxen
panted and gasped for breath. And what was visible of men and
animals above the morass was dripping with sweat. The dense
swarms of biting flies above the column bit into the lads' or the
oxen's flesh at one place, tore a piece out leaving a shining
stream of flowing blood behind them, flew off, bit their way in

at another point, tore out another little scrap, and flew off to come down again at yet another place.

While the spans were standing still the lads were hard at it with all their strength, digging out and bringing up the troza, which was completely submerged and had become trapped in roots and lianas. When it was fully freed, the long line of spans was driven on. It advanced maybe twenty paces, then the troza was sunk in the mud again and disappeared from sight. The oxen, still pulling their hardest, hauled the troza a few paces farther before they stopped, and by then the troza was so firmly rammed into the morass that even twice the number of spans could not have pulled it farther. The whole column stopped again with curses and groans. The troza had to be dug out once more. And when it was finally brought to the surface, the lads succeeded in hauling it another twenty paces before it was submerged again and had to be dug out again.

The muchachos who were walking beside the oxen, driving them on and pulling up and dragging out the towing chains all the time so that they did not get caught under roots and sunken bushes, were standing in the morass rather than beside it. With one careless step they could fall under the oxen's feet. The animals, pulling forward with all their strength, tortured by thousands of insects, half blinded with the infernal damp heat and by the strain of the work, maddened by the yelling of the boys driving them and the continual pricking of the goads, trod mercilessly into the morass any lads who carelessly fell under their feet. Every fifty meters a lad disappeared under the feet of the oxen. The column could not be halted at that very second, for if the muchachos tried to stop even the two spans nearest to them, the spans in front pulled them on and those following pushed from behind. Only their great skill in maneuvering their bodies and the suppleness of all their limbs saved the lads that fell under the oxen's feet.

That was why the first advice a new boyero got from the

experienced ones was always: "Boy, take care that you don't get under the feet of the oxen! But if you are down, don't wait for the column to stop but wriggle out quicker and smarter than a hunted iguana." The reason for that advice was that new boyeros didn't go near enough to the spans when the column was on the move, and therefore those novices slowed down the day's work considerably.

Every span had to have a boy of its own to keep the column moving and to watch the towing chains so that they didn't get caught. But that made it necessary for them to go so close to the working oxen that most of the time the boy was half under the body of one of the two oxen, and needed only to let one foot slip into a hole from which an ox had just pulled its foreleg, and then he was already lying full length under both animals. Every muchacho had to look out for himself, for his own life. No one could help him; for every one of them had three times as much work to do as is normally expected of a man.

2

With each new troza that was brought to the tumbo the morass grew deeper. If it might still have had a certain density and firmness when the passages began, with the dragging of the heavy trozas, the stamping of the feet of twelve or fourteen pairs of heavy oxen, and the movement of the lads' legs, the morass grew pasty and muddy, like dough. The more it took on the consistency of dough, the deeper the trozas sank in the mud, the harder and more tiresome it became for the animals to drag their feet out of it, and the more strength which should have been devoted to the work of hauling had to be wasted just to keep moving through that deep and sticky mud. Not only that. The softer the dough, and the deeper it became softened and broken up, the more the heavy cakes and lumps of it clung to the troza and to the legs of the animals and the lads. The legs of the oxen began to look like elephants' legs while the troza tripled in weight. As soon as the troza was pulled to the surface the lads naturally scratched off the excessive burden of mud. But the passage hardly went five meters farther and already the troza had grown to twice its size and weight.

But what good was it to weep! If the troza was to earn money it had to be sold, and if it was to be sold it must be taken to market. How it gets to the harbor is not the purchaser's affair but the vendor's. The vendor would prefer to bring the caoba out of the jungle with tractors that run on steel caterpillar tracks. But where the tractors could carry it there is no caoba growing. The high price of gold is due to the rarity of that metal and the difficulty of obtaining it. The high price of mahogany, in contrast, is due to the difficulty of transport. It takes less trouble, less time, and less money to bring pine wood from the interior of Finland to a port in Central America than to deliver caoba from the Central American jungle to the same port. That is why lumber that comes from the woods of Russia, Sweden, and Finland is many times cheaper in the seaports of America than wood from the primeval forests of those American republics.

3

When the sixth troza of the day stuck on the way to the tumbo, deep in the morass, the oxen felt it their duty, for their own self-preservation, to quit work for the day.

While the lads were doing all they could to dig out the sunken troza, one span after another began to lie down. When the troza was at last free, every span was resting, lying in the mud. The boyeros knew that neither pricking the oxen with the goads nor whipping them would get them to go on working. They had already worked two hours longer than they usually did. But since they formed part of such a big team, their herd instinct and their social consciousness had made them forget for a time that they were overworked. Now, however, that same herd instinct persuaded them all to lie down and refuse to work anymore.

A panting Vicente, lungs gasping and covered in sweat, went up to Andrés: "At last we've finished work today. I can't go on."

"None of us can go on, Nene. But it's only the oxen that will have a rest, until one o'clock tonight. Not us. We're going to the campo now, to eat. But then we have to work half the afternoon before we can rest."

"We can't shift any trozas without the oxen," said Vicente.

"Quite right, my child." Andrés chuckled. He too was panting like all the other lads. And his body too was streaming with heavy sweat; in many places it was pink where it ran down on him, because it was mixed with the thin streams of blood that flowed where he had been stung. Yet, despite his exhaustion, he could still laugh with Vicente, and he repeated: "Of course not, Nene. Without oxen we can't shift any trozas. I see you know how to use your head."

"But I'm saying, Andrés, if we don't have any oxen then we can't haul any trozas and don't need to go on working."

"It may have been like that on your finca, my son. Not here. Here you work as long as you can still stand. And when you can't stand any longer, then you work crawling on your arse. But you just have to work. El Gusano told me yesterday that we're clearing the trails on the other side of the ditch, where they've already been felling, and have to cut away the thicket to get the trail open. The caoba is ten times richer on the other side. But the trail is even more marshy."

"Even more marshy and muddy than here?" asked Vicente in astonishment. "How is that possible?"

"Everything is possible here. And on the other side, because of the slope of the land, the marsh is so soft that the trozas can sink ten meters deep in the ground when they're hauled, so we shall have to build calzadas. And that's what we shall be doing this afternoon until we all fall down and just sleep where we drop."

"Calzadas, what's that then?"

"You'll learn this afternoon, and when you're building the calzadas you'll also be learning that every job here is the same in its terrible difficulty and strain. There's never any easy work here, and no rest at all."

4

After the muchachos had had a breather for five minutes, they began to unyoke the oxen. The heavy bars of the yokes, each of which weighed twenty kilos and which had weighed down on the animals' necks since two o'clock in the morning, were unstrapped and removed. Released, the animals were able to turn their heads, which must have felt as if they were paralyzed, and began in their relief to lick the wounds made by the biting flies and other insects and to scratch and scrape their painful skin with their teeth.

At last all the oxen were unyoked. They still lay there in their teams, where they had lain down. Their bodies had sunk into the mud during their rest. They seemed to feel at ease in the mud, which was cooler than the blazing hot air that enveloped them; the mud not only cooled their bodies but also eased the terrible itching of the insect stings; and masses of garrapatas, large and small ticks that had bitten into their skin, felt themselves in danger of their lives in the parts of the oxen's bodies that were surrounded with mud, and began to pull their powerful pincers out of the skin, crawl along the bodies, and come to the surface. Instinct gave those creatures the feeling that they were lost if the mud dried on the oxen's bodies and solidified in the heat so as to squash them and kill them. But the oxen too knew instinctively, also maybe from experience, that lying in the mud and then letting the mud dry and solidify on their skin freed them from hundreds, indeed thousands of parasites.

A number of the lads had gone with their drinking shells to a spring some two hundred meters away, to one side of the trail, which trickled out of a crack in a rock. There was not much water, and to be able to use it the boys first had to dig out little hollows so that they could collect the water in them. Each of them scooped his shell in the hollow, rinsed his mouth, and then stirred a little lump of pozol into the muddy water that he had scooped up again into his shell.

Most of them, however, were too tired to go over to the spring. They preferred to stretch out and rest on the side of the trail where it was a bit dry.

5

All of a sudden, breaking out of the thicket, El Pícaro appeared before them. He sat on his horse and looked at the team.

The lads went on lying where they were.

"Not eleven yet, and finished the day's work already?" he shouted.

Pedro, rolling a cigar, said: "The oxen won't do any more with us."

"Of course not, if you've overworked them. If you'd looked after them better and lifted the trozas quicker and higher out of the mud, the poor beasts wouldn't have needed to haul so bloody hard, then they wouldn't be so overtired. Lazy buggers, that's what you are, and I suppose I shall just have to sort the lot of you out, to give you a bit of guts. Half the lot of you will be hanged for two hours this evening, to freshen you up. You're not here for a holiday and for convalescence, you're here to work! Off you go, the oxen to pasture! And at twelve tonight get down to it and get the rest of the trozas hauled up. Por dios, it's a sin before God and man how you loaf about here, and a disgrace that strong brown whoremongers like you should lie around on your filthy arses in the middle of the day and not work. The oxen to pasture, off you go now! And when you've guzzled your filthy muck in the camp, then it's over to the other side, to clear the trails. Damn and blast it, I'll get it across to you what it really means to work here. I ought to give every one of you twenty right now, to get a little life into the team. Aren't you really ashamed of yourselves, overworking the oxen so much that the poor brutes can't so much as grunt anymore? I have the Santa Purísima as eternal witness that you're lousy and shitty slavedrivers, a stinking mob of Indians, that's what you are, sons of mangy bitches and cabrones!"

He looked all round to get a good view of the area and find a new inspiration. And he found it.

"Los yugos, the yokes, goddam it, you don't need to leave them just lying in the shit when you're unyoking. Too stinking lazy to take them a couple of paces to where it's dry!" Fidel half raised himself on his arm, without getting up from where he was lying, and said: "Why should we take all the trouble to drag them through the muck and bring them over here when we've got to yoke them up again tonight in the same place they are now?"

"Shut up or I'll give you a good beating, you insolent swine," shouted El Pícaro.

"Just so you know why we left the yokes lying where they are now," said Fidel. Something in his voice made it clear that he was not speaking to explain; he was speaking to annoy El Pícaro. El Pícaro recognized that well enough. But like all capataces, and like all whippers and torturers, El Pícaro was very careful not to drive a situation too far when he knew he did not have the upper hand, when he was in a situation where he could not escape his fate if serious trouble broke out. He saw well enough that because they were so overtired the muchachos were in such a state that the very slightest provocation could have been enough to make one of them get up and attack him, drag him off his horse, beat him like a dog, and then bury him in the morass. What good would El Pícaro's revolver have been to him? Of six shots, even if he had been able to fire six shots, in such excitement four would have missed. And once the six shots were fired, he was lost.

He said no more. He lit a cigarette deliberately and turned his horse. He rode back a few paces, then gave his horse a blow with the whip and at the same time dug in his heavy spurs to make the horse jump to the other side of the trail, where he would be nearer to the camp. The horse jumped. But El Pícaro, who had not been watching the work there at all, but had only observed the men resting, underestimated the difficulties of the trail. He had been sure that the mud was only on the surface. He would have had hard work to wade slowly across the trail on his horse.

But with the lads watching he wanted to show that the trail was no more trouble than lots of others. And so he jumped with his horse so deep into the morass, softened and stirred up as it was, that he sank up to the saddle in thick mud as if he'd been shot in.

The horse tried to stamp its way out, but the more it kicked the deeper the animal sank.

6

The muchachos went on sitting quietly.

El Pícaro didn't shout to them for help. It would have been fatal to his dignity. He slipped from the saddle and now found himself up to the hips in mud. He untied the lasso, made a loop, tied that round the horse's muzzle and the end of the lasso round his wrist, and pulled himself out of the mud, cursing and swearing.

The horse, relieved of the weight of its rider, struggled desperately in the morass until it found firmer ground on roots or big stones and was able to get itself half a meter higher. Meanwhile El Pícaro had reached the side of the ditch, and from there, standing on less muddy ground, he pulled the horse over to him with the aid of the lasso, which gave him a hold on the horse's head and also showed the horse the direction.

By now he looked, if not entirely but certainly on the surface, like all the lads looked. From the part of their black, wiry hair down to the soles of their feet the lads were covered with dark grey paste, which, since they lay down to rest, had slowly begun to dry on their bodies. Their hair was matted and crusted, and the only item of clothing that any of them wore— ragged white cotton pants—were thick with mud and soaked. No one could have known for certain that those pants were made of cotton; they might just as well have been a garment consisting of nothing but mud. Seen as a whole, each of the lads looked as if he had been wrapped in dark grey dough from top to bottom, ready to be put in the oven and baked to make a pastry man. And El Pícaro's horse now looked like a grown-up gingerbread horse. He himself only differed from the lads in that his hair was not matted and his face was only splashed with mud. But since he was wearing shirt, pants, leather gaiters, and boots, he had much more trouble freeing himself from the mud that clung to him.

With his hands he scraped the wet sticky mud from his clothes, then from the saddle and the sides of his horse.

"Damn it all," he shouted furiously, "how the bloody hell was I to know that the goddam mud was so goddam deep here and so filthy?"

"If you'd asked us, we'd have told you," Santiago called out to him. And Fidel shouted, loudly and rudely: "Since you know everything else, we thought you'd be bound to know how deep the lodo here was."

Then Andrés joined in: "If we'd been able to bring all the trozas up by midday, we'd have done that for sure. Now at least you know why we couldn't get them up."

El Pícaro was very proud of himself because he had succeeded in getting out of the mud without help from the lads. Now he changed his tone and said: "I'll exchange half the spans for the night for well-rested ones and give you six more spans. Take all the spans to the camp now and then on to the big pasture, a mile behind the camp. I'll find the spans for you. Who would ever have thought the mud was so deep and thick here!"

"On the other side of the ditch, where they're felling now, it's twice as deep," said Matías, "and the trail is twice as long as this one."

"Yes, I know," said El Pícaro, mounting his horse. "I'll send to Don Severo and ask him for more spans."

El Pícaro rode off, not so proud and cutting as when he came. And as he rode off he could really have been taken for a knight from some old legend who, bewitched by a wicked sorcerer, now found himself in a state of putrefaction and would suddenly become the petrified knight, and frighten future generations.

"He looked so ridiculous," said Santiago grinning, "that I thought he would try to drag himself out of the shit on his own ears."

Fidel added grimly: "If he'd torn off his bloody head, that would have been a comfort to me."

"Why a comfort?" asked Prócoro, turning round the other way and looking at Fidel.

"Why a comfort? How can you ask such a dumb, ignorant question, man? Because then I shouldn't feel it my duty to chop his head off one day. I just can't get rid of the feeling that I shall do that one of these days. It haunts me day and night, if I just see the mugs of those two, Gusano and Pícaro. They make it so easy and pleasant for us to have such lovely and thrilling feelings and to pray to the good God in heaven devoutly to send a suitable occasion for that chopping really soon."

15

When the oxen had rested for a good while, when they no longer felt the yoke on their necks and so knew that their work was over for the day, they readily allowed themselves to be roused and driven to the camp.

"Where's Eulalio, then?" asked Andrés suddenly, as he got the team moving. "I haven't seen him for at least an hour. Damn it, it's just occurred to me that he wasn't with the team during the last hour." Several of the lads shouted into the jungle, calling his name.

After several such calls they heard Eulalio answer in a feeble voice: "Aquí estoy, compañeros." Two of them ran over to him.

He had sat down, leaning against a tree. His face looked greenish, and a light foam hung on his swollen lips. The leg that had been bitten by the culebra was a smoky reddish purple color. It was swollen, burning, and distended, and looked as if it was going to burst. "Damn it, compañeros, I can't walk," said Eulalio in a tired voice.

Two of the lads picked him up and carried him on their shoulders to the camp, following the column.

As they arrived there three boys were driving the oxen to the pasture, where the zacateros, responsible for fodder in the camp, had piled up leaves, dried maize plants, and grass, which was cut in the mornings in some of the more open places in the jungle. But the oxen were too tired to feed. They nibbled for a bit at the thin grass of the pasture. Then they looked for shade under the trees which grew here and there in the area, and rested. Later in the afternoon they would plod over to the stream, drink themselves full, and then, properly rested, seek their fodder comfortably in the cool of the evening.

The cook hadn't got the lads' food ready for them. And that gave them a chance to throw themselves down on their mats in the boyeros' hut, where they instantly fell asleep.

2

Andrés went to El Pícaro's oficina. El Pícaro was swinging in a hammock, hung under the projecting roof of the hut that served him and El Gusano as oficina and as dwelling. El Gusano was with the fellers to ensure that none of them got sleepy but made every effort to produce three or, even better, four tons.

"Jefe," said Andrés to El Pícaro, "come over to our choza at once. Eulalio is lying there and he can't walk."

El Pícaro, who was smoking a cigarette which consisted of raw tobacco cut small and rolled in ordinary packing paper, went on smoking undisturbed and asked lazily: "What's the matter with him? I suppose he doesn't want to build calzadas this afternoon. I'll make him walk all right."

Andrés didn't reply. He remained standing in front of the portico, holding his muddy palm hat, all holes, in his hand.

"Bueno, vengo," said El Pícaro at last. "All right, I'm coming."

He slipped out of his hammock and went over to the choza where the boyeros slept when they passed the night in the camp.

Very often, of course, especially when they were working a long way from the campo and the oxen were in a pasture that was nearer to their place of work, the boyeros and gañanes slept in huts put up quickly from small tree trunks and palm leaves and so lightly built that they lasted only as long as the lads had to work in the neighborhood.

As El Pícaro went over to the hut he passed the kitchen. The kitchen was a palm shelter set on piles. Only on the side from which the wind generally came had a wall been built, which consisted of thin trunks woven with lianas and hung with leafy branches outside. Cooking was done on the ground, where there were several fires burning with dented tins and enamel pots hanging over them, and where small and big earthen jars were now standing. The cook, an Indian like all the workers there, had an eight-year-old boy to help him. He also had his aunt, who was certainly twice as old as he and with whom he lived in a sort of marital relationship. But that woman never helped him cook. The livelong day she only ate and smoked—extraordinarily thick cigars which she rolled for herself and for him. And when she was neither eating nor smoking, she lay in a hammock hung from two of the beams that held up the roof. It was well known in the campo that that old, fat, deeply wrinkled aunt, who did not smell very agreeable since she seldom washed, would spend a quarter or half the night with any of the boyeros or hacheros for an appropriate amount of raw tobacco, aguardiente, or a chain of glass beads. The cook had no objection. But he expected that, if she was paid with aguardiente, he should get the bigger half. Then he drank excessively and beat his aunt unmercifully, shouting out to the whole world that she was an incorrigible old whore and one day he'd strangle her with his own hands.

"Hey, you dirty swine!" shouted El Pícaro to the cook. "Why isn't the goddam fodder ready for the muchachos yet? I'll cheer you up a bit when the músicos come, you'll see."

"La comida, the food, will be ready in a second, jefe, for sure," the cook answered.

"If it isn't, I'll smack you in the face with my whip, you cur, you stinking son of a whore."

The cook went over to the little kitchen boy who was poking the fire and blowing on it to make it burn better. "You rascal," he shouted at the boy, "if you'd looked after the fire better the bloody food would have been ready long ago." He picked up one of the branches that lay by the fire and brought it down mercilessly on the boy's back. The boy jumped up and ran away. "You come here at once, you vicious little devil!" the cook shouted after him. But the boy stayed a safe distance away. From there he shouted: "If you hit me anymore I'll go and be an ox-boy."

"Come here," said the cook, now very conciliatory, "I won't hit you."

The boy went back into the kitchen. The cook patted him affectionately on the back and murmured in a low voice: "I didn't mean that, Pablito. I had to beat you up a bit when El Pícaro was here, so that he'd think it was your fault, do you understand? Otherwise he'd have hanged me or whipped me, and then that old witch would laugh at me. You know what she's like. You didn't mind a couple of smacks, Pablito, eh?"

"No, of course not, Don Filemón," said the boy, pacified, and got busy again.

3

El Pícaro had entered the hut. Eulalio was lying on his mat and groaning. Some of the lads were kneeling beside him. They gave him some water to drink and cooled his head and his leg with water.

"What's the trouble, then, muchacho?" asked El Pícaro.

"He was bitten by a rattlesnake when we were clearing the dry ditch of bushes," explained Andrés.

"That looks bloody bad," said El Pícaro, feeling the leg. "It's beginning to turn blue above the knee, too. There's nothing else for it, Eulalio, but to saw your leg off."

"Yes, I think so too, jefe," answered Eulalio, resigned to his fate.

"Perhaps it's better simply to chop the leg off," cried Pedro. "That will be quicker."

"You're a burro, an absolute ass," said Santiago to Pedro. "If we chop the leg off and it's not chopped cleanly, the bone can split, and then it will be weeks before the bone heals."

"What do you say, Lalio?" asked Andrés.

"It's all the same to me how you get the leg off. It hurts so terribly, it can't hurt any worse whether it's chopped off or sawed off. All I want is to get rid of the damned leg. Because I can't stand it much longer. It's eating its way right up to my hip, that cursed poison."

"You ought to have told us sooner that you'd been bitten," said Cirilo, "then we might have been able to burn it out. We burned it out too late, that's the trouble."

"Leave me alone with your good advice," moaned Eulalio. "I didn't know any sooner myself that it had bitten me, goddam it. And now cut the goddam leg off or saw it or chop it so that I can get some peace, and stop croaking all that silly rubbish."

"Andrés," called El Pícaro, "come over to the oficina with me."

The two went off and after a few minutes came back with a bottle of aguardiente, a crosscut saw, and some rags from an old shirt.

El Pícaro looked round, took one of the drinking shells, poured the water out of it, filled the shell to the brim with aguardiente, and said to Eulalio: "Drink that down so that you don't feel this too much." Eulalio swallowed the spirits in one draft. Then El Pícaro took a rag, dipped it in another of the shells which he had filled with aguardiente, washed down the saw, and then washed Eulalio's leg clean above the knee and moistened it thoroughly with spirits.

"We must bind the leg below the hip," said Andrés, "so that

he doesn't bleed to death. And we must have hot fat from the kitchen to grease the wound. Then sugar on it, thick."

"Salt, you mean," said Pedro.

"Brown sugar, I said, and sugar it is," Andrés insisted. "And you, Matías, go to the cocinero, the cook, and bring all that over. Bubbling hot fat, and sugar. The sugar well pounded so it's like powder. Off with you, run!"

4

Meanwhile Eulalio, after the drink of aguardiente that he had put back so fast, had fallen into semiconsciousness; he seemed only vaguely aware of what was going on around him.

"Who is good at sawing?" asked Andrés, looking around.

"I'll do it," answered Santiago. "I've had practice. Before I was carretero I worked as a butcher with Don Benigno in Ocosocoantla, and I know how you have to saw bones."

"Good, then you do the sawing," ordered El Pícaro.

Santiago picked up the saw, tested the teeth, and said: "Hold his head still and his arms, and the other leg too, so that he doesn't begin to struggle. And here at the thigh, too, where it's bound, and someone else lower down the leg. But hold really tight."

"You must leave a flap of flesh, Santiago," said Andrés, "so that there's something left to fold over the bone."

"I know that, you ox. But quite right, we'd forgotten the stitches. Run over to the old whore and bring a good strong darning needle and some strong thread, long enough to go round several times, to sew up the flap properly."

Needle and thread were to hand in an instant. El Pícaro dipped it all in spirits and held it ready. One of the lads stood close by with the bowl of hot fat and another with the sugar.

Eulalio gave a sob, tried to sit up, but was firmly pushed down onto his mat, with all his limbs held down. He groaned a few times, grunted and swallowed, as he watched with his eyes open what was happening to his leg. He seemed for much of the time not to be fully clear whether it was his own leg being dealt with or that of one of the lads around him, each of whom had a specific task to fulfill.

Everything worked out to the full satisfaction of all the helpers.

When the lads could at last go and eat, Eulalio had fallen asleep, having knocked back a second good drink that El Pícaro fed him.

The lads' midday meal was nothing significant. But since there was nothing better, it had to do. Rice, boiled with green and red pepper pods, a few little bits of sodden leather, or carne seco as it was called, bone-hard dried meat, black beans with green peppers and sprinkled with a few drops of rancid fat. And after that, to wind up with, a brew called coffee.

The meal had hardly been bolted down when El Pícaro was already in front of the hut: "Come on, muchachos, off with you, get the calzada built. Andrés, you know where. El Gusano showed you the new place yesterday where they will be felling next week."

"Sí, jefe," answered Andrés.

The lads set off, armed with machetes.

5

Andrés, Pedro, and Santiago paced out the route that El Gusano had defined as callejón. El Gusano had only roughly laid down the direction of the trail. It was now the task of the experienced boyeros to work out the trail that would offer the least difficulties in the transport of the trozas. Reckoned from the felling area to the floating ditch, the route was about ten kilometers long. Of those ten kilometers, five were marshy. The three prospectors were trying to avoid the marsh and find another route. But however they tried, the route chosen by El Gusano always turned out to be the best. All the others without exception led over rocky mounds and over more than twenty ditches, some dry, some marshy. Those ditches were formed by erosion by the waters of the tropical rainstorms, and cut deeper in the ground every year, now often so deep that it would take hours to take even a single troza over the ditches. The drawback was that not one of those ditches had a direct connection with any of the rivers used for floating. They flowed into marshes, morasses, and lakes or into underground channels, caves, and gullies. It might be possible that one of those many ditches did deliver its water to the river in some way; but to find that out and make the necessary investigations would certainly have taken some weeks. And it was possible that after weeks of exploration they would learn that the ditch flowed into a hollow ending in a crevice, or that it ran off completely into open country over a great field of detritus where the trozas would not float anymore but would remain caught up amid masses of stones, and lost.

It was not in any case the three lads' task to undertake an exploration. The felling area had been indicated to them, also the tumbo where the lumber was stacked ready to be floated off at the start of the rainy season. All they had to do was to clear of jungle growth the trail on which the trozas were to be hauled.

The rest of the boyeros and the boys had already begun to cut the varales, the roots from which the calzada was to be built.

It was only because caoba was ten times more plentiful in the new area than in the area where felling had been carried out that morning that it was worth spending a week building a new calzada, a paved track. As soon as all the trozas from the area where they had been hauled that morning were finally at the tumbo, which would probably be midday two days later, the boyeros and their boys should not have had any more work for a whole week other than preparing the trail in the newly opened area. During that time the oxen could rest and feed well so as to be good and strong at the end of the week. The care of the oxen was always the prime consideration on rest days, for they cost a lot of money and were harder to obtain than Indians, who could be picked up when they were drunk and saddled with a fifty-peso fine for disturbing the peace, and then, since they couldn't pay the fifty-peso fine, sold to an enganchador, who resold them to the monterías.

6

When Andrés came back from his inspection he told Pedro, with six of the lads to help him, to clear the trail of bushes and undergrowth which would be in the way during transport.

He himself, with the rest of the lads and the boys, began to build the firm path. It was only where the ground was marshy, or so soft and wet that it silted up when no more than three or four trozas had been hauled across it, that the calzada was laid.

Trunks the thickness of an arm, three to four meters long, were laid side by side on the surface of the trail. Those trunks were then woven together with lianas, bast, and straps of bast. That formed the paving. On a calzada like that a troza could easily be hauled over the morass with two spans of oxen; and the faster the oxen went, the faster progress was made. Since the troza was not dragged over the naked earth and the oxen hauling it did not tread on the earth, the morass was not deepened. But purely through the weight of the oxen passing over it and of the trozas hauled over it, and eventually as a result of jolts and kicks on the varales, it happened inevitably that after a good number of trozas had been hauled, the calzada began to sink. Generally it sank on one side first, and of course on the side where the ground was softer and more marshy. If the calzada had been sloping to one side at the start, then the troza traveling over it would have slid to that side. But because the oxen were still pulling, the troza dug under the firm path sideways on and tore it up. Or else the spans could not keep going on the sloping, slippery path, slipped down to one side, and pulled the troza into the morass, so that the same troubles and problems occurred as with trozas hauled all the way through the morass.

For those reasons it was not enough just to build the calzada; it had to be continually repaired and renewed as long as there were trozas being hauled over it. But the building and the subsequent repairs caused so much extra work and kept so many lads from more important work that calzadas were built only if a great number of trozas were to be hauled that way, or when the passage of a smaller number of trozas over marshy ground would have caused more time and trouble altogether than the building of a calzada and its maintenance.

"So now you see, Nene," Andrés explained to the boy, "why calzadas are built only in exceptional cases. You've seen well enough today what things are like without calzadas. And we haven't finished yet. At twelve tonight it all starts again, and again tomorrow morning until ten or eleven, as long as the oxen keep going. It means two damned hard days for us and for the oxen. But if we'd wanted to build a calzada there to begin with, that would have taken four or five days, and for so few trozas it wouldn't be worth it."

"But then we shouldn't have had to work so terribly hard," said Vicente.

"That's never the question here, whether or not we're over-worked. The only question is, more production or less. And one way or the other, we muchachos are the ones who pay, the ones who always have to pay."

7

When the sun was low and the swiftly falling night announced itself with a cool breeze, Andrés called: "Muchachos, we'll stop for today. We've got to be up again at twelve." Prócoro reminded Andrés that El Gusano had said they should work on the trail until the sun was right down.

At that, Fidel said: "We don't care a juicy shit what the cabrón said. We're going now, I've done enough slogging."

"Who is the cabrón, and what sort of shit was that?" called

El Gusano, suddenly there among the lads. Unseen by the workers, El Gusano had ridden up, and because the ground was soft no one had heard his horse's hooves.

Fidel stepped out and said rudely: "I said cabrón, I said it. And we've all slogged quite enough for today." As he stepped forward he had taken his machete firmly in his hand, and now held it as if he intended to hit out at El Gusano at the slightest movement he made toward Fidel.

El Gusano saw the gesture. He raised his arm with the whip. It wasn't certain whether he was going to whip the horse or whether he wanted to get up close to Fidel with the horse and grab hold of the lad.

But in that same second he saw that all the lads, already prepared for the journey home, were standing together in a group, that they all had machetes in their hands and were all looking at him. He didn't know whether the lads intended just to make a challenging impression or whether they seriously thought of attacking him. He thought it wisest not to decide the question definitely there and then. He casually dropped his arm with the whip and said: "You could surely have done a bit more today to get the trail ready quicker. Maybe you're right, you're tired. But you'll all be up at twelve! I shall be calling you. The trozas from up there must all be at the tumbo tomorrow. Don Severo has ordered that expressly."

Without waiting for an answer, he turned his horse and rode off.

16

 The muchachos tottered back to the camp completely exhausted by fifteen hours of hard work in the depths of the jungle. It was dark by the time they arrived.

After an hour they went to the cook to get their evening meal: black beans boiled with green pepper, tortillas, and coffee.

As they ate, Pedro asked: "What's our compañero Eulalio doing? Has anyone been to see him?"

"Yes," said Andrés, "I've been to see him and given him some coffee. He looks half as if he's getting better and half as if he's going to pass out. I can't make him out."

"When we've eaten we'll go and see what we can do for him," said Matías, spooning up his beans in a bit of tortilla and pushing them into his wide-open mouth.

Fidel took a drink of coffee and said: "There's nothing else we can do there now. His leg's off, and if we saw any more of him there'll be nothing left of the boy."

The lads were squatting on the ground in front of the kitchen as they ate, with a dim light from the flickering fires of the kitchen hut and two smoking lanterns that the cook had hung on two of the hut's beams.

While the lads were still squatting there the hacheros also came to the kitchen to get their food.

Often, when the cutting fields were too far from the campo, the fellers, like the boyeros, took a light meal with them when they left in the morning and warmed it up near where they were working. In such cases they got their full meal in the evening. The so-called full midday meal, or la comida, differed from the light meal the lads got in the morning and evening only in that besides black beans there was rice and a little bit of dried meat or an ailing canned sardine. It must of course be said now that the meals there were much fairer than in the armies of civilized countries. El Pícaro and El Gusano got not one wretched bean more to eat than the muchachos. And even Don Severo got the same food when, as now, he was in the working area; maybe it was just a little cheered up with one or two cans of sardines in the week. Only the staff in the Oficinas Centrales, the headquarters of the montería, where the shop was and where the traders came, could manage anything better.

2

When the caoba gave out in the area and the lads started to work more than an hour's distance from the camp, the camp was abandoned and a new camp built at the center of the new exploitation area, an oficina for the contratista or the supervising capataz, a new kitchen and new dwelling huts for the men. Since all those buildings were of the most primitive kind and no other material was used but what was offered by the jungle, it took barely a day to put up a new camp. And it was abandoned again when a new, more distant area was opened and exploited. Only the headquarters of the montería remained invariably in its original place.

It had to stay there because it formed the center of the concession. The concession was lost to the Company or entrepreneurs if, according to the circumstances, the center was deserted for six or twelve months and no one worked in the concession area. The government then had the right to regard the concession as given up and to award it to a new entrepreneur. Of course it often happened that three, five, even ten years passed before the government received official information that the concession had been given up. The companies and entrepreneurs paid taxes only on production that was shipped. The nonreceipt of those taxes might be due to shortage of production in the concession, resulting maybe from shortage of caoba or shortage of workers. In no way need the reason be that the concession had been abandoned. And whether it was abandoned or maintained could only be ascertained if the government sent a commission. That was very expensive; and the government could never know whether the commission really found the montería or merely went through the motions of finding it. The headquarters of the Company or the entrepreneur at the seaport, or possibly in San Juan Bautista, issued only such reports, biased according to particular conditions, as were useful to the businesses themselves. Those businesses were often nothing more than purely speculative operations which disguised themselves more easily through the holding of a concession.

The Montellanos of course were not thinking of giving up their concession. On the contrary, they exploited it down to the last tree they could ever find. And if they had come across a concession that had been abandoned without having been fully exploited, they would have started work on it with such crazy frenzy that one would have believed they wanted to swallow up the whole jungle.

3

It was a really big crowd of lads who now squatted at their evening meal round the kitchen hut, guzzling their food and tossing down their drinks greedily and noisily, chattering, clattering their little bowls and cans, standing up and squatting down again somewhere else, shouting, whistling, humming, arguing. Some of them collapsed completely as they squatted down and began to fall asleep over their drinking shells and earthen bowls.

Several lads got up and went over to the huts to throw themselves down on their mats.

Then El Pícaro came up to the group of boyeros. He wasn't seen until he was quite close to them, for it had been quite dark for a long time. The light of the fires and the two lanterns, which seemed to be wondering all the time whether they should now really give some light or whether they would do better to go out with one last sorrowful flicker, extended only a few paces in the heavy darkness. El Pícaro was still covered from head to foot with mud and mire. Even his face and his hair showed ample traces of the elegant ride he had tried to make through the morass. But the mire had dried by now and hardened, and hung solidly on his clothes like armor. In many places the mud crust was already beginning to drop off and peel off, or crumble into dust. El Pícaro was evidently waiting for the next downpour to go and stand under the rain fully clothed and get the mire washed off his clothes, his boots, and his thick hair without having to make too much of an effort himself. It wasn't, of course, that he liked having the dirt on him. The only reason he was still going about encrusted with mud was that those were the only clothes he had. Even the four shirts that he owned were all equally full of holes and equally muddy, because hardly a day went by on which he did not have to ride or wade through mire, and often enough he fell flat in the mud. The other reason he was still wearing that shirt was that up to then he had not found a minute to wash or to look for a shirt that looked better than the one he had on his body. On top of all that, he was just as tired as all the other men and at that time of night could summon neither the strength nor the ambition to wash himself and peel off and rub down the muddy coat from his shirt and pants. The jungle, and work in the jungle, allow no privileges—the master is like the slave, the officer like the soldier; come the evening they are both just as tired, and the last spark of ambition and love of cleanliness are lost to both as soon as they have put down their meager rations.

El Pícaro remained standing among the boyeros. Some of the muchachos looked at him drowsily to find out what he wanted and what new orders he was going to give. But most took no notice of him.

"You could stand up and say 'Good evening, jefe' when I come here," he began.

Not one of the lads moved. Only Vicente, half scared that El Pícaro might perhaps give him a blow, said half aloud: "Good evening, patroncito." But then he saw that none of the lads had opened their mouths to greet El Pícaro and he was ashamed of himself and had the feeling that he had let his comrades down. But no one found fault with him, for no one would have wanted El Pícaro to give a pair of hard cuffs to the skinny body of that pathetic little slip of a boy, who was completely worn out by tiredness and overexertion.

What El Pícaro said could also be heard over among the fellers, for he shouted it loud enough with the idea that everybody should hear it.

When El Pícaro stopped speaking and no one but Vicente stirred, Celso said to the group in which he was squatting and eating his beans: "Bueno, great, that nobody got up and only that little mite of a boy opened his mouth; for I can swear to you right now, if any one of you had said 'Good evening, jefe,' then I'd have smashed his face to bits tonight."

"Hey, what's that you're saying?" shouted El Pícaro, who had heard Celso speaking without understanding what was said.

"I said I'd bash his face in," was Celso's answer.

"Whose face would you bash in?" asked El Pícaro.

"Anyone who opened his mouth at the wrong moment," replied Celso, and hid his face behind his tin can, from which he now took a long drink of coffee.

In the uncertain light El Pícaro couldn't see clearly who it was that had spoken. But he seemed to have something else on his mind; for he forgot what Celso said immediately and took not the slightest trouble to think about what Celso meant.

He looked back at the boyeros now, rolled himself a cigarette, went over to one of the fires and lit it, and returned to the place where he had been standing. Then he puffed out a cloud of smoke and said: "A pair of you come over to my oficina. I'll give you some spades. It will be best if you bury Eulalio right away. He's dead. We couldn't leave him lying until tomorrow, he'd be stinking by then and foul up the whole area. You all know where the cementerio is, the burial ground. A goddam thing here, we can't ever have the men at full strength. And Don Severo is after me about it all the time. I thought he would get over it. In a week he would have had a wooden stick tied on his goddam stump and work well with the fellers and be able to reduce his account. But damn it all, everything goes wrong here." He beckoned to some of the muchachos to follow him to the oficina.

4

The lads got up and went over to the hut where Eulalio was lying. "Nothing more to do for him," said Matías. "He really is dead. We could have saved ourselves the trouble of sawing off his leg. The bloody poison must have been up in his hip already when we cut his leg off. Maybe he'd had a second bite higher up, which we didn't see. I'm sure that's it."

"He makes a nice blue body." Santiago had a look at Eulalio in the dull, smoky light with a touching reverence that was like an unspoken prayer. But when he began to become conscious of his feelings, he shook them off with a quick movement of his head. In order not to give the least impression to the muchachos, who were standing all round and didn't know what to do or say, that he could possibly even be crying, he said in his usual ironic tone: "And now we shall have to dig up his sawed-off leg again when we've already buried it, so that we can put it with the rest of his body; for if one fine day the angels came to wake him up, he'd have a lot of bloody trouble hobbling around on his stump looking for his leg."

"Don't you think, Santiago," said Andrés to that, "that Dios will make him just as welcome even if he does come hobbling on one leg?"

"I'm not so sure of that. Maybe Dios will get a bit of a shock when he sees him in his pants, all ragged and covered in a thick coat of mud. And anyway, a miserable ox-drover like him, and all of us, whipped, with calluses all over us, torn to bits by hanging, covered with filth and caked in mud, uncombed, those rolled-up pants so full of holes they can see your arse from behind and your prick from in front, and then to appear up there with all those popes and cardinals and bishops and prelates and those nice clean angels that flutter round them, no, camarada, that's something I can't believe, that Eulalio will be welcome there and accepted as equal. No one can tell me that, and if anyone does tell it to me, then he's not telling the truth."

Andrés had knelt down by Eulalio and was endeavoring to close his eyes, which would not stay shut. Then he gave a signal to the lads, and they pulled Eulalio on his mat into the middle of the hut. The muchachos placed their smoky working lanterns round the body, two on each side of the head and two on each side of the feet, as they did at home on their fincas or in their villages. Now all they needed was candles. But since no one there had any candles, the smoking open wicks of the lanterns had to do that devout service.

"Dios will surely not find fault with him or with us, nor will the Madre Santísima, if we only burn our wretched linternas here instead of candles, because we have nothing better," said

Pedro, as if he wanted to pray to heaven for forgiveness that they could offer no better burial ceremonies to the departed.

Vicente and some of the other small boys squatted down and began to sing litanies. Of those litanies they did not understand a word correctly, for they were singing what they had only learned through hearing it so often. Because it was one-third corrupt Latin, one-third worse Spanish, and the last third a mixture of different Indian dialects, even God in heaven must surely have had accursed difficulties in understanding what those lads down there in the jungle wanted from him. But the singsong came from their full hearts and must surely have been more honorable than ninety percent of the singing droned out beside open graves in a civilized language that everyone there could understand, and what's more with expressions from which, without being an astrologer, it was easy to read that everyone, singers and mourners, had only one thought: "Oh, for God's sake, if only we could stop standing around here and go and down a good cognac."

"That's right enough, it will be enough to drive you round the bend before that old windbag gets out of breath."

"Oh, damn it all, has he still got something to say? It's just starting to rain, and my wife has got her new hat on, and that cost me a mint of money. God knows why I let myself be persuaded to drag myself to this funeral, it would have gone just as well without me. God be praised, now he's started to cross himself and talk about dust and ashes and chucking three pinches of earth into the grave. There, I've got a drop of rain on my nose, it's really beginning to rain, and I haven't brought an umbrella. The sun has been shining all day and now it has to come on to rain. Now I shall have to take my hat off too and look at the greasy hatband and sniff the lining."

5

Andrés pulled out the two mats that were under the one Eulalio was lying on, while Fidel and Matías lifted the body. Andrés then laid the two mats over the body, after the lower mat had been rolled up on each side of Eulalio.

"Where have you put the leg?" cried Matías.

"Here it is," answered Prócoro, and pushed it against the stump. Cirilo observed casually: "It was high time we dug that leg up; the dogs would have started to scratch it up soon."

"You ought to have buried it in the campo santo," said Sixto.

"We didn't have time for that this morning. The Gusano was after us, we had to get off to build the new trail up there."

The top mat was now rolled up in the same way. Several of the lads had brought lianas and long bast straps. The body, now completely wrapped in the two petates, was tied up so that it would not slip out of the mats.

Now that he looked like a long parcel, all the lads knelt down, crossed themselves, and joined in the boys' singing. Each of them sang in his own way, and there were certainly no three who could sing one and the same litany or the same Ave, even if they had wanted to. But no matter what words they sang, or how uncertain and confused the tunes in which they expressed their feelings, they were all thinking of Eulalio; Eulalio whom they had seen among them yesterday perfectly well, and who today had passed away to go to another montería as boyero. Handling oxen and hauling trozas to the tumbo, those were the only things Eulalio really understood.

There was no doubt about it among any of the muchachos; wherever Eulalio was going or where he would end up, he would be a boyero again and have to haul trozas. Maybe he wouldn't be whipped as much as he was by El Gusano and not hanged as often as Don Severo ordered; maybe there was sometimes good meat in the food and more black beans and fresher tortillas; maybe he got a new shirt and good white cotton pants and occasionally his drinking shell was filled with good old comiteco; but he must haul trozas every day, from twelve o'clock at night to eleven in the morning, and build calzadas in the afternoon. That was certain. And that was the unshakable belief of all caoba men. For Eulalio had left without working off his debts. As long as they were not discharged to the last centavo, he had to haul trozas wherever he might be going. People came and went, but the debts persisted. Countless thousands of peons, agricultural workers, lived on the fincas, the holdings, and the feudal estates as serfs and had to work off debts they had inherited from their father, who had in turn taken over the debts his father left. "The faithful repayment of the father's debts is the sacred duty of the obedient son, so that the father has to suffer less time in purgatory and finds rest on the other side." That is what the cura said whenever he came to the finca and consecrated the weddings of the peons and baptized their children in the finca chapel. And consequently all the muchachos who were there singing litanies were absolutely certain in their belief that Eulalio would have to go on hauling trozas; for that there could ever be any existence for a peon, here or on the other side, where he would not need to work, where he would have no debts which he was obliged to work off, would have been incomprehensible to them. The work might perhaps be less hard, the food better, and the treatment milder; but they had to work. Because Eulalio knew no other sort of work but handling oxen and hauling trozas, that would continue to be his work, and that was how things happened perfectly naturally. "Una vez peones, para siempre peones. Fate made us common, and land workers, so we shall go on being peones to all eternity. Ni la muerta nos libra. Not even death frees us from our fate."

One who thinks that way, one who has been taught to think that way, he alone is the true proletarian.

He is the proletarian implied in all the propaganda; he is the proletarian about whose lot there is conflict and bloodshed in all proletarian struggles for freedom; and he is the proletarian whom no revolution will ever liberate.

6

The lads stopped singing, crossed themselves, then the departed, and then themselves again. Then they were ready to pick up Eulalio and go off with him.

And then El Gusano came into the hut. He looked round, looked at the package on the ground and said: "You don't really need to burn so many lanterns. Hell only knows when we shall get more kerosene. Torches from branches would have been just as good."

"Yes, we would have done that too, jefe." Santiago stood up, blew out the lantern that he had in his hand and two others that were standing just by his feet. Without taking any more notice of El Gusano, he said: "Vámonos, muchachos!"

The lads became very active, took the bundle on their shoulders, and marched out of the hut.

During all that hustle and bustle they pushed and shoved El Gusano here and there as if he were a piece of furniture that was in the way. He had come in as the one in command, who meant to let no occasion pass without making it clear that he was the one who gave the orders. But in this matter there was nothing for him to organize, no one had asked him or El Pícaro for any sort of advice or help. He tried to make it look as if he felt he must take charge of the burial or concern himself with it in some way or other. When the lads were finally on their way out, he was going to follow them. He acted as if he were the senior person present and had to give a worker his final escort, not as one bereaved, as a mourner, but in order not to let the men forget that they could not, indeed might not, bury their dead without his orders.

But the men so quickly formed a close group, ran here and there and continually shoved into one another, that there was no room left to be able to join the procession. Quite unexpectedly he found himself several paces behind it; he didn't know how that had happened, for up to then he had seemed to be in the middle of the muchachos.

No one turned to look at him. The lads suddenly adopted a very rapid pace, so that he would have looked ridiculous if he had tried to catch up with them, like a dog that has been left behind. He stood still and gazed after the funeral procession.

The little group was soon swallowed up in the night; for a few seconds he could still see the glow of the smoking lantern as it swayed to and fro, became smaller and smaller, and then all of a sudden disappeared.

7

The muchachos carried only one lantern. They had put out all the others as they left the hut and laid them down on the ground. The contemptuous meaning of their gesture had been so clear that even El Gusano could not mistake it. Not one drop of kerosene would they take from him as a gift as they carried their comrade to his grave. The only lantern they still carried was essential because of the extreme darkness.

When they had gone a little way and reached the thicket, they began to cut down branches and boughs and burn them as torches.

The cementerio was only fifteen minutes away from the camp. So long as a new camp was not set up too far away, the men made use of the burial ground that had been laid out when the first man died in the new semaneo. The campo santo for a newly opened semaneo was always laid out a long way toward where the next fields were to be cut. Thus the burial ground, once laid out, served for a long time. Only if the new camps were set up too far away in new territory did a new campo santo have to be arranged so that not too much time would be lost in burials. All the lads' time belonged as undisputed and legal property to the owner of the concession. And the less time spent on superfluous work like the interment of a muchacho, the more time there was for useful work. It generally happened in a new camp that somebody had to be buried after three days.

Whether many or few lay buried in the campo santo which they were just reaching, it was hard to say. There were a number of low mounds scattered irregularly over the area. Broken and weatherbeaten little crosses made from roughly hacked tree trunks were stuck in the ground here and there. There were hollows to be seen on all sides, from which one might conclude without thinking any more about it that a body must have rotted there, one meter down or even less, so that the surface of the earth had crumbled. Pigs and dogs had scratched at most of the mounds and hollows. Often enough the dog had been brought by a worker because it could not be parted from its master. And when its master died, the dog looked for him under the ground. But that was exceptional. The dogs that hung around in the camps in dozens were always hungry, and, like the ever-hungry tame and wild pigs, they had to find out for themselves where and how they could get food if they wanted to live. If they couldn't get food from the living, they must take it from the dead. The dogs, and even more the tame pigs, were too scared and too lazy to go hunting in the jungle to catch something. The wild pigs of course were at home in the jungle, but they tried, even more than the tame ones, to lead a comfortable life, as a pig is entitled to by nature. In the conflict over those little prizes the wild pigs were always victorious over the tame ones and over the hungry dogs, and they left the field to the defeated only when they couldn't touch another thing because their stomachs were stuffed full.

8

A hole was dug in a few minutes. Some of the lads began singing their litanies again, but this time less from a heartfelt impulse than because they didn't really know anything better to do while the hole was being dug.

"If we'd had our old medicine man here," said Prócoro to Valentín, who was standing beside him, "Eulalio wouldn't have died so miserably. Por Dios, how many people in our village have been bitten by cascabeles and are still alive. I know half a dozen boys, all of my age, and all of us often let ourselves be bitten by a rattlesnake for fun, and played with it. Then we gave a shout and ran to the brujo, to the gristly old medicine man, and he gave us a dose and everything was all right again."

"You don't need to tell such fibs here," Valentín retorted. "On the finca where I grew up everyone died who was bitten by a cascabel. There's no cure for it."

"And I'm telling you all the same that there is a cure for it, one that always helps," asserted Santiago, joining in the discussion. "I know for certain, from half a hundred people I know, that there's a good medicine against culebra bites. And there's even one kind that you can take in advance. And when you've taken it you can go out hunting culebras and catch the snakes in your hand. They can bite you like mad and it does nothing to you, absolutely nothing."

Cirilo now called out above their voices: "You all know a lot of shit, that's what you know. You're all burros, stupid asses. Anyone who's bitten by a culebra like the one Eulalio was bitten by, he always passes out."

"If he always passes out, why didn't you say so this morning?" said Fidel. "Then we shouldn't have had to hurt poor Lalio so much sawing off his leg, if he was bound to die."

"I'm not saying," Cirilo corrected himself, "that you shouldn't at least try everything you've ever heard of, everything you know, to keep somebody alive. It does often help if the leg or the hand is cut off. But then it has to be done at once and not when the poison has already reached as high as the navel. Then you don't need to trouble."

"Goddam it all!" thundered Andrés to the lot of them. "Goddam the whole lot of you here! Keep your goddam traps shut, can't you!"

9

"What's the point of all this damned quarreling?" A new voice was heard that seemed to reach the group from the deepest darkness. "He's dead, and he had a painful death, and now let him finally decay so that he gets his rest at last. If you all go on shouting and arguing much longer, he'll get up again, crawl out of the package you've tied up so bloody badly, give you all a couple of socks on the jaw, and wrap himself up again. What sort of funeral is this, here in the middle of the night, with the corpse just by you and you're all fighting over whether he was given the right or the wrong treatment. He was treated wrong by you oxen, that's why he passed out. If he'd been treated properly he'd still have his leg and could go out with us tonight to haul trozas."

It was Celso, one of the oldest and most experienced hacheros in the montería, who had come to see how the funeral was going. There were only two of the fellers present; all the others had stayed in the camp and were sleeping, because with all their strength they were even more exhausted than the boyeros. And as the dead man belonged to the boyeros, it was felt to be their ceremony only; the fellers didn't feel they had to take part in an occasion that did not affect them. It was the same when the fellers buried their dead: they did not think it was necessary to be disturbed by the boyeros in their entertainment.

"That's just what we're arguing about, Celso," said Cirilo, going over to him. "It's all been done wrong. If he'd been properly treated, and at the right time, then he'd be leaping about here like a young kid."

Celso went nearer to the hole where they were still digging to make it sufficiently wide and comfortable. In a superior manner he took the spade from the hand of one of the two lads who were digging. "Cut another foot wide here, and then one here, and the whole bloody shit is finished."

He threw out two spadefuls of damp black earth on one side and two more on the other, then climbed out. "Lay him in there now. It's deep enough to keep the jabalís, the wretches, from digging him up and eating him. And if the brutes, the damned creatures, do eat him up, it won't hurt him anymore."

Matías and Sixto picked up the package, swung it to and fro, and then let it fall in the hole.

Celso, standing on the other side, said: "He's lying damned awkwardly in the hole, with his bottom on the ground and his head and legs sticking up in the air. But I reckon he'll have time enough to get used to that uncomfortable position." And he made the sign of the cross on the package, then crossed himself, took the spade, and threw several heaps of earth into the hole. He passed the spade to one of the lads and said: "I didn't come here to do all your work for you. If you've got a stiff, you can bloody well bury it yourselves." Stretching his limbs, he said: "How tired I am. Hell and the devil, I'm as tired as a dog. And how I'd like to bash those two coyotes over the head with the spade."

Looking round him in the flickering, smoky light of the torches, he felt for the half-cigar that he had put down on a branch when he seized the spade. He found it, lit it with a smoldering twig, and disappeared into the thicket to go back to his choza.

While the hole was being filled in, the boys and some of the lads sang through their litanies again; they knew only four lines, and they repeated them over and over again without ever agreeing on a common language and even less on one and the same tune.

When about a foot of earth had been piled on the package, two muchachos jumped into the grave and trod down the earth with their bare feet. Then they laid branches over it, threw some more earth on it, and trod that firm again. Finally the grave was smoothed out.

The little mound was so insignificant and made such an inconspicuous impression that you might have thought a two-year-old child lay buried there, and that they had been economical with the earth at that.

Meanwhile Santiago had cut two pieces of wood with his machete and bound them together with the broken end of a liana to form a cross.

As soon as the little mound had been trodden firm, he stuck the cross in the soft earth.

The muchachos stood silent for a minute, crossed themselves three times, and Andrés said, half aloud: "Madre Santísima, Holiest Mother of God, bless his poor soul. Ave María, Purísima."

And they all repeated: "Ave María, Purísima en el cielo, Madre de Dios, Virgencita Santísima, ruega por nosotros and give him your blessing and eternal peace. Amén."

Then they stood for another minute in silence, looking at the little mound. Matías knelt down and pushed the cross in a little further, as if he felt it had not been stuck in the earth properly. Then he gently scraped more earth round the cross and pressed it down with his fingertips.

When the lads saw that it was all over, they turned and made their way back to their huts.

From the far distance sounded the muffled howling of a family of monkeys, monos gritones, passing the night in the crowns of the mighty trees. It echoed through the jungle like the roar of an angry mountain lion. Gruesome and terrifying, it seemed to tear the night apart, but it did not disturb the jungle. It sang and fiddled, chirped and whistled, whined and whimpered, rejoiced and lamented its ever-unchanging song with the constancy of the roaring sea.